6/15

AGNES AND THE

RENEGADE

A Men of Defiance Novel by

Elaine Levine

Published by Elaine Levine
Copyright © 2014 Elaine Levine
Cover art by Hot Damn Designs
Editing by editing720
All rights reserved.

Print Edition ISBNs:
ISBN-10: 0985420561
ISBN-13: 978-0-9854205-6-7
Last Updated: 02/18/2014

Ebook Edition ISBNs:
ISBN-10: 098542057X
ISBN-13: 978-0-9854205-7-4

DEDICATION

For Barry, always

And to Melvin and Evelyn--the best parents a writer
could ever have

ACKNOWLEDGMENTS

Many thanks to Aggie M., who didn't mind having her name borrowed for this story. Before I knew anything about what became of Chayton or who his heroine would be, I knew what it sounded like when he said her name, "Agkhee."

A special shout-out goes to my sister, Barb, who never fails to believe and encourage. And to my friend, Melissa Mayhue, who always knows when to do a coffee intervention.

If you happen to find yourself in Fort Collins, Colorado, be sure to stop in at the Moot House. They let Melissa and me sit in a corner booth for hours once a month as we talk murder, mayhem, and time travel conundrums.

I never forget that writers without readers are simply diarists. Your participation in my fiction is what makes me a novelist. So to all of you who buy my books and take the time to drop me an email, chat with me on Facebook and Twitter, write reviews, and share my books with your friends and reader groups, I thank you. None of my fiction would be possible without you.

BOOKS BY ELAINE LEVINE:

~Red Team Series~
(This series must be read in order)
1 The Edge of Courage (2012)
2 Shattered Valor (2012)
3 Honor Unraveled (2013)
3.a Kit & Ivy, a Red Team Wedding novella
(coming 2014)
4 Twisted Mercy (coming 2014)
4.a Ty & Eden, a Red Team Wedding novella
(coming 2014)
5 Assassin's Promise (coming 2014)
5.a Rocco & Mandy, a Red Team Wedding novella
(coming 2015)

~ Men of Defiance Series ~
(This series should be read in order)
1 Rachel and the Hired Gun (2009)
2 Audrey and the Maverick (2010)
3 Leah and the Bounty Hunter (2011)
4 Logan's Outlaw (2012)
5 Agnes and the Renegade (2014)
6 Dulcie and the Bandit (coming 2015)

CHAPTER ONE

Defiance, Wyoming Territory, May 1879

Aggie put the last pin in her hair with shaking hands. She could hear voices downstairs in the boardinghouse's large kitchen. Her landlord, Logan Taggert, and his family had arrived. When she'd queried him about the possibility of leasing his hunting cabin for a summer spent painting, he'd quickly accepted. She'd been clear about her gender, age, and experience. All her work had been as a student under Theo Hamilton, her teacher, mentor, and adoptive father. She'd never stepped out on her own before. And truthfully, had Theo not died the winter past, she would still be his student. She wondered whether she would satisfy the Taggerts' expectation of an artist tenant.

She gave a cursory look at herself in the mirror above the dresser. Her light brown hair was too silky to stay neatly coiffed without an excess of pins. Her blue eyes were unexceptional. She wasn't particularly curvy, either—a fact that had never bothered her before and didn't now. She was used to assessing the world and its inhabitants and rarely gave any thought to her own appearance. It wasn't as if she would be doing a self-portrait any time soon. She smiled when she thought of the ones Theo had done of himself in the second half of his life. She treasured those portraits now. She hoped she didn't seem too waif-like for her new landlord; if Mr. Taggert thought she wasn't equal to the difficulties of life in a remote cabin, he could still turn her away.

"Miss Hamilton! The Taggerts are here!" Maddie, the boardinghouse proprietress, called up to her.

"I'll be right down!" she answered. Her dress, one of only three she was bringing with her, was a simple cotton in a purple, two-tone checkered pattern. It buttoned up the front, and had a hem, cuffs, and a collar of ivory cotton. She tugged on her sleeves and straightened her spine. If her landlord and his family did turn her away, it wouldn't be the end of the world.

Theo had left her a modest inheritance that included their new warehouse in Denver and its apartment, plus a small annual stipend. The arrangement she'd made with the Taggerts suited her needs—and budget—perfectly. The cabin she'd leased from them was in an isolated spot near interesting land features. For the sum she paid, they were to keep it fully stocked with food supplies and provide her with the use of a horse for the summer.

Without the Taggerts' help, it might not be a good idea to go to such a remote location as their isolated hunting cabin. If they withdrew their support now, she would have to find other subject matter for her work—perhaps a sampling of frontier towns like Defiance.

She slipped the strap of her art bag over her head, picked up her carpetbag, draped her linen duster over her arm, then grabbed her wide-brimmed Plainsman hat and hurried from her room. Her trunks and crates of art supplies were already downstairs, ready for loading. She came to an abrupt stop in the kitchen when she saw the Taggerts; she'd thought they'd be much older, but they were close to her age.

"Miss Hamilton, I'm very pleased to meet you!" Mr. Taggert came forward to introduce himself, his wife, and their foster daughter, White Bird. All three of them greeted her warmly, easing her worry. Both Taggert adults had blond hair and Scandinavian features—she with warm, brown eyes and he with cool gray eyes. Their foster daughter, who might have been nine or ten, looked nothing like them with her warm olive skin, big dark eyes, and thick black hair.

Mrs. Taggert took Aggie's hand and squeezed it. "I had no idea you were so young."

Aggie looked between her and Mr. Taggert. "Is that a problem?"

"No, of course not." Mrs. Taggert smiled. "We're always happy to help artists. Your portfolio was impressive. We can't wait to see the work you'll do

3

out here."

A little tension eased from Aggie's spine.

"I hope you don't mind, Miss Hamilton, but I did an inventory of the supplies you've packed," Mr. Taggert said. "I think we should stop at the general store to pick up a few more things. And I noticed you don't have a gun."

Her tension returned full force. "No, I don't. I don't know how to use one and would likely not, even if I needed it." She glanced at the adults in the room. "I thought you said the area where your cabin is was settled and…peaceful."

Mrs. Taggert and White Bird looked up at Mr. Taggert, who gave them a reassuring smile that came a heartbeat too slowly. "It is. I'm only thinking of snakes or mountain lions."

"Oh. Well, then, no. I'm not coordinated enough to shoot a snake. And by the time I happened to see a mountain lion, it would surely be too late." A terrible thought entered her mind. "Unless you mean for me to hunt for my food, which I can't do."

Mr. Taggert laughed. "Not at all, Miss Hamilton. Our agreement included weekly provisions. The gun would be for your protection. The cabin's ten miles from us at the ranch."

A little shiver of doubt cooled her enthusiasm—but not her determination. "I understand. However, my funds are limited for such purchases. I would prefer not to buy a gun at this point."

"Understood. If there's trouble of any sort, we'll

bring you up to the house." Mr. Taggert loaded her things into the bed of the wagon. She and White Bird sat on the back bench while Mr. and Mrs. Taggert sat up front. They took their leave of Maddie, waving to her as they pulled forward into the town. It had poured overnight, and though the sky was now a clear, brilliant blue, the street was clogged with mud. Mr. Taggert kept the wagon to the side of the road, where the horses' hooves and the wagon wheels could get some traction.

They drove only a couple of blocks before stopping in front of a general store. Mr. Taggert helped them all down. Aggie followed Mrs. Taggert and White Bird into the store. A rich scent filled her nostrils as she entered—tobacco, burlap, licorice, wood smoke. The store held the chill of the night in it; the heat from the woodstove was comforting. She took another deep breath, adding coffee and tea to the list of fragrant scents. She strolled around the store, taking note of the goods available.

Mrs. Taggert waved her over. "Miss Hamilton, these are our friends Jim and Sally Kessler." Aggie nodded at the older couple as Mrs. Taggert continued, "Miss Hamilton is an artist. She's rented the hunting cabin south of our house for the summer."

Mrs. Kessler had an odd expression. "The one out by the bluffs?"

"That's the one." Mrs. Taggert nodded.

The shopkeeper's wife's eyes widened. "Is it safe?"

"Of course it's safe. We wouldn't let her have the cabin if it weren't."

"But"—Mrs. Kessler looked at her then back at Mrs. Taggert—"but *he's* out there."

Mrs. Taggert sent Mrs. Kessler a meaningful glance, nodding her head almost imperceptibly toward her daughter. The shopkeeper's wife dropped the conversation, smoothly switching to Mrs. Taggert's shopping list.

Aggie wandered around the store, preoccupied with Mrs. Kessler's whispered warning. Who was the man she was worried about? In what way was he a danger? After a few minutes, Aggie went outside, seeking the fresh air to clear her mind. The Taggerts wouldn't have rented her their cabin if the situation there were dangerous. And where they lived was not that far away. If an active danger was present, it would affect them as well—surely they would not remain in the area?

As she leaned against the railing on the boardwalk in front of the store, she drew deep and calming breaths of the warm morning air. She knew the day would heat up rapidly, drying the quagmire in the middle of the road, here and on the trails they would travel today.

The general store was on the edge of town at the convergence of two roads—one led back into the residential area where Maddie's boardinghouse was, the other led around a bend and into the business district. It was a quaint and bustling town, with its petite white church, small cottages, and newer brick homes.

She could tell Defiance was a thriving outpost. The railroad spur stopped there once a day, making travel down to Cheyenne, and from there to Denver, easily accomplished. Telegraph wires followed the train tracks and led to several business establishments, including the general store. The town was remote, but it was connected to the rest of the world. Its modern conveniences made her feel better about having chosen it as her base of travel for the summer.

As she leaned lazily against one of the boardwalk's support beams, she watched a rider come into town. An *Indian*. He rode a black-and-white spotted pony, moving with its rolling gait as if the horse was an extension of himself. The horse had a yellow circle drawn about one eye. Other symbols decorated its hip. A couple of feathers were tied at the top of its mane.

Although the horse was decorated, the man was not. Straight black hair spilled around his shoulders. His face was unpainted, his clothes simple—a fringed deerskin tunic over leggings and moccasins. The Indian sat on an unusual pad and a colorful blanket. The reins and halter were not the usual tack, but were made of finely braided rawhide. He looked over at the store and saw her. Aggie's entire body tightened as his eyes locked with hers. Without cause or provocation, a chill slipped through her mind—not of fear exactly, as he hadn't threatened her. More a warning, an awareness.

As she watched, he took his horse to the hitching post, moving from the pink wash of the morning sun into the blue shadow of the store's building. She noticed he didn't tie his horse, just let the reins fall forward in front of it. He collected a thick package he'd brought, swung his leg over his mount's neck, and slid off its back. She couldn't look away from him as he started up the stairs. Nor did he look away from her.

She studied him, remembering everything about him, cataloging his features as she often did when studying a new model. When she got to the cabin, she'd paint him, she decided. His face was narrow, his cheekbones high, his chin broad, his mouth wide. His nose was straight, triangular. His eyes were as black as his hair. His brows were straight slashes over dark, almond-shaped eyes. He had no hair on his jaw, and none that she could see through the ties of his tunic or on his forearms. His skin was a warm brown, even in the shade of the boardwalk. Tall and lean, he walked toward her with the limber prowl of a wolf. Though he had no weapons on him, she didn't doubt he was capable of terrible violence.

Aggie shifted to pull her sketchpad from her bag. When her attention was diverted, men she hadn't noticed before gathered around her Indian. He gave each of the three a dismissive look before his gaze returned to her. They shouldered into him, blocking his forward progress.

"Keep your eyes to yourself, chief," one warned.

"You got no business looking at a white woman," another said.

The Indian's expression hardened, as if he knew what was coming. His gaze was on her, but his focus was with the men. Then one of them shoved a fist into his stomach, hard enough to lift him off his feet before he doubled over. Another man kicked his legs out from under him. Her Indian looked up, holding her gaze as he fell to his knees. He didn't fight back, didn't try to protect himself or deflect their blows.

"No!" Aggie shouted, jumping to his rescue. "Stop this! He did nothing wrong." She tried to pull one of the men away from him but was shoved back against the railing. She hit her head on the support beam and cried out. Her Indian did fight back then. He punched the man who'd struck her, hitting him in the groin. When the man bent over, her Indian captured his face and slammed him against the wooden slats of the boardwalk. The others intensified their fight until the door to the store slammed open. Mr. Taggert entered the fray, pulling men off her Indian, giving him a chance to regain his feet. Others joined the fight, so his reprieve was short-lived. It seemed just the two of them against far too many men. Mr. Kessler came out of the store with a shotgun. He walked to the edge of the boardwalk and fired into the air. Twice. The fight had spilled down the steps and out into the street. Men were so covered with the wet muck of the muddy road that they were barely recognizable.

One of them was the sheriff. She hadn't noticed

him join the fight. He was cleaner than the others, so perhaps he'd come to break it up. As she watched, the sheriff gave Mr. Taggert a hand up from the muck, then he reached one down to her Indian. He accepted the help up, then swiped the sludge from an arm, but it did little to clear it off his buckskin tunic. She braced herself for when his gaze returned to hers, but he didn't look at her again.

Chayton stood in the middle of the road with the town's slime dripping off him. The sheriff was pulling men out of the mud, dispersing the crowd. Chayton hated these people. Hated the town. Hated *her*, the one whose blue eyes never flinched upon seeing him. Had the men not stopped him, he might have done the unthinkable: he might have touched her. Never, in the long, empty years since his wife Laughs-Like-Water was murdered, had he ever been drawn to another woman. And never to a white woman.

He shut that thought away. He wasn't drawn to this one; she'd been rude to stare and he'd merely wished to teach her a lesson.

Logan's wife, Sarah, came out of the store, hot on the heels of his daughter, White Bird. The girl rushed to the railing, gripping it in a white-knuckled hold. She smiled at him and looked ready to fly down the stairs and come to him. He let himself watch her a second longer, seeing in her the image of her mother, so beautiful and kind-hearted and brave. And, thanks to white men like those who'd just attacked him, so dead.

He turned his back on his daughter, halting her forward motion. Such a display of emotion was unseemly and dangerous among the people of this town. It would be best for her to forget he ever existed. Logan walked to the stairs where Chayton's pack of deerskins lay. "You want the usual trade?" Logan asked in Chayton's native *Lakȟóta* language.

Chayton nodded, irritated to need yet more help from his friend.

"I'll bring it out to you at the bluffs tomorrow. You best head on back. We'll be right behind you if you hit any trouble."

Chayton drew his horse away from the others at the hitching post. With a quick hop, he leapt up to his pony's back. He sent a last look toward his daughter, who was regarding him now in a calm, disinterested way. He nodded at her, then turned his horse toward the edge of town, letting him stretch out and speed away from the pit white men called a town.

CHAPTER TWO

It was late afternoon when Aggie began worrying they'd somehow gotten off track—the cabin was such a long way from Defiance, more than half a day's ride. The spring rains that had churned Defiance into a mud pit had made the plains blossom in color. The road was barely distinguishable in the lush spring growth of grasses and wildflowers. They went over a small rise, and at last she saw her cabin about a half-mile from the road.

The cabin itself was tiny, made of mud brick covered with stucco. On one side of the front door, firewood was neatly stacked. On the other side sat a bench. A well stood halfway between the house and corral. She could just make out a small outhouse behind the house as they drove up. Her agreement with Mr. Taggert included his providing a horse and its feed. Though the corral was empty, a six-foot-high pile of hay was stored inside a small fenced pen near the corral.

Mr. Taggert helped them out of the wagon. Aggie looked around at the sea of prairie colors surrounding the cabin, finding herself eager to start working.

"Well?" Mr. Taggert prodded, a hint of tension on his face.

She smiled at him. "It's wonderful. Exactly what I was looking for."

Mrs. Taggert drew her foster daughter back against her, and her hands folded over the little girl's pinafore. "White Bird and I came down a few days ago to straighten the cabin and bring fresh linens, but let's go inside to be sure you have everything you need."

Mr. Taggert opened the door for them, then started to unload Aggie's crates and trunks. It took a minute for her eyes to adjust from the bright sun to the dim interior of the cabin, but when they did, she was thrilled with what she saw. The one-room cabin was larger than it seemed outside. In the far corner was a large bed with a pine headboard and footboard. The bed was made, and a stack of additional linens and blankets sat on the foot of it. There was a dresser with a pitted mirror and a large bowl and pitcher on it. Catty-corner to the door was a fireplace with a swinging iron pot arm. A square table with two mismatched chairs was pushed against the wall near the door. Another stack of linens was piled on it— tablecloths, dishtowels, and potholders. The walls inside were whitewashed stucco that had crumbled in some places, revealing the earthen bricks. A dry sink stood between the fireplace and the stove with a big tin washbasin on it. The cabinet held a full complement of the necessary pots and utensils. Cutlery was neatly arranged in the drawers. Stacked next to the fireplace was a pile of splintered wood for the oven. An ax hung to the right of the front door. Three kerosene lanterns were placed strategically about the room.

"This is wonderful, Mrs. Taggert. I think everything I'll need is here."

White Bird lifted the bed skirt. "We brought you a tub, too, because the creek out back isn't very big."

"And we had a small keeping box put in under the table," Mrs. Taggert said as she pointed in that direction. "It's insulated with sawdust. It won't keep dairy goods cool for long, especially not with the summer heat coming in, but it will let you get a few days out of the dairy items we send down each week."

Aggie smiled; her cabin was perfect. The best thing was that there was enough space in the middle of the room for her to set up several easels and spread her work out, space to let her paintings dry and set.

"We'll let you get settled now," Mr. Taggert said from the doorway. "I'll bring your horse down tomorrow. If there's anything else you need, let me know or ask my men when they bring your supplies down each week."

Aggie made a simple supper of eggs and biscuits, then went outside to eat later that evening. She sank onto the bench in front of her house, exhausted but happy. The opportunity to spend a summer in this place didn't exist even five years ago. It wouldn't have been safe for a white person, alone, here in what had been the heart of Sioux country.

When she finished eating, she set her plate aside and listened to the sounds of nature around the cabin. It was quiet but not silent. Crickets, robins, larks, and sparrows chattered, busy in the fading light. A large hawk soared, his plaintive cry hovering overhead. The breeze, which was a tad too stiff to be called a breeze, made a sound as it cut around the cabin—not whine or a sigh, but maybe a bit of both. Down by the creek, the old cottonwoods' big leaves flapped in the wind, slapping against each other.

The evening was cool, the sun low in the sky. The heat she'd expected when they left Defiance had never quite arrived. She wondered if the weather would step back into winter or jump forward into summer. Either was possible this time of year. She pulled her shawl tighter about herself. She'd eaten late—it had taken her a while to organize her gear. And she'd spent hours sketching the Indian she'd seen in town. She closed her eyes and let herself dwell in the heat of his gaze. No one had ever looked at her the way he did. What would have happened had the fight not broken out?

When she opened her eyes, the evening's gloaming light had softened the world around her, coloring the clouds and land in pastels far more beautiful than anything she could paint.

She walked a small circle around her house, looking at the expansive land surrounding the cabin. Off to the north, she could see a line of sandstone bluffs. Perhaps that would be the first area she would go exploring once Mr. Taggert brought her horse.

After her walk, she prepared to retire for the night, drawing water from the pump to fill the pitchers in the house and the water kettle for the morning. She made sure the front door was barred, then did a quick sponge bath and changed into a nightgown. The windows had shutters that could be closed from inside the house, an oddity she thought might have been left over from the Indian wars, which put her in mind of the man she'd seen in town so many hours ago.

She brought a lamp to her dresser, then retrieved her charcoal and sketchpad, setting to work, filling more pages with the things she'd seen in town. Her Indian. The way he'd looked on his black-and-white pony. The men who'd attacked him. The fight. And afterward, his cryptic, angry conversation with Mr. Taggert.

At some point, she fell asleep, the sketchpad still on her lap, her pencil still in her hand. When she woke, she didn't know whether she had dozed a few minutes or if it had been longer. She doused the lamp, then lay still and listened, wondering if something had awakened her.

In the dark isolation of her new home, sounds were amplified. The wind in the eaves outside. Distant coyotes. Strange screeches and calls she hadn't heard during the daylight hours—any of which might have been what roused her. She shut her eyes, trying to force herself to relax and go back to sleep. As eerie as things sounded, she reminded herself there was no such thing as ghouls; everything out there was natural, not unnatural. She had nothing to fear.

Her cabin had three windows: one over her bed on the south wall, the other two on the front and back walls. There was no window on the north wall because of the fireplace. The windows were closed but not shuttered. She lay on her side, her gaze bouncing between the east and west windows. She didn't know what she was on the alert for; perhaps it was the complete lack of human noise that irritated her senses. In the warehouse where she'd lived with Theo in Denver during the last year, the streets were alive well into the wee hours of morning, and then again throughout the day. It was an industrial section of town, but a night never passed when there wasn't a fight or drunken brawl of some type, or even just the noise of people passing by.

She missed Theo. She'd been so frightened when he brought her from the orphanage. He'd shown her around his expansive Georgetown art studio where he lived in Washington, D.C., then told her he expected her to see to the cooking and cleaning for the two of them. She was only twelve, but she'd helped in the kitchen at the orphanage since she'd arrived four years earlier. He'd chosen her because of her domestic skills, he'd informed her.

Aggie sighed, closing her mind to the memories that would not aid her now. She'd become expert at adapting to major life shifts. She'd done it when her parents had died and she'd gone to the orphanage. She'd done again it when Theo brought her to his home. This was yet another new beginning. Each had led to something better. This would, too.

The moonlight dimmed briefly, darkening her room. She sat up in bed, wondering if she'd imagined a shadow moving outside. She blinked and shifted her gaze from the windows in the main area of the cabin to the one above her bed. As she watched, something walked in front of it, briefly blocking the light.

Something tall and solid.

She gathered herself close to the wall, hoping whoever was looking in wouldn't see her. But they could from the other windows. Summoning her courage, she slowly raised herself to look out of the window over her bed. The moonlight was bright, casting sharp shadows over the outhouse and chopping block. Everything was calm and still outside. Perhaps the shadow she'd seen had been a cloud slipping over the moon.

She closed the shutters and bolted them. It took her senses a moment to acclimate to the new darkness now that most of the moonlight was blocked by the shutters. She held herself still and tried to calm her breathing as she watched the other two windows, her ears straining for any unusual sounds. She needed to close and bolt the shutters on the other windows as well, but she dreaded crossing the room. For several minutes, while she waited and listened, there was no movement and no strange sounds outside. In fact, everything had gone very, very quiet.

Gathering her courage, she climbed off her bed and crossed her cabin, hurrying to the first window. She paused against the wall, then spun around and slammed the shutters closed. After running to the other side of the cabin, she grabbed the shutters and was about to repeat the action when a face appeared in the window. A painted face. An Indian warrior's face. She screamed and banged the shutters closed, dropping the bolt over them. She backed away from the window, scrambling into the center of her cabin. Her gaze bounced around the small space as she sought safe refuge, but there was none to be had.

Oh, God. She was alone, all alone, hours and hours from the nearest ranch.

She closed her eyes and saw again the terrible image of the face on the other side of the window. Her heart was like a sledgehammer in her chest. How many of them were out there? She'd thought this land was settled, but clearly it was not. What were their intentions? If they wanted to get inside her cabin, there was little she could do to stop them.

She stood in the center of the cabin's only room, wondering what she should do. Not knowing how many there were, she wasn't safe attempting to escape from one of the windows. And there was nowhere in the small cabin that she could hide. She was heaving air in rapid, terrified gasps, adrift in the darkness of her cabin.

If they were coming in, it was most likely they'd come through the door. She moved the two chairs to the same side of the table, then huddled beneath it. If they got in, she'd run out while they were looking through the cabin.

A terrible noise cut into her terror. They were banging on her front door. It was barred by only a foot-long piece of wood that dropped into the handle on the jamb. It wasn't a wide piece of bar that went across the entire opening. Obviously, it had been made to secure the door from the wind, not marauding Indians.

The banging sounded again. The door rattled and jumped. Someone was bludgeoning it with an ax. Oh, God. Aggie watched helplessly from her cover under the table. The wood wouldn't take much more abuse.

And it didn't. After the next blow, it swung open. Aggie shut her eyes, instinctively worried the intensity of her gaze would draw the intruders to her hiding spot. The first one through the door moved quietly on moccasined feet—quietly but not silently to ears straining for the slightest sound. Those feet came straight toward her. The chairs scraped the floor as they were thrust aside. The table over her head was lifted and tossed into the room.

The warrior grabbed her arm and yanked her to her feet. Aggie cried and pleaded, resisting his relentless grip as she drew back against the wall, then fear paralyzed her, freezing her in place. She didn't struggle, didn't fight him. It was futile. She looked toward the door, wondering how many others would come in with him, and was surprised to see he was alone.

The warrior held her pinned to the wall with a hand at her throat. She couldn't see the details of his expression in the dark interior of her cabin. The paint that banded his eyes heightened his devastating effect. She could make out the whites of his eyes and his flashing teeth. She realized he was shouting at her. She couldn't hear much beyond the racket of her own heartbeat thundering in her ears.

He took his knife out of its sheath and held it to her throat. Aggie closed her eyes and prayed her death would be swift.

Chayton looked at the woman he held. Her tears spilled down her face and splashed off his wrist. He could feel her rapid heartbeat and knew her terror, but she didn't fight him, didn't beg and plead. He wondered if Laughs-Like-Water had faced her last moments like this. Or had she fought to protect their children, fought to the bloody, brutal end?

He should kill this woman. Her life for his wife's. That she was in his valley, unguarded, meant she was a gift to him, his to do with as he wished. If he killed her, he might be able to purge the guilt shredding him for being absent when his family most needed him. He touched the flat of his blade to the woman's neck and pressed it upward over her face.

He could feel her body trembling against his. The dark was a kindness—it hid her eyes. If he could see them, he knew they would be blue eyes, eyes that had watched him so boldly, owned by a woman who had stood against the men of her people to defend him that very morning. He'd watched Logan bring her to his valley earlier in the day.

He pressed his knife to her hairline. And hesitated. This woman's death wouldn't be enough. A hundred women. A thousand men. He could kill them all and it wouldn't be enough. If he surrendered to the bloodlust eating his soul, there would just be more dead. And still no Laughs-Like-Water, still no freedom to move in the lands of his people, and still his people would remain locked away in the unsustainable and soul-deadening life of the reservation.

The woman's breath puffed against his face, sweet and hot, pulsing as fast as her heart. He released her and stepped back from her, sheathing his knife. She didn't move. He turned and bumped into the table. He picked it up and threw it against the opposite wall. It bounced off her stove and shattered when he kicked it.

Chayton braced his foot against the door and yanked his ax free, then walked out into the night.

Aggie didn't move from the spot he'd put her in for several long minutes after he left. She knew him. She'd drawn him; he was her Indian from the morning. Had the men not stopped him, would he have attacked her then? Did they know what she hadn't? She'd been mesmerized by the lethal energy that surrounded him, blinded to his perilous nature.

A minute passed. He didn't return. She eased herself away from the wall and pushed the door closed. It hung a little skewed and wouldn't close properly. The latch was gone. Aggie dragged a chair over and propped it against the door. There was no door handle, just the latch and a strap for the latch from the outside. The wood block was in pieces on the floor. The chair wouldn't stop him from coming back and finishing what he tried before, but at least there would be a bit of warning.

Her legs were shaky when she crossed the room. She picked up the quilt from the bed and wrapped it around her shoulders, then lowered herself to the floor at the foot of the bed. If he came back, she'd wiggle beneath it.

And if that happened, she hoped and prayed he'd believe she'd left.

CHAPTER THREE

Chayton sat on his black-and-white paint at the wide break in the sandstone bluff—a ridge that ran in an east-west direction for miles. His valley was on the south side of it, Logan's land on the north side. His friend would be traveling this way to bring him the goods he had traded skins for in town yesterday.

As he waited, Chayton's long-simmering frustration fed on itself, growing ever more virulent. His friend had brought someone to his valley. Not just someone. The white woman from town. The one whose eyes had haunted him through the night, taunting him with both her bravery in town and her terror last night.

After a while, Chayton saw Logan leading a horse packed with goods toward the pass. When he drew even with Chayton, they silently eyed each other. Chayton turned his horse and led him along the path they both knew so well. At the rocky base of a steep climb up a bluff, Chayton dismounted. He never took his mount up that way, which minimized wear of the habitat—something that had worked in his favor the times posses from town had come hunting for him.

"What's on your mind, Chayton?" Logan asked in English as they began unloading the packhorse.

Chayton carried two more loads over to the stack of goods they were making on the ground before he answered in *Lakȟóta*. "You brought a white-eyes to my valley."

Logan studied him. "It's not your valley. It's mine."

Chayton's rage broke free. "This is the land of my people. It has been so since my grandfather's grandfather told the stories of his grandfather's grandfather."

Logan nodded. "An ownership that ended with your generation. I bought the land."

"You cannot buy my land."

"It was no longer your land."

Chayton faced Logan. "Leave. And take the *wašíču* with you."

"I had to buy it when the government opened it up for sale. If I hadn't, someone else would have. They would have taken your horses. They would have hunted you down. I bought it so you would have a haven and your horses could continue to thrive in the Valley of Painted Walls."

"I do not want the woman here. If you will not remove her, I will."

"It is only for a summer. She's an artist. She has

come to paint the landscape. It would be unacceptable if you caused her harm. She'll be gone by the time the leaves fall."

"Or sooner."

"Chayton, she is my guest. I ask you to guard her and help me see to her safety and comfort. She has come up here from Denver. She is not familiar with our country. She has no malicious designs on you, and, in fact, has no weapons."

The two men eyed each other again. "We will see how long she stays."

* * *

Aggie heard a horse outside. She jerked awake. It was light already. She had no idea what time it was; she'd slept little during the night, only shutting her eyes once dawn chased the darkness away. She couldn't risk opening one of the shutters to see who was there—if it was the Indian again, she'd waste the few seconds she had to get hidden. She had lifted the bed skirt and started to crawl under the bed when she heard a man's voice call out.

"Miss Hamilton? Oh, God! Miss Hamilton!" Mr. Taggert burst through the door.

She wiggled back out from under the bed. "I'm here."

Mr. Taggert hurried to her side and crouched down in front of her. "Are you hurt? What happened?"

Aggie was never so glad to see another human

being as she was right then to see Mr. Taggert. She shook her head. "I'm not hurt. Just scared to death. The Indian from town came here last night."

Mr. Taggert lifted her to her feet and gave her a thorough once-over. "Did he hurt you?"

Aggie rubbed her throat. "He pinned me to the wall. I thought he was going to cut my throat or scalp me, but, obviously, he did neither. He broke your table. And the door—"

"Do you want to come up to the house?"

Yes. But if she did, she wouldn't paint. And if she didn't paint, she'd have no income from the sales of her paintings to supplement her small stipend—she might even lose Theo's warehouse. "No. Just tell me, is he crazy? Is he going to do that again? Am I safe here?"

Mr. Taggert released her and walked back to the door. He put his hands on his hips and lowered his head. The fact he didn't immediately answer her question was not comforting. He looked outside, squinting into the morning light. "His name is Chayton. At one time, he had the gentlest soul I'd ever seen in a man. Now, I don't know." He looked over at her. His expression was hidden in the shadow of his hat's brim, but the tension around his mouth was clear. "Let me bring you up to the house. Then I'll go have a talk with Chayton."

Aggie shook her head. "You go have a talk with him. If, afterward, you think I should leave, I will. If you think he's safe, then I want to stay here and keep

27

to the original plan."

Mr. Taggert gave her a hard look, then nodded. "Agreed. I brought you some dairy items for the keeping box. And I've got your horse. I'll bring them in, turn the horse out in the corral, then go see about Chayton."

Aggie drew the edges of the quilt tighter about her shoulders. "What if you can't find him?"

"Don't worry about that. I'll find him."

"Thank you."

* * *

Chayton had been expecting Logan to return after visiting with the blue-eyed *wašíču* woman. He stood beside the rocky slope that led up to the bluff where his cave was. Logan tied his horse by a scrub pine and came straight toward him.

"What the hell's wrong with you?" Logan shouted. "Since when do you make war on women?"

"I did not harm her."

"No? You terrified her. She's my guest, Chayton. I gave her my word she would be safe here. I left her alone because I thought you would help me see to her welfare. Instead, you bust down her door and wave a knife at her." Logan shook his head. "You gotta get your head squared away. You're a guest here, too."

Chayton thought back to their conversation earlier in the morning. "I am not a guest here. The land was sold illegally. How can your chiefs sell something that does not belong to them?"

Logan sighed and sat down on a large boulder. "Chayton, the world is not the same as it was when we met."

"No, it is not. I have no home, no land, and no people. You and the *wašíču* have everything that belonged to my people."

"Chayton, you have people on both sides of your blood." A chill rushed over Chayton's skin at Logan's words, even in the glaring heat of the noon sun. "I've corresponded with your grandmother."

The horror of Logan's revelation made it hard for Chayton to breathe. "Why?"

"When I went to the reservation to trade with you last summer, you weren't there. When I asked around, I learned your grandmother had sent a delegation to retrieve you, but that you hadn't left with them. I thought perhaps you'd gone on your own to see her. I wrote to her hoping to find you."

"It is because of her that I could not stay with my people. The soldier in charge at the Agency believed I was *wašíču* and forced me out. That old woman took what little was left of my life. Why would I go to her?"

"Chayton, you are half white."

"I am *Lakȟóta*. My mother lived and died *Lakȟóta*. She was not *wašíču*."

"Yes. But she was born white, taken on a raid, forced to live among your people."

"She was not forced to do anything. She loved my

father and bore him four children."

Logan shook his head. "You're missing the point. You have choices. Return to the Lakota, live in the white world, or live as a recluse here. The choice is yours, but you cannot scare my guests."

A curious thought entered Chayton's mind. "Is the woman your second wife?"

Logan's eyes widened. "No, she is but a guest. And an artist. I'm hoping she will paint some landscapes that I can buy, both for my house and for my trading posts. Hurting her hurts me."

Chayton crossed his arms and considered Logan's demeanor and request. "I will allow her to stay the summer."

Logan nodded. "Thank you. I'll let her know she'll have no further trouble from you." Logan stood and set a hand on Chayton's shoulder. "Please consider at least meeting your grandmother. She is of an advanced age. It would mean a great deal for her to finally set eyes on her grandson. I watched the hell my father went through when he was searching for my brother. It eats at a person to know your flesh and blood is out there somewhere in the world, alone."

"It would mean nothing to me. My grandparents are dead. My parents are dead. My sister and brothers are dead. My wife and son are dead. I have lost my people. I am dead, too."

"Your daughter lives."

"Yes. And I will continue to provide meat for her until the *Wakȟáŋ Tȟáŋka* brings me to rejoin my family and my people."

"White Bird is thriving in her life with us. Perhaps I will introduce her to her great-grandmother."

Chayton glared at Logan. "You will keep her away from my grandmother."

"When you asked us to foster her, you asked that we teach her to live in the white world. We have done that. And we have helped her remember her Lakota heritage. Such a balance is important. Her great-grandmother is part of her world, an important part that she should not have to miss out on."

Chayton turned to leave. There was no point saying the same thing over. "I have spoken on the matter of my grandmother," he said as he walked away. "You will tell your guest that I will not interfere with her visit to my valley provided she stays to the south of this ridge. I do not want her to near my cave or to go into the Valley of Painted Walls."

"I will make that known to her."

Chayton climbed to the ridge above the cave where he lived. From that vantage point, he could see the wide plains that spread far into the southern horizon. He did not want to think about his last days at the Agency. Yet though he closed his mind to the subject, the memories still seeped out of the tears in his heart.

The sun was like fire. He looked at the crops wilting in the long, straight rows and knew, with an unshakeable certainty, that the earth would not feed his people this winter. It was the middle of the summer and there had been no rain for a cycle of the moon.

31

The women and children gave the crops what water they could, but the ground was endlessly thirsty.

"There he is!" a couple of the soldiers who worked at the Agency pointed him out to a group of white men.

Chayton squared his shoulders as he faced the men.

"You the one they call 'Chayton'?"

"I am."

"Your mother was Lucy Burkholder?"

"No."

"Shit. What was her Indian name?" the man said to one of the others. "Spotted Horse. Spotted Woman."

"My mother was Spotted Horse Woman."

"Thought so. He's the one. Bring him."

Chayton resisted, pushing back at the first man who tried to take hold of his arm. The fight escalated fast, but with so many of them, his hands were quickly and tightly bound. The man holding the other end of the rope was mounted and quickly took off at a trot, forcing Chayton to jog behind his horse. Twice he fell and was dragged for a short distance before he was able to right himself and get back on his feet.

By the time they reached the officers' quarters where the Agency office was located, he was drenched with sweat. The salt seared the scrapes on his chest and arms. A crowd of his people had gathered, following them to the office. It was a terrible thing to see one of their own dragged away. He lifted his chin to show them his courage, hoping it would calm them. If white men were allowed to come onto the reservation and drag him away, whom might they take next? Any of his people could be subjected to that treatment. A woman or an elder would not survive being dragged across the reservation.

He put his back to the crowd to shield them from the bloody mess of his skin. The men pulled his rope and led him into the adobe building. The little room was crowded with white men—soldiers and civilians.

"We found our man," one of the white men announced. "Can you confirm he's the one known as Chayton whose mother was Lucy Burkholder?"

Chayton looked at Captain Blake. He was known among the Lakȟóta as a dishonest man. He took the best of their provisions for himself and his favorite men. Treasured items among Chayton's people often showed up in his possession. Anyone who complained or registered an offense against him was beaten—or worse—disappeared.

Captain Blake reached into his pocket and pulled out a golden locket that had belonged to Chayton's mother. It had been sacred to her, part of her medicine pouch. Chayton had seen it many times. He looked around at the men in the room, beginning to wonder if this wasn't a random act of cruelty but something far more sinister.

The white man took the locket. Opening it, he stared at the tiny images it contained, then at Chayton. He shook his head. "I don't see it. He looks all Indian to me. However, I'll take this locket and him and let Mrs. Burkholder sort it out." The man pulled an envelope out of his pocket and dropped it on the captain's desk. "Your reward. Mrs. Burkholder thanks you."

The men yanked on his rope and started for the door. Chayton dug in his heels. "What is happening?" he asked one of the soldiers who spoke some Lakȟóta.

"In English, Chayton. I know you can speak it."

Chayton made a face. "I will not speak the language of these pig-eaters. What is happening?"

"Your grandmother has been looking for you," the translator said in English so that the others in the room could understand his answer—and the question Chayton had asked. "Be glad someone wants you. She's your ticket out of here."

"My grandmother died many winters ago," Chayton said, continuing in Lakȟóta.

"Not your white grandmother."

"My mother was Lakȟóta. I am Lakȟóta. I am not leaving my people."

The man translated for those in the room. The captain scoffed. "Your people have been given a death sentence. It's only a matter of time before they starve to death. If you stay here, you'll not only watch them die, you'll die with them. Your grandmother is offering you an alternative to such a dire fate."

"You say that as if you cared, but we know you steal our provisions and feed us rotten meat."

The captain looked at the translator. "What did he

34

say?"

"Tell him," Chayton challenged the man.

"He said he's not going."

"I said," Chayton switched to English, "that you steal our provisions and feed us spoiled meat and grains thick with worms."

The captain's eyes narrowed. "Get him out of here." It took three men to pull him out of the office. Even bound, they could not control him. The fight spilled onto the grounds outside. Chayton was handicapped with his hands still tied, but his legs were free. He put up a vicious fight. His people came to his aid. Violence spread into the crowd. Men and women swarmed the white-eyes who'd come for Chayton.

Some men retrieved their horses and attempted to grab Chayton's rope. The crowd grew tighter, closer around him, spooking the horses. They reared up and stomped down, then bucked to clear room. Hooves slashed into the crowd. A mother screamed then started to wail. Others joined her wailing. The horses stepped back and the crowd cleared a little space around the kneeling woman.

Chayton's heart stopped. So many had been injured in the melee that the ground drank their blood. He pushed his way through the crowd, moving to kneel next to a woman crouched in the dirt. The little boy she held hung limp and lifeless in her arms. Chayton stared in horror, barely aware of others also wailing, until the whispers that Two Bears, a revered

Elaine Levine

keeper of history, had also died in the crush.

Chayton's chief came over to him. Setting a hand on his shoulder, Stands With Horse asked what was happening, why had the white men come for Chayton?

"They say my mother's mother has ransomed me and that I must return to my mother's people." Chayton looked around at the weeping people, seeing the shock and horror and fear on their faces. "I am with my mother's people. I am where I belong."

"You are Lakȟóta. *And you will always be* Lakȟóta. *But you are also white. You must go with these men."*

"Never."

"Look at what has happened here, Hawk That Watches. See what has happened today." His chief lifted his hand and showed the destruction. "If your mother's mother is wealthy enough to pay a ransom, she is wealthy enough to send much worse trouble to us. You have to go."

Chayton stared at his chief, uncaring of the tears drawing streaks on his filthy cheeks. "I cannot live without my people."

"And your people will not live if you stay."

Chayton wiped his cheeks. The pain of that memory was as raw today, almost a year since his departure, as it had been the day it happened. He'd left with the white men that day. For four days, he'd traveled with them. On the fifth day, he'd slipped away and returned to the only refuge he knew: the Valley of Painted Walls. He'd hidden there for

36

months, never showing himself to Logan when his friend came looking for him. Logan had seen his pony among the herd and knew he'd come to the valley. It wasn't until the autumn that Chayton had sought Logan out, bringing meat for his daughter and skins to trade for winter supplies.

Logan had been relieved to see him, then. And though their friendship wasn't as it had been before Chayton's world had collapsed, Logan offered Chayton trades for his skins that were heavily skewed in Chayton's favor. Logan had been a true friend, white or not.

Chayton had no choice but to respect his wishes with the white woman now in his valley.

* * *

While waiting restlessly for Mr. Taggert to return, Aggie went out to the small corral to have a look at the horse he'd brought her. He was a handsome sorrel gelding that did not shy away from greeting her. She filled his water trough and gave him some hay, then returned to the house to put it to rights after last night's invasion. She straightened the splintered wood that had spilled across the floor and piled the broken table and its pieces outside the front door. When everything was back in order—as best she could make it—she made herself some breakfast, then took her sketchpad out front and sat on the bench.

The drawings she'd made of Chayton in no way

hinted at the murderous inclination he'd displayed last night. In her sketches, his eyes were bright, illuminating the fevered activity of his mind, full of curiosity, determination, and even anger. It was curious that she'd noted his capacity for violence when she'd first seen him in town, but she had not drawn him that way.

It was early afternoon when Aggie heard riders approach. Tamping down an instinctive flash of anxiety, she went outside to see the Taggerts accompanying a wagon with lumber and a couple of men.

Mrs. Taggert dismounted quickly and hurried to her, wrapping her in a tight hug. Absurdly, Aggie felt a flood of relief. Mrs. Taggert took hold of her arms and leaned back to look at her. "I'm so sorry, Miss Hamilton. I don't know what got into Chayton. I've never known him to behave like that. Life has not been easy for him since his wife was killed." She shook her head. "Were you hurt?"

Mrs. Taggert was slim and seemed so fragile; Aggie didn't want to cause her any undue stress. "He scared me. Terrified me, actually. But he didn't hurt me. He broke your table, though."

"We brought you a replacement table." Mr. Taggert nodded toward his men. "Sam and Wylie are going to rebuild your door. While they do that, I thought Sarah and I could show you around the area and point out geography you might find interesting for your work."

Aggie gave Mr. Taggert's men a nod, then stepped aside so they could bring in her table. "Does this mean that you were able to talk to Chayton?"

"I did. He'll be keeping his distance. I don't expect any more encounters with him. He has given his word and he'll keep it."

Aggie felt strangely let down by that news, but better safe than sorry. Mr. Taggert's friend was fascinating, but also dangerous, rather like a mountain lion or a bear--a fearsome creature best observed from safe distances.

Mr. Taggert saddled her mount, then led the group on a long ride across the changing terrain. The tour took them north to the cliffs and buttes of the sandstone ridge she could see from her cabin, then east to the rolling hills of short grass and wildflowers, through a meandering creek bed to the south, and finally west toward the beautiful Medicine Bow Mountains in the far distance. Every direction provided awe-inspiring vistas. She was itching to get started with her work.

When they returned to the house, a brand-new plank door protected her little cabin, and the workmen had already left. The afternoon was fast approaching evening. Aggie dismounted. Mrs. Taggert gave her a worried look. Aggie smiled at her. "Thank you for the tour. It was good to learn where Chayton lives so I can stay away from that area."

"If you have any concerns at all, we showed you the path up to the ranch—come up at any time," Mrs.

Taggert told her.

"Thank you both. It was nice to have your company today. I'm grateful you were able to resolve the situation with your friend, Mr. Taggert."

"Please, call me Logan." He nodded toward his wife. "And Sarah. We're not formal people."

"I will. And I'm Aggie." She waved to them as they took their leave.

Aggie rode out to the hill by the bluffs early the next morning. She'd decided during the tour that would be the spot where she would start. She tied her horse off with a long lead at a copse of cottonwoods down by the creek, then climbed the long way up the gravelly hill. Standing on top of it, she made a slow circle, absorbing everything she could from her vantage point.

She spread out a blanket, then lifted the art bag over her head and put it aside. She sat on the blanket and closed her eyes, letting herself connect with the land, opening her mind to the stories it might tell. Those whispers of a place's story would bring a majesty to her work. She laid back, covered her face with her straw Plainsman hat, and listened to the ground. She went still, tuning herself in to the earth beneath her. Its life force, in that spot, was thousands of times slower than her own. In the time the earth took to inhale, she'd taken dozens of breaths. When she'd calmed her breathing, slowed her beating heart, and opened herself to the earth, she could hear what it wanted to tell her. The stories it told of the lives that had been on this hill, under the sun, in the wind, weathering the snow and rain.

After a while, she sat up and reached for her sketchpad. She drew the landscapes in each of the four directions. She sketched the grass, details of the ground between the clumps of grass, sagebrush, yucca plants, tiny but vibrant wildflowers—all the elements that would form the texture and content of her paintings.

What she didn't have yet was the mood for the pieces. Early afternoon was the worst time to study a place. So much sunlight might be good for photographs, but the glaring light didn't work for oils. The best time to see a place was during the softer light of late afternoon to sunset, predawn to midmorning, or anytime a storm was in the air.

Now that she'd identified the location where her work would begin, she would do a few pencil studies in preparation for getting the work on canvas. She made a plan to be here before dawn and in the evening for the next few days to see what the sky told her about this beautiful land.

Chayton crouched in the recesses above the hill where the white woman sat. Weaponless, she was defenseless as a babe in a cradleboard. She wore a wide, flat-brimmed straw hat that obscured her features from his inspection, but he remembered those eyes. Blue, like flax. Her hair was a mixture of tones, brown and red and some lighter strands—blending like the colors of wet river stones. It was straight, like his. Today, she had it in a wide braid that fell halfway down her back. She wore a white shirt that buttoned in the front, decorated with strips of lacework his wife would have thought beautiful. The woman's shirt was tucked into the waist of her simple brown skirt. She wore ugly black boots and stockings.

She didn't seem aware of her surroundings, except through her frequent, mindless stares. Perhaps she wasn't right in the head. Maybe that was why Logan was so protective of her. But if that were the case, why were none of her people with her? He watched her just sitting there. Sometimes she would bend her head to one side, holding still for so long, he wondered where she'd gone in her head. She wasn't asleep, but she wasn't awake. Logan had mentioned she was an artist, but not that she was deranged. After a while, she put her hat back on, took a pad of paper from her satchel, and started to scribble on it.

He watched her for the entire time she sat on his hill. Hours after she arrived, she returned to her waiting mount. The horse caught his scent and whickered, shifting to look up at him, but she ignored his warning.

Foolish, foolish woman.

CHAPTER FOUR

The site Aggie had selected to start her work was an hour's ride from the cabin. In order to get there before the early spring sunrise, she had to leave her cabin at 3:00 a.m., which she did for an entire week, driven more by instinct than time, as she had no watch. Some days, she sat on her hill in the wee morning hours and watched the light move over her vista, catching the nuances of blue and yellow, shadow and sun, watching as the light told its story.

On those days, she would return to her cabin late morning to do chores and to sleep through the insipid light of the afternoon. In the late afternoon, she repeated the journey, watching the harsh afternoon light soften to pink and salmon and lavender, seeing the mood of her vista change until the shadows swallowed it.

Then one day, as she knew would happen, she didn't make the trip at all. It was time to paint.

She stretched a canvas and set it up on one of her

largest easels, then spent the night filling it with the images she'd stored away on her sketchpad and in her mind, working through the night by the weak light of her three lanterns.

* * *

For days, the blue-eyed white woman didn't leave her cabin, except for brief visits to the little hut Logan called an outhouse and for stops to see to her horse in the corral. Was she ill? Chayton waited in the shadows of the cabin grounds, watching as the long spring evening faded into the night. Prior to this new behavior, she would go to sleep when darkness fell. But once again tonight, light glowed inside her cabin. It never went out.

He walked around the house and came to the front door, which was open. Looking inside, he saw the woman standing before a white board, painting. The smell in her cabin was heavy and astringent. He stood at her threshold for several long minutes. After their first encounter, he'd kept himself out of her sight, though she'd rarely been out of his.

He was uncertain how she would react to him, given his last visit. Very slowly, he moved out of the shadows and took a cautious step inside her cabin, uninvited. She did not look at him. He stood unmoving, waiting for her to acknowledge him. If she screamed or startled in any way, he'd make a quick exit. Still she didn't look at him. He moved to stand more directly in front of her. She had only to look up from her board to see him.

She did not. He moved slowly closer to her, ever ready to run for the door, drawn toward her as if an invisible cord tightened between them.

With only the meager light from the lanterns, her hair looked dull and brown, nothing like it did in the sunshine. It was so fine it escaped from her braid. Her face was pale, dusted with faint little spots over her nose and cheeks. Her lashes were long and dark. Her brows arched over her eyes like narrow wings. Her mouth was soft looking, rounded. Her neck was slim, as were her shoulders. Her breasts made slight mounds in her shirt.

She was humming, the sound haunting in the enclosed space where she lived. Some paintings were set about the room. He walked over to them. The hairs lifted on his neck as he saw on the boards scenes from his hill—the mountains to the west, the ragged line of cottonwoods to the south, the wide, green prairie to the east. Each scene was captured on its little board in a perfect miniature of the actual space, as if she'd caught the land in her hand and set it free on this little surface.

A breeze crept inside and stirred the heavy smells in the room. Chayton wrinkled his nose, then followed the scents to the table beside the woman. A couple of thin pieces of wood stuck out of a glass jar. He bent and sniffed them—and found the source of the piney scent that was so astringent. Several small metal tubes were scattered about the table. He picked one up and sniffed it. It was squishy. He squeezed it, feeling the give in the tube as color coiled out from the opening. Chayton pinched the dark blue thread of color, then spread it between his fingers and sniffed it. This was the other heavy smell, thick like an oil of some type. He wiped his fingers on his sleeve. Deciding he liked the color, he pinched off another bit and swiped it on his other sleeve.

Still the woman took no notice of him. He stepped behind her to observe her work. Half of her white surface was covered with a black sketch of a scene, the other half was coming alive with the pigments she applied to the board. She was a being possessed by a spirit, creating.

He moved to stand beside her. How could she not know he was in her cabin, touching her things? And then it happened—she looked up at him. He held still, bracing himself for the chaos that was sure to break loose when panic hit her.

It didn't. She looked him over from head to foot, then reached out to touch him. Her hand moved like that of a blind person, over his chest, his necklaces, and the decorations on his tunic. Her fingers lifted to his neck, over his choker, to the bare skin at his throat. She stared at his neck, at the way her fingers touched him. Once again, the skin between his scalp and back tightened.

The woman was not quite right. Her body was there in the room with him, but her mind was not. No sane woman would touch a warrior who was not of her family.

Her fingers lifted to touch his jaw, his cheek. She looked up at his face, his eyes. He was breathing heavily, shocked how good it felt to be touched by someone. A woman. A person not seeking to hurt him, someone who didn't fear or condemn him. Her eyes were the blue he remembered, but darker in the dimness of her cabin. Her expression was soft. He realized then she wasn't seeing him; she was seeing something else. She was with him in this room...and she wasn't.

Suddenly, he knew what was going on; he'd interrupted this woman in the middle of a vision. A terrible transgression. He backed away fast, out of her reach, out of her cabin. Pinning himself flush against the wood siding beside her door, he waited for something to happen—the earth to shake or the skies to rage and smite him. He wasn't sure what he'd witnessed, but it was unlike anything he'd ever experienced.

The woman was an Other. A *white* woman was an Other. No wonder Logan was so protective of her. He closed his eyes, regretting his desire to kill her that first night.

Chayton hid where he could watch the cabin unobserved. The blue-eyed Other worked until the light of dawn. When she left the cabin to go to the outhouse, he went into her cabin. He poured water into a tin cup, then left two pieces of jerky next to the cup on her workbench. He went around the side of the house, watching as she fed and watered her horse, then returned to her cabin to stand before her painting.

Reaching for her brush, she found the jerky. She bit into a piece. He was relieved when she sipped from the tin cup before resuming her work. He wasn't certain whether her visions worked in the way his did, fueled by a lack of sleep and the deprivation of food. But she was such a slight woman, he didn't know how she could survive the multi-day span of a vision unfed or unwatered.

He did not want to care for a woman, or a *wašíču*, but Others were sacred. For some unknown reason, the *Wakȟáŋ Tȟáŋka* had selected this woman, and being a warrior, he could not dishonor that choice. He sighed, knowing he would protect the female as she answered *Wakȟáŋ Tȟáŋka's* bidding, even if it meant doing women's work like cooking and serving her food and seeing to her horse.

When she showed no signs of stopping her work, he left to set up a rabbit snare so he could make a rich soup to nourish her for her journey that evening. Once the snare was set, he tended to her horse and his, grooming them, exercising them, testing the level of training her horse had received. He was a large quarter horse, in fine health. Chayton smiled as he thought how proud his people would have been had he gained such a fine animal in a raid.

That thought, as with all like it, was immediately

followed by the knowledge that he no longer had a people. He had nothing. No one.

Not even this valley.

* * *

The marathon didn't stop for days. The cabin's air was rich with the heavy scent of linseed oil and oil paints, cut with the sweet, astringent scent of turpentine, even with a cross breeze from the open windows. When Aggie grew fatigued, all she needed to do was fill her lungs with the fragrance of her work, and she'd be right back in a place in her mind where the truth of her work lived. Sometimes, she propped herself up on a chair. When she remembered, she ate a bit of jerky or raisins. Twice she refilled her water bucket, but after that she wasn't aware of being thirsty and didn't seek out water.

On the morning of the fourth day, Aggie became aware of several things simultaneously. Her shoulder hurt. She was lying on her side on the hard cabin floor. The door was open and a cool breeze swept across the floor, tickling her hair. Her foot was hooked in the rungs of her stool, which lay on its side at her feet. There was a cup of water next to her face, upright and within reach.

And a man crouched in the doorway, watching her. She looked at him again. Not just any man—he was the renegade Indian who'd frightened her so terribly her first night. She blinked, holding her eyes shut for a long interval, hoping he would be gone when she opened them. She wasn't strong enough to fight him off. He was still there when she opened her eyes, regarding her with a steady, unblinking gaze.

He couldn't be there. He was too violent to be there. She couldn't make out his features, backlit as he was by the bright morning light outside her cabin. He wore fringed leathers. His hair was braided and wrapped in wide leather strips that hung in front of his shoulders.

She shook herself, certain he was a lingering part of her strange reverie. She'd dreamed of him while she worked, touched his body, his face. She needed to wake up and rejoin the world. She pushed herself up into a sitting position and braced herself while her mind righted itself. She'd been painting for days on end.

Canvases of varying sizes were propped on every surface, drying. She looked to her left to see if she'd managed to set her palette down before collapsing. It rested on the table next to the easel she'd been working on. Good. At least she hadn't wasted the paint on it. She sent a quick glance to the door and was relieved to see no one there. Tired and distraught from her extended period of hyper-creativity, she'd imagined the Indian then. She was always emotional coming out of these episodes.

She remembered the first time she'd succumbed to one of these extremely intense working sessions. Theo had been away visiting a client, delivering his latest commissioned piece. Aggie had spent years spying on him every time he'd been at work, memorizing his methodology; the original sketch he'd done for the piece, the way he transferred the sketch to the stretched canvas, the way he painted the background before the foreground, the color selections he used, even the arrangement of colors on his palette.

While he was gone, she'd found an unused canvas that was much smaller than the one he'd used. She'd recreated his entire work, a quarter of the size of his original. Then, as with her latest bout of painting, she'd worked until she was unconscious. She'd always been so careful not to disturb Theo while he was working, and when he wasn't working, he had very little interest in making conversation with the little waif he'd brought home from the orphanage.

She hadn't regretted leaving the orphanage for Theo's studio. The work he did was fascinating. And he'd been very grateful for the food she cooked and the way she kept his living space neat. She'd watched the way he lost himself in his work, his concentration unshakeable. She'd learned early on stews and soups were the best foods to feed him because she could keep them warm until he was ready for breaks during his work.

When he came home that day and found her collapsed on the floor, a replica of his work on her easel and his paints opened and spread about, well, she'd been terrified how he would react. She was only sixteen. If he put her out on the street, she'd have nowhere to go. He'd stared at her much as the Indian had just done as he squatted by her door, as if she were a different kind of animal. Not a human. She'd felt ill that morning.

Theo had walked to the palette tray that was flipped upside down, its expensive paints spread against the floor, wasted. He picked it up and set it back on the table. She'd started crying silently. How very badly did she want to stay with him and learn from him, though she knew he'd never take on an apprentice—especially not a female student. He scraped the mess off the floor and tossed it in a waste bin. Then he took hold of her arms and lifted her to her feet.

"Follow me," he'd ordered. He pointed out several different areas on the floor where oil paints had smeared into the rough wood planks of the studio floor. "See this? And this? I speak from experience when I say it is much better if you put the palette down before sleeping."

"I'm sorry…"

He glared at her, fervent emotion slicing across his usually stoic demeanor. "Never apologize for your art. We'll begin your lessons tomorrow. Clean up in here before you leave."

For the next several years, she'd spent long hours practicing his techniques, learning about color selection and creation, composition—everything he'd taken a lifetime to learn. He'd brought in his artist friends to teach her their techniques. And then, in the last few years of his life, she'd increasingly had to help him with his commissioned pieces as his arthritis had grown severe, twisting his hands into painful knots. The disease was insidious, stealing his ability to create art, which for him was like a slow suffocation. They'd moved west, hoping the drier air would ease his symptoms, as so many people reported it had for their ailments. She and Theo were not so fortunate.

The night before he died, he showed her his will, listing her as his sole heir. He left her everything, including the new Denver warehouse where they lived. He'd told her now that she knew how to paint, it was time she went out to find the stories she wanted to create. He'd told her that he'd made his way in the world painting the stories others commissioned, but he wished she would find the stories *she* wanted to paint. He said they'd come from the soul and would be so very much more powerful than the work he did.

They'd argued that point. She'd always been a fan of his work. It was important to give a voice to those who couldn't create. Yes, his work had been commissioned, but it was all very important. It was their last argument.

God, she missed him, she thought as she looked her palette; she'd remembered to set it down. She smiled, feeling weepy again. The tips of her fingers were sticky, the oils still tacky. She sighed in disgust.

Remembering the dream of her deadly visitor, she flashed a glance toward the empty doorway, feeling a strange mixture of relief and loss that she'd only imagined him. She reached for the tin cup sitting in front of her and emptied it. She pushed herself to her feet, then went to clean the paint off her hands with a little rag dipped in turpentine. She was slowly returning to the real world. How long had she been lost in her creative bubble? Theo had shown her how to stave off those artistic seizures by giving herself time with her art every day. In the busy weeks since his passing, she'd not been able to do that, so she wasn't surprised she'd succumbed as she had.

Outside, she drew deep breaths of fresh air as she checked on her horse. She remembered feeding and watering him twice, but wasn't sure how long it had been since she'd last seen to him. He was munching on a fresh pile of hay. His water trough was full. She frowned as she looked into the corral, trying to remember if she'd been out earlier in the day.

Aggie sighed. Looking down at herself, she realized she was in the same clothes she'd been in for several days. Her painting apron, a heavy canvas smock, was covered with fresh stains on top of the old. At least she'd had the sense to put it on before she went under. It was time to clean up, take stock of her work—see if any of it was usable. Sometimes, the early pieces on a project weren't. They ended up being mere studies of a subject. She reminded herself not to judge them too harshly—even her studies sometimes brought a fair price. She needed a volume of work to select from if she hoped to get into a show at the end of the summer.

She fetched the water buckets from the house and filled them at the pump. She moved the small paintings from the dry sink and the larger one from the stove so she could heat water for a bath. The paint was still curing, so she couldn't stack the canvases against each other. She'd painted four works. Not a bad start. While the water was heating, she dug out the toolbox she'd brought with her. Taking out a hammer and a box of nails, she picked places along two bare walls where she could hang the paintings to dry.

She dragged the big tin tub into the center of the room, then poured several buckets of well water into it while she waited for the water on the stove to boil. She drew the shutters closed on the windows and locked the door, then lit a couple of kerosene lamps. She stripped down to her underclothes and poured several pots of hot water into the tub. She put more water on to heat, then gathered a towel and bar of soap, dropped her chemise and drawers to the floor, and slipped into the tub. Most days she only sponge-bathed, so dipping her entire body into a full bath was luxurious and decadent.

She leaned back against the edge of the tub and looked up at her four paintings. There were several different ways to examine art. One was to gauge its emotional impact; how does it make one feel? What was the mood of the lighting in the work? What was the message or story the work wants to tell? Another was to look at it critically from a stylistic standpoint. Did the work adhere to the conventions of its genre?

Was the subject accurately represented within that genre's technique? Were the colors right? Was the texture, the depth, the content right?

Aggie closed her eyes and cleared her mind, mentally selecting the filter she would use to see the paintings. Light. How was her use of light? The room was dim, shuttered as it was to the morning light. She got out of the tub and moved the table under the paintings against the wall, then rearranged two lamps on it to illuminate the work. She added a third lamp, then stepped back into the tub and studied the paintings.

She'd done two of the western vista she'd selected, with the distant mountains as seen from her hill. One captured the area at sunrise, the other at sunset. She'd done another large work of the southern vista, looking at the sagebrush and creek bed. The fourth, a smaller canvas, was of the eastern view, the grasses and endless sky as lit by the setting sun behind her on the hill. These four works were done in a realistic style, almost photographic in their accuracy. But unlike photographs, whose content spoke only through shades of gray and sepia tones, these works showed a slice of the infinite range of colors painted across the sky and the earth. They did a good job of using the light at their particular times of day.

Aggie took up the soap and washcloth, switching her focus from the paintings to giving herself a thorough cleaning. She rinsed off, then shut her eyes as she selected another filter to examine her paintings through. Had she selected the right composition—the correct content and angle for the story she wanted the paintings to portray?

The water was rapidly cooling. She got out of the tub and fetched a pot of newly heated water and poured it into the tub, then stepped back in and faced the paintings with her eyes closed. Sitting up, she opened her eyes, looking at each work in turn. Of the four, the only one she liked the content of was the smaller, eastern-facing work. The others needed something in the foreground that would anchor the great distance represented by the space between the viewer's perspective and the horizon. She tilted her head, considering whether something could be added to the works to fix the deficiency. She'd take a ride out there later today to see what options she might have. Maybe a close-up of sagebrush.

She leaned back, sinking under the water to wash her hair. She let the water close in over her face. Holding her breath, she listened to the sound the water made in the tub as she moved around, clearing her mind for another look at her work, relaxing for a few seconds until a thought slammed into her mind.

The Indian!

She hadn't been alone this morning, hadn't dreamed or imagined his presence. He'd been there, watching her. And he'd given her water. She sat up, splashing water out of the bath. The door was still barred, the window shutters still closed. She was alone now, but she hadn't been this morning. She looked over at the tin cup sitting on the table. It had been on the floor when she woke, next to her. She remembered lying down on the floor by her easel. She hadn't fetched any water before giving in to the exhaustion weighing her down. Her door had been closed then. When she woke, he was there, hunched down, staring at her.

A chill swept down her damp skin. She'd narrowly escaped a disastrous outcome by awakening when she had.

CHAPTER FIVE

When she went out to the hill the next morning, the air was already hot. Aggie settled her horse in the shade from the cottonwoods along the creek bed below her hill. The Plainsman she wore kept the blazing sun off her face and neck. She took her art bag and blanket up the hill. She was looking for some natural elements to add to her landscapes and wanted to do a study of some of the vegetation.

There were two clumps of mature bushes. Sage and rabbitbrush. The rabbitbrush had the silver-gray leaves of the sage, but in a different pattern. Both were on a draw that went up her hill. She went to it, kneeling in front of the rabbitbrush to get a perspective of the plant in the foreground and the rolling prairie in the background.

Looking down at the bush from above, she realized she was still too high up for the right perspective. She went down on all fours. Her eyes shifted focus from a close inspection of the rabbitbrush to a wider view of the distant ground. She turned her head this way and that, changing her height, looking at the details around the bush.

Something beneath her hand moved, drawing her attention back to the plant. She held still, fearing she'd knelt on a snake. Seeing no reptile beneath her, she wondered what she'd felt move. She pushed a bit of dirt aside and realized her hand was on a pair of big, brown hands.

Aggie shrieked and fell back on her bottom as a man separated himself from the landscape. The renegade Indian. He rose to his knees, covered in dust from the top of his head to his lean, bare chest. A stripe of burnt umber crossed from temple to temple, covering his eyes and brows. Another reddish stripe covered his mouth and went from cheek to cheek.

She stared at the man before her. He looked like someone who might eat children. For dessert. When he was already full. Just for the meanness of it.

Steeling herself to face the frightening warrior, Aggie pushed to her knees. Only a few feet separated them. Had he not moved earlier, she would never have seen him, even with her hands right on top of his. How often had he been there when she went to her hill? Had he seen her studying the rabbitbrush? She blushed at the thought, realizing how ridiculous she must have appeared.

"Hello," she whispered, praying he was more the man Sarah and Logan thought him to be than the devil he'd shown to her. He stared at her, giving no indication he'd heard her, then barked a shrill call, baring bright, white teeth in his savagely painted face.

Aggie jumped, then scrabbled back as fast as she could, which was neither fast nor far because of her cursed skirts and the rabbitbrush around them. A low thundering began. She thought it was her pounding heart at first, but a horse came out from behind a copse of trees down by the creek, running at full speed toward them. She feared she might get trampled until Chayton, naked except for his breechcloth, ran down the hill toward the east and away from her. The horse turned to follow him, slowing slightly as it came even with the renegade. The man increased his speed and reached up to grab a fistful of mane, then vaulted onto the horse's back, lying low atop its bare back as the horse sped away.

Aggie watched him ride off into the far distance, then closed her eyes, locking everything she'd just seen away in her mind, keeping it fresh, like an unopened picture book. After a few minutes, when she'd sorted and cataloged every color, texture, and nuance, she made her way down to her horse and returned home. As soon as she got the horse settled, she sat outside on the bench by her front door and sketched out several scenes. All of them had the Indian hidden in them, hidden in plain sight, only there if the viewer had the eyes to see him.

She set the sketchpad aside but couldn't tear her gaze from what she'd drawn. Perhaps he wasn't real. Perhaps he was a spirit man, a ghost of the people for whom this land had been home. She'd asked for that, hadn't she? She'd opened herself to hear the story the land wished to tell. Perhaps the land had given her more than its wind and its colors and its heart. Perhaps it had given her a teacher who could show her the people who'd lived where she now lived.

The Indian was her answer.

One of the many things she'd learned from Theo was that an artist must choose what a piece of art would say. A painter couldn't tell every story in a single work of art, but he or she could tell one story. Some artists told the story of light, others the story of darkness and shadows. Some told the story of motion. Some painted the seasons.

In this collection, she would tell the story of Chayton.

She knew now what she needed to do to fix the first four paintings she'd done--knew exactly what they were lacking.

She refilled the water in the house, then took a piece of jerky for herself as she got things set up inside for another painting session, hopefully one that let her stay coherent while she worked. What she needed to do was merely fine-tune the work she'd already done. And add her spirit man. He would be in every work she did here. Only those who knew to look for him would find him. Perhaps only those who were permitted to see him would.

It was the wee hours of the morning before she'd finished the alterations to her paintings. She forced herself to lie down for a few hours. In the morning, she would head back to her hill and seek out her warrior.

* * *

She searched for him for three days without any success. Had she spooked him? Perhaps he'd left her valley. Perhaps Logan had ordered him to keep his distance, and that was why finding him was so difficult. Resigned to the fact that she might never see him again, she returned to her cabin to paint him as he'd been the day he'd hidden in the draw. She stretched a four-foot canvas for this work. She sketched out where the silvery-leafed rabbitbrush would go, the Medicine Bow Mountains in the far distance, and her phantom warrior standing over her.

She spent days with that painting alone. The man in it seemed so real. She surprised herself with how much of him she remembered. His dark, unsmiling eyes spoke to her from the depths of the canvas. It was as if he were real, there with her. Sometimes she would even look over her shoulder, expecting to see him. She felt a quickening inside of her, a warm, melting sensation she'd never felt before. She knew nothing about the man she painted, but her imagination filled in all the blanks. She wished she'd been able to find him. His absence preyed on her mind—almost as if she missed him, which made no sense at all to her.

When she finished with that work, she hung it on the wall, rearranging the other works so the warrior's painting had a central place of honor. She looked at it throughout the day, in the drifting light of the sun, studying and analyzing it, deciding it was one of the best pieces she'd ever done.

Chayton stood on the rocky slope of her hill, his face painted, his hair braided and wrapped, all of him covered in the dust he'd hidden himself beneath. He wore only a fringed breechcloth and the necklaces she'd seen him wear the morning she woke after her painting marathon. He was proud. Regal. A warrior left over from another time.

* * *

A knock at the door startled her the next morning. "Mornin', Aggie," Logan greeted her.

"Good morning to you! Won't you come in?" She set the dishes back in the washbasin and dried her hands.

Logan lifted his hat off as he stepped inside. "I was heading in to town and thought I'd stop to see if you needed anything." She saw him sniff the air and knew he smelled the heavy oils and turpentine. He looked at the paintings hanging on the walls.

"You've been busy." He pointed to the landscapes with the hand holding his hat. "I know that hill." He frowned as he looked at her work, moving in to examine more closely. "You've seen Chayton. Is he bothering you?" he glanced back at her.

"No."

Logan stared at the paintings with her hidden warrior. "You're a hell of an artist, Aggie." He looked around at the cabin's small room. The latest painting featuring Chayton was on an easel with its back to the room. He walked around it, then stopped and stared as if struck by it. She swallowed nervously, but held her silence. He, of anyone who would see that work, knew Chayton best. He would see its shortcomings as even she couldn't. Long minutes passed. Finally, he began absently slapping his hat against his leg, giving the tight confines of the cabin a critical glance.

"You're going to run out of space here fairly quickly." He frowned. "Do you have enough light in here?"

"Everything is fine here. I'll make it work."

"For now, perhaps." He nodded. "Sarah wanted me to ask you to come up to the ranch for Sunday dinner."

The invitation took her off guard. She clasped her hands together. "I don't want to seem ungrateful, but I don't have time to take a day off. I haven't a calendar or a watch. I don't know what day of the week it is or what time it is. And to tell the truth, when I get working, I lose all sense of anything. I wouldn't like to make a commitment I can't keep."

Logan nodded, then sent another look around the place. "I think it's too dark in here." He walked outside, moving to the corner of the house. "I have a big tent I'm not using this summer. If you like, I could send some men down to set it up in that field. You could put up several easels in there."

"Is it sturdy?"

"It is. Fully wind-tested. It was used as a church in Cheyenne when they were building the railroad. I traded for it several years ago so I could have a tent to set up a shop in when I do a show at different fairs and rodeos."

"Well, then, yes. I think that might be very helpful. Thank you for offering it."

Logan ran a hand through his hair, then set his hat on his head. "May I ask you something? I don't mean to pry, but I'm curious. Why the feverish rush to produce work? It isn't as if you have a time limit on the use of this cabin."

"No, but I do need to earn a living. I find only about twenty percent of my work is show-worthy. I need to complete enough of my best work to support an exhibit on my own, otherwise I will have to share the space." She looked at him levelly. It was the truth, just not the whole truth. The chances of her landing an exhibit, shared or otherwise, were pretty slim. She had to produce her very best work. Period.

She'd been able to find only one gallery willing to consider showing her work, an offer that came loaded with caveats for volume, quality, and timing—even though the gallery owners were Theo's long-time friends, the very people who'd enticed Theo to move from the East Coast to Denver. As far as the art world was concerned, she was an unknown. None of the most powerful art collectors even knew Theo had taken on a student, much less that she'd spent the last years of his life handling his remaining commissioned works.

She desperately wanted to do more pieces featuring Chayton, but she'd been unable to locate him. She mentioned it now to Logan, hoping he might tell her where to find his friend. "I ran into Chayton the other day and haven't seen him since. I'm afraid he's moved away."

Logan smiled. "He's not gone. He's not going anywhere while his daughter is still here."

So it was his daughter they were fostering. She'd wondered about that. Aggie sat on the bench in front of her house, wrestling with an inner debate over asking something that was none of her business. "It's my turn to appease my curiosity. Of course, you don't have to answer, but why is White Bird with you and not him?" As soon as she asked the question, she wished she hadn't. She shook her head. "I'm sorry. It's none of my business."

"It's okay. I don't think many white people understand what's happening with Indian children. They're taken away to a boarding school at a very young age. Five or six years old. They often don't see their parents or families again for years. Chayton asked that we raise her instead, teach her to live in the white world, as the schools would. He knew we wouldn't erase her ties to her culture or language—

67

and we would love her as our own."

Aggie's shoulders slumped as she considered how great Chayton's sacrifice was. "I hope he at least gets to see her often?"

Logan shook his head. "He doesn't interact with her at all and very little with me. He provides a deer or elk or some other large game every few months. We trade hides for supplies whenever he needs anything."

"Where does he live, exactly?" Logan had shown her the general area, by the bluffs. But she needed directions so she could make a visit to him.

He frowned. "You're full of questions."

She nodded. "I'm hoping he might sit for me."

"Good luck with that." He shook his head. "He's like the wind: often there, but never seen." He looked off to the west. "It's best to keep with the landscapes if you wish to make your quota. He's too elusive for you to chase, and the terrain can be dangerous. Besides, he prefers to be left alone." He went toward his wagon and climbed up to the bench seat. "The offer for supper stands. Come up to the ranch anytime, whenever it fits with your schedule or you want a break from work. Sarah would be very happy to see you." He waved to her, then continued down the road.

Two days later, Aggie walked through the tent Logan had sent down. It had probably held twenty or so parishioners when it served as a church in Cheyenne. His men had also brought tools and lumber to build her additional easels and rig up racks for her to hang her finished work. They were screen-like wooden stands and would support several pieces on either side of each panel. This was almost as useful as Theo's big warehouse.

Intent on finishing the study she was doing of the sage and rabbitbrush, Aggie rode out to her hill. She had pastel chalks with her so she could capture the colors and light as they defined the scrubby bushes. She spread a blanket on the ground, then sat down next to a thick bush. Crossing her legs, she settled in for a short sprint.

She drew a detailed sketch of a leaf, a single branch, several branches together, and then the whole bush. As usual, she wasn't aware of time passing. When she finished the study of the rabbitbrush, something slipped into her consciousness. She held still, wondering what it could have been. There was no sound, no scent, but something was behind her. A chill wrapped around Aggie's spine. She slowly twisted around to see who or what was there.

Chayton stood beside the creek bed, near her horse. He was tall, she realized—something she hadn't noticed before. She waved to him, then turned back to the sketch she was working on. She wasn't going to let him know that anything about him frightened her, though in truth, her hands shook too much to continue working.

A minute passed. Then two. She itched to turn around and see if he was still down there, but then there was a sound behind her. He'd crossed from the grassy area near the horses to the gravelly slope of the hill. She had no doubt that he could move without a sound, so the fact that he didn't hide his footsteps seemed a kindness. Still, she did not turn around. Her breathing grew more rapid as he approached, closer with each step.

Though of course Chayton was only a man, Aggie felt as vulnerable as if a mountain lion was approaching. Her hands tightened on her sketchpad. Her gaze slowly focused on the image she'd been sketching. It was of him, a charcoal drawing of his face. Good heavens, but his eyes looked sad. And when had she switched from a sampling of the vegetation to drawing him? Oh God, and now it was too late to flip the page. He was standing right behind her. The hairs lifted along her neck. She held still, but he didn't. He stepped around her, walking slowly, quietly now.

She watched his leather-clad legs as he moved in front of her. Her dratted eyes cataloging the light on his leggings, the stains, the wear, the fringe that was present and the places it was missing. He wore moccasins that conformed to his feet, the leather simple and unadorned. When he didn't move, she lifted her gaze, moving up his body. His leggings attached to the thong about his hips that held his breechcloth. He wore a leather vest that was open over his chest. In front of the vest was a bone breastplate with a leather strap in the middle that was beaded in vibrant colors of blue, white, red, brown, and orange, colors that matched his elaborate wrist cuffs. He wore several necklaces, the uppermost of which was a wide choker of long bone beads. A beaded strap around his chest supported his quiver of arrows. His black hair was loose, except for a long beaded braid on the right side of his head. Eagle feathers dangled from the back of his hair, another toward the top of his head.

His cheekbones were high, his dark eyes judging her. His face paint was different today. He wore only two vertical stripes of black from his temple to his chin, over his eyes. His black gaze was on her, his expression utterly closed to her. And yet some things could never be hidden from the eyes of an artist trained to see the stories that no words could ever communicate. What she saw in his eyes was startling.

He was as afraid of her as she was of him.

Why, why she ached for him, she'd likely never know. But her eyes filled with tears, making his image waver in front of her. She made no attempt to hide the moisture that spilled over her eyes and trailed slowly down her cheeks. It didn't matter anyway. She'd likely never speak to the renegade.

He looked at the markings she was sketching. She looked at him, studying him. He wore a brightly beaded, fringed sheath that housed a wide, long knife. Several pouches hung from his waist, others from his neck. His shoulders were broad, with lean, supple muscles in his arms. His waist was narrow. His hands and lower arms were heavily veined. His skin was a sun-kissed bronze.

She made a facile calculation of the pigments and tones she would need to paint his skin as it was now in the bright orange afternoon light. She bent her head to the right and shifted her weight so that she could see how the shadows touched his body.

When she lifted her gaze, he was watching her. She returned his gaze, listening with her eyes to the sound of his soul. When she could no longer bear the pain she felt from him, she blinked. He looked away, staring into the far eastern horizon. She wondered what he saw there, perhaps across not just distance, but time.

Her mind captured that image of him. She closed her eyes, seeing how he would look on a canvas, feeling what visitors to the gallery would experience when they viewed the painting of him. When she opened her eyes again, he was gone. She set to work, sketching out exactly what she wanted to show in an oil work.

It was late evening when she returned home. She set about her chores—cleaning the horse corral and feeding the horse, making dinner. She ate, bathed, then tried to sleep, but every time she closed her eyes, she saw Chayton, standing on the hill in front of her. Deciding sleep was too elusive; she pulled her painting smock on over her nightgown and walked barefooted to her painting tent.

She rolled out a four-foot length of white canvas, then walked to the end of the table to look at it in perspective, seeing her subject in the raw fabric. She considered doing a close-up of Chayton's face, then thought how he would look full-bodied in the four-foot work. She wanted this piece to impart Chayton's essence, the spirit of his people—his capacity for terrible violence, his preference for peace, and his sorrow, as aching and hollow as the wind.

She pushed the roll of canvas longer, longer even than the six-foot table. She had to pull the second table over to support the overflow. She cut the canvas at eight feet—only because her longest stretchers were seven feet long.

This would be a work that impacted its viewer as soon as he entered a room, one the viewer could never forgot. It would assault the viewer with the truth of his own soul, the cost of his own choices, the emptiness of his own losses, and the bitterness of dreams he would never fulfill.

She would paint Chayton, but he was a mirror to all humanity.

The work continued for a week in long days, interrupted only by occasional breaks for food or sleep or chores. The canvas was too large for any of her easels. She had to rig up a support structure for it with chairs from the house and the framing of the art stands that Logan's men had made. She painted the top half while standing on a table in front of the piece.

At last, when it was finished, she cleaned her brushes and moved everything out of the way so that she only saw Chayton's portrait. She'd captured him perfectly: the pride in his stance, his athletic build, his facial structure, his complicated adornment, his fringed leather clothes. He stood on the steep slope of her hill, the rocky ground his backdrop. The work was as precise as a photograph and as eloquent as a stage drama. She hadn't manipulated anything about it. Not the colors of the earth or the sky, not any of his features. The piece was just truth. His truth. His story. The absence of herself—as a woman, and especially as a white human—in the work let her art say what thousands of voices couldn't.

Life hurts.

God, she wished Theo could see it. She slumped to her knees, her strength failing her after the long days of painting. She'd taken care to give herself breaks this time, but she needed air. And sunshine. She gave the work one last look, deciding that she wouldn't sell it. She'd include it in her show, if she was lucky enough to get one, but the work was too meaningful to exchange for money.

Which made no sense, because she desperately needed money, if she wanted to keep Theo's studio.

CHAPTER SIX

Aggie started a stew from her supplies of dried ingredients for lunch a few days later. Hearing a horse out front, she wiped her hands on a tea towel, then went out front to see whom it was. Logan dismounted. She waved to him, waiting while he finished tying up his horse. "What brings you out today?"

"I promised Sarah I'd swing by and check on you while she was gone. How are you getting along?"

"I'm quite well, thank you. Is Sarah on a trip?"

"We have friends down south of Defiance. She and White Bird went down to visit them."

"I have a fresh stew cooking. Would you care to join me for a bowl?"

"Thank you, no. I won't stay—just wanted to see that you're getting along all right." He looked toward the large tent that was set up next to her house. "How's the tent working out for you?"

"Wonderful. It was a brilliant idea. I'm so glad you suggested it. The light is perfect in there. Bright. Diffused. It's pleasant to work there anytime, but especially in the afternoons."

"Mind if I have a look at your work? I'll admit I've had to keep myself busy so that I don't come down and pester you." He grinned at her.

Aggie laughed. "Of course, you're welcome to go see. I just finished another painting. I'd like to get your opinion of it."

Logan flashed a smile at her, then headed toward the tent. Aggie followed him inside. Chayton's portrait was set up directly opposite the entrance. Logan ducked inside, then came to an abrupt stop. She slipped in next to him as he stared at the painting, his face going lax in disbelief. She couldn't tell if he liked the work, but he certainly had a visceral reaction to it—almost to the point of not breathing.

After a while, he looked at her. A muscle was knotting and releasing in the corner of his cheek. She thought she saw moisture pooling in his eyes. He turned on his heel and left the tent, striding over to sit on the bench in front of her cabin. He sat with his hands on his knees, staring off into the horizon. Aggie sat next to him, keeping company with him in silence.

"What price will you be setting on Chayton's portrait?"

"I won't be selling it."

Logan's cheek tensed as he looked at her. "I'd like to buy it. Name the price you want."

Aggie shook her head. "It's not for sale."

"Let me trade for it, then."

"No. I will give it to you. For White Bird. She

should have it. But I'd like to put it in the exhibit, when I can arrange one."

"Thank you. Your talent is extraordinary." He looked at her and smiled. "When can I take it?"

"It needs to dry, and then I need to seal it with a varnish. It may be a few weeks. I don't want to risk damaging it."

Logan walked back to the tent. Aggie followed him again. "Why is he so sad?" she asked. "What happened to him?"

He took a long minute to answer. "What didn't? His country fell to invaders. His village was attacked and his family slaughtered. His parents had been killed by soldiers years earlier. He had to surrender his daughter to us or she would have been forcibly taken from him for school. His people are dying on the reservation where they're locked away like untended cattle. Everything happened to him, any of it more than enough to kill a man." He looked at her. "I'm glad you can see him as he is."

Aggie had to blink away her tears. No wonder Chayton made so compelling a subject.

"You mentioned when we first corresponded that you're trying to get into a show with a friend of your father's. If that doesn't work out, I will make your gallery exhibition happen," Logan announced in a solemn voice. "Let me be your patron."

Aggie's gaze flew to him. She studied his face, trying to read his level of intent. "How? How will you make that happen?"

"I'm an art collector. I have contacts. Where do you want to present your work?"

Her heart was beating uncomfortably fast. "Denver, I think. Some place close would be easiest. And it's a hub for western tourists these days."

"How are your supplies holding out?"

"I'm running low on some paints. I didn't anticipate doing such large works."

"Give me a list of what you need. I'll put an order in for you. If you have a preferred vendor, include that information. I'll use him."

Aggie hurried to her worktable. Her hands shook as she took out her sketchpad and flipped to a blank page. She took an inventory of her supplies, jotting down items she was running low on. When she finished, she looked at the long list. It was too much. She shouldn't accept his patronage. Now knowing what she was capable of, he would insert himself into her work, order her to do things differently or commission pieces that weren't part of what she wanted to paint right now. Unlike Theo, who'd supported them through commissioned work, she felt driven to produce from a different creative force. "I don't think I can do this, Logan."

Logan still stood at the entrance to the tent, observing Chayton's portrait in a trance-like state. "Do what?"

"Accept your patronage. It's too much."

"Aggie, name a successful painter, just one, who succeeded without a patron?"

She pressed her lips together, unable to refute his argument. "I won't sacrifice my art. I won't—I can't—paint what I'm not moved by."

Logan smiled. "Agnes Hamilton, you've given my family the greatest work of art we will ever own. Being your patron is an honor. Why would I interfere with a genius like yours? How do you do it, anyway? How do you create something so real? In paint?"

"I don't know." Aggie looked at Chayton's portrait. "I see things in detail and I remember them exactly as I see them." She handed her list to Logan.

He glanced over the list, then nodded. "And your food supplies? Are you well stocked?"

"Logan—"

He held up a hand. "I don't want you worrying about anything but work. Leave the rest to me." He left the tent and went to his horse. Once he'd mounted, he looked down at her. "I'm grateful that the postmaster in Defiance answered your letter when you were researching likely locations. I'll let him know that when I'm in town next." He turned his horse toward the road that would lead back to his ranch. "If there's anything you need, I expect to hear from you."

She waved at him, then watched him ride away. Her head was buzzing. With Logan's support, she could do more of the large canvases. And she wouldn't have to worry about running low in food or art supplies or spending time traveling back to Denver for the supplies she needed.

A patron! She found herself a patron!

She was jumping out of her skin, too excited to concentrate on work. She wanted to go find Chayton and tell him the good news. A bad idea, certainly, but one she couldn't resist. If he was still in the area, then she still had a chance of getting him to sit for her...if she could just find him.

Excited at the prospect of seeing him, Aggie banked the fire in the stove, then hurried outside to saddle her horse. It was late afternoon when she got to her hill. She rode around the creek, looking for Chayton or his horse. She didn't see signs of either. She dismounted and tied her horse near some cottonwoods and climbed the hill, looking for Chayton in all the recesses, behind the short clumps of brush. He wasn't there.

"Chayton!" she called, cupping the sides of her mouth so that the wind wouldn't steal her words. "Chayton!" She turned around and shouted his name in the direction of the sandstone bluff. There were caves up there. Maybe that was where he lived.

She stood at the top of the hill, wondering if he was there, watching her, ignoring her. The wind gusted about her, pulling at her hat and tugging the ties of her apron. The sun was hot and would have been unbearable if not for the cool air that blew. She shut her eyes and listened as the wind blew around rocks on the gravelly slope below her. It was a selfish companion, the wind, whining and crying but never listening.

Chayton was nowhere to be found. Feeling a little

dejected, Aggie went back down the hill. Perhaps he was out hunting. Perhaps he'd gone on a trip somewhere. Perhaps he was ignoring her. And who could blame him? She'd invaded his valley, fixated on him. How often had Theo extolled the virtues of balance? He'd hold her face in his large hands, smile down at her, and whisper, "Everything in its own time, in its own way, my love."

A lesson he himself failed to heed at the end of his life. Maybe that was a conscious choice. Maybe his corporeal pain was a mere shadow of his soul's pain and opium was its only relief.

She sent a last look around her hill. Chayton wasn't a friend. He wasn't an enemy. He wasn't anything to her. Still, he haunted her. She'd asked for the land to tell her its story, and he'd appeared. What it meant, why it was, well, such things weren't hers to understand.

Early the next morning, Aggie heard a wagon approach on the road near her home. She was already at work in her tent, sipping a cup of coffee. Sam and Wylie were on the front bench. She walked out of the tent to greet them. Sam pulled to a stop in front of her cabin. He hopped off the wagon. Seeing her, he lifted his hat. "Ma'am. Mr. Taggert wanted us to bring you down some supplies. Milk, cheese, butter, some berries that Rosa, their housekeeper's daughter, picked for you."

"Oh. Thank you! Please tell the Taggerts how

grateful I am for their generosity."

"You bet, but we've more to unload. Mrs. Taggert thought you might need more furniture in the tent. She had us gather it together before she left town."

"More furniture?" Aggie followed them out to the wagon. A wide bed, similar to the one in her cabin, took most of the space in the wagon bed, complete with mattress and a crate of linens. A small commode with a towel rack stood next to it, along with a few other items Aggie couldn't see.

"If you don't want it, we can take it back."

"No—I do. I think that would be very helpful. Let me show you where to put it." She led the way into the tent, hurriedly moving the table and empty easels out of their path. They tucked the bed into one of the low sides of the tent, putting the commode next to the headboard. They set up the washbowl and pitcher on it. When they went to take the crate it had been in with them, she asked if they would leave it. All of those containers came in handy. They brought in several more lamps, a wide shelving unit, and a screen that separated the resting area from the working area of the tent. They brought in a sturdy set of stepping stairs that would be perfect for her to reach the top of a large painting, if she did another. There were several different crates of linens, pillows, and other items that Aggie couldn't wait to dig into, a few chairs, a tall stool.

"Mrs. Taggert sent along netting to keep the mosquitoes out if you sleep here at night." They hung the circular turret from one of the tent supports.

Wylie made a face. "She sent this here rug, too. Didn't want you to be uncomfortable in such rustic surroundings. Help me get this rolled out under the bed," he said to the other man. "Shoulda put this out first." They lifted one end of the bed and kicked the carpet out under it, then repeated with the other.

"What happens if it gets wet? Or gets paint on it?" Aggie asked, worried that she would ruin something of the Taggerts'.

"Mrs. Taggert said you weren't to worry about any of that. She makes these rag carpets every winter and has a stack of spare ones up at the house. If there's anything else you need, you're to let her or the boss know." They sent a look around the large tent. Aggie could tell when their gazes encountered Chayton's portrait; they both stiffened, then moved closer for another look.

"You've seen him," Sam said, sending her an awed glance. She nodded. He exchanged a long look with his friend, then glanced at the painting again. "He ever bother you?"

Once, yes, but there was no point telling these men about that. Logan had taken care of it, and it hadn't happened again. Aggie shook her head. "I've tried to find him so that I can get him to sit for me. He's elusive."

"No one in town can ever find him when they go lookin'. He ain't gonna show himself unless he wants to. Best leave him alone, ma'am. For your own good."

83

The two men shared another look, then took their leave.

Aggie spent the morning getting her new space in the tent organized, then decided to make it a chore day since she'd gotten off track from work anyway. She straightened the cabin, cleaned up after the horse in the corral, did her laundry, bathed, then made a feast of a dinner for herself with the fresh fruit and dairy products Sarah and Logan had sent over. She topped off the big meal with a decadent berry pie, which she ate a slice of sitting alone at her little kitchen table.

The solitude she'd sought out here was a blessing and a curse, in near equal parts. It gave her endless freedom to create, but it was never comfortable becoming aware of being alone. At her warehouse in Denver, she had neighbors of the other business owners and their workers. People were all around her there. She wondered how Chayton lived alone as he did.

She rose early the next morning and set to work on a small landscape. Though she took breaks during the day, she never let her mind fully separate from the painting she was working on. It wasn't until the light grew dim in the tent that she realized how late in the day it had become.

She cleaned up her workspace, stretched, then headed to the cabin. Dinner would be a simple plate of bread with fresh butter and a thick slice of cheese. And pie. Her stomach growled in anticipation.

The door to her cabin was open, as it usually was

during the day, but she'd no sooner stepped inside than she became aware that something was odd. She froze in place at the threshold as her gaze dashed around the uncluttered space. Nothing looked different. She walked into the back area where her bed was and ventured a quick peek beneath it. Everything was as she'd left it that morning. Her bed was still neatly made. Her quilt folded at the foot of the bed. No one was hiding beneath it.

Unnerved that she hadn't been able to find whatever had triggered that odd sensation, she returned to the kitchen. Lying on the dry sink, where her pie had been, was a dead rabbit. Skinned, gutted, and ready for cooking, a small pool of blood drying around it. Aggie felt lightheaded as she stared down at the small bit of game.

He'd been here. Chayton had come here while she worked. How could she not have heard his horse? And, darn it, he'd taken her pie. She retrieved her cast iron Dutch oven. Not wanting to waste the meat he'd left her, she prepared a quick stew with carrots, potatoes, spices, and the rabbit. She fetched some wood for the stove from the pile outside, sending a glare around her. Was he still nearby, watching her?

Hopefully, he'd bring her pie dish back.

She'd go up to the caves tomorrow and find him. She was done with his cat-and-mouse game. Yes, she'd made a promise to Logan to stay south of the sandstone bluffs, but Chayton had come into her house, so turnabout was only fair play.

CHAPTER SEVEN

Aggie climbed up her hill the next morning, then walked the mile between her hill and the sandstone bluff, near the invisible line she'd promised not to cross. She assumed Chayton made his home somewhere up there, else why would Logan have warned her to stay away? Perhaps he lived in the caves. Or maybe another little cabin just out of her sight.

It was difficult to find a way up the steeply sloping rise. There was no clear path, and the ground zigged and zagged around boulders and brush in an upward climb. She lost track of how long it took. She was focused more on keeping her skirts out from underfoot as she had to use her hands to climb over and around boulders as she neared the top. The higher she climbed, the rougher the terrain became.

At last, she made it to the level where there were some caves. They looked too shallow and small to accommodate a grown man. She edged her way around the ledge, hoping there were more caves, larger ones, around the bend in the sandstone wall up ahead. With her luck, there would be no caves, just an abrupt end to the ledge she was on and no way to turn around. Still, she pressed forward.

"Chayton!" she called. "Chayton! I know you're up here!" Her voice echoed in the deep gorge that stretched far into sandstone bluff. The canyon was longer than she'd expected viewing it from the plains below. "Chayton! Quit hiding and come out!"

Aggie stepped into a cave that she hadn't seen from below, but couldn't tell whether it was where he lived. There was no bedding, no fire remnants, no piles of clothes or tools. Perhaps there were more areas in the far back where Chayton made his home.

Her eyes were becoming acclimated to the dark interior of the cave. She'd decided to push in a bit farther when she sensed something move in the shadowy depths of the space. The hairs rose on her neck and scalp as she heard a heavy breath, then a scream from a mountain lion. She stood paralyzed with terror. The mountain lion moved forward slowly, unfolding itself from a ledge where it had been resting. It leapt down to a lower ledge. It was scenting her, its mouth open, its breath rolling in rumbling growls from its chest.

Aggie silently began to pray as she started edging backward. The lion roared again. She screamed and squeezed her eyes shut. And then something slipped in front of her, standing between her and the lion. A wall of rawhide. She gasped and pushed against it, only then realizing it was a man.

He spread his arms and pushed backwards, inching her toward the cave entrance in slow, emphatic steps. Aggie gripped fistfuls of his deerskin tunic in her shaking hands. She could hear the mountain lion advance. The man spoke in a soft chant, his words a rolling singsong of calming tones. The cat screamed at them. The sound bounced around the cave walls, growing amplified. She buried her face in the man's back, between his shoulder blades. He did not seem tense. They reached the cave opening. When Aggie felt the hot sun on her back, she needed no prompting to turn and hurry down the trail, retracing her steps around the wall of the bluff.

She didn't look behind her until she'd reached the side of the bluff that overlooked her hill. Chayton followed her—she was relieved to see that no mountain lion followed him. He waved his hand toward her hill below and gave an abrupt order in that language she couldn't comprehend. She didn't have to understand his words to know what he was saying— and she didn't need to be asked twice.

Aggie made her way down the boulder-strewn sandstone bluff. As difficult as it was climbing up, it was even harder going down. Chayton moved ahead of her and showed her the steps to take. She followed in a numbed panic, feeling the aftereffects of shock. She was cold, even in the hot sunshine. And she was light headed. Chayton looked back at her, his expression aggrieved. She lifted her chin and continued on, forcing herself to put foot after foot to get to her horse. By the time they'd walked the mile separating the bluff from her hill, she was feeling much more herself.

When they reached her horse, Chayton indicated she should mount up. Just when she thought he was making her go alone, he called for his horse, with that high-pitched shout he'd used the first time they'd come face to face.

His horse trotted over to him and paused for him to swing up into the saddle. They walked the horses back to her cabin. Once or twice, Aggie looked at the warrior, wanting to strike up a conversation. He hadn't given any indication that he knew English, and she didn't know Lakota, so she held her silence. Besides, he did not look at her or in any way encourage her to break the silence.

Once at her house, he came to a stop near the corral. "Thank you. For saving me," Aggie said after dismounting. He didn't acknowledge her comment. He merely turned his horse and started back the way they'd come. Aggie scrambled up the corral fence.

"Chayton!" she called after him. He paused to look back at her. "Be careful with that mountain lion!" He turned away, but she stopped him again. "Chayton! If you bring back my pie dish, I'll make you another pie."

Maybe it was a trick of the light, but she thought she saw the start of a smile in the hard lines of his face. She started to climb down the fence, but it was his turn to stop her.

"Woman!"

She lifted herself back up to see over the fence.

"Why you were looking for me?"

"I wanted to thank you for the rabbit. And I wanted to talk to you. I thought maybe I could get you to sit for me."

"Sit for you?"

"Yes. So I can paint you."

"No." He turned and continued the way he'd come.

Aggie found it hard to concentrate on her work the next afternoon. The day was sweltering hot. No breeze stirred the air. The tent felt like a breath held in a dragon's mouth. She went behind the screen and took off her dress, leaving only her layers of thin cotton underclothes—chemise, drawers, and petticoat. She'd forgone her confining corset and the weight of several petticoats when she arrived. Often, she didn't even wear her stockings or shoes. She was here to work, not entertain. Theo had told her again and again that art was all that mattered when she was working. It was a lesson she'd taken to heart. She pulled her smock on over her underclothes. The apron was heavy and hot, but at least her sides would be cooler. She pinned her hair up in a sloppy attempt to get the heavy mass up off her neck. She tied the front and back entrances to the tent open, hoping to get some exchange of air. Returning to work, she forced herself to focus, reminding herself of all that was at stake if she didn't make this exhibit happen. Her time was running out.

She was working on a pastoral painting of Chayton's horse grazing near the creek. She had hidden Chayton behind the brush. It would take a hunter's eye for anyone to see him. But his pony, decorated with special markings in ocher and sienna, was a clear indicator the horse was of value to a warrior who would not be far away.

She was nearly finished with the work when a shadow moved across her feet from the western opening of the tent. She ignored it at first, thinking the tent flap had come loose from its tie. But after a while, her gaze was drawn in that direction.

Chayton stood there. In her tent. Watching her. She straightened, then felt the tightness in her back and neck from leaning in to work on her painting. She set her brush and palette down. Her fingers were tacky with the oils. No matter how she tried, she could not paint without wearing the sticky colors.

She pressed her palms against her smock, digging her fingers into the heavy linen to get the worst of the pigments off them. "Hello."

He looked away from her without returning the greeting. Instead, he walked into her tent, moving from canvas to canvas, studying each, lingering. She held her breath when he stepped in front of the large portrait of himself. After a minute, he looked back at her, a question in his eyes.

Aggie came to stand near him. "I'm giving this

work to Logan, for your daughter." She looked at the painting, then at him. "Do you like it?"

His nostrils flared. He turned to face her. His gaze swept the length of her body, down then up. She became aware of standing before him barefoot, in only her undergarments and her painting smock. He lifted a hand to touch the pads of his fingers to her bare arm, stroking her in a light touch from her wrist to her shoulder. He looked at her collarbone, then touched the bare skin exposed there.

He murmured something unintelligible to her. "I don't understand," she whispered, struck by the emotion in his eyes.

His gaze lifted to hers. His hand encircled her neck, his fingers slowly tightening his grip as he said, "You are the soul of everything I love in the skin of everything I hate." His hand squeezed her neck in a hold that was almost painful. He studied her eyes, which did not waver from his. His hand eased from her throat. He gestured toward the many paintings on easels and drying on the framework Logan had set up for her. "What are you doing here, painting me?"

"I came to paint western landscapes." She glanced around the tent at her work. "I asked the land to tell me its story. It showed me you. So I painted you."

"Why?"

"The land cannot weep. But you can. Its story comes through you."

Chayton's face was set in a rigid hold that gave no hint of his emotions. He lifted his hand and touched his fingers to her forehead. He tapped her, then dragged his fingers slowly down her temple to her cheek to her chin. "Who are you? What are you?"

"My name is Aggie Hamilton. I'm an artist."

"You tell stories." He said as he stepped away from her to walk among her paintings again. "Why do you do it?"

"I tell visual stories because they are important. We should never forget some things, but forgetting is the easiest of all things we do."

He looked back at her. "No, it is not." He started toward the tent exit, saying as he left, "I have brought back your pie dish."

Aggie watched him step out into the sunshine, watched how the light hit his hair and feathers. She followed him outside. "I made a coffee cake this morning. Would you like to have a piece with me?"

He paused, facing her as he studied her. "I will eat."

Aggie smiled at him. She led the way from her tent to her house. Inside, she poured water into the basin and washed her hands. She still had paint on them, but they were otherwise clean. She wasn't finished working for the day, so it didn't make any sense to scrub them more thoroughly. She gathered dishes and turned to the table to find Chayton standing outside the threshold of the front door. He looked annoyed.

"What's wrong?" she asked.

"You have invited me to eat with you, but you have not invited me inside. It would be rude of me to presume an invitation."

"Oh." Aggie straightened. "You've already been in my home. Several times. I didn't think that was a boundary you recognized." He said nothing further, nothing in his defense. She smiled. Perhaps Indians didn't tease. "Chayton, please come in. And forgive my rudeness. I rarely have visitors and often forget my manners."

He stepped inside, then promptly ignored her while she put coffee on the stove and stoked the fire. She fetched the butter from her keeping box, along with blueberry jam, watching him from the corner of her eye as she worked. He was moving around her small cabin, looking at each painting.

"What are you going to do with these?"

Aggie leaned against the doorjamb. "I hope to arrange a show in Denver. I'd like to be able to sell some of them."

"My wife was an artist. She traded with Logan every year."

"What was her medium?" Aggie asked, but her question confused Chayton; he frowned at her. "What type of artist was she?"

He stroked the beaded strip of rawhide that bound the two sides of his breastplate together. "She did beadwork. She decorated all of our garments. All summer she would prepare the finest skins and all winter she would work them into items for trade and for us to wear."

Chayton looked at her, his eyes swimming. She

wondered how long he'd been mourning his wife—the pain seemed as fresh to him as her own loss was to her. "When did she die?"

He faced the painting in front of him. She could see his struggle for control. "Four summers ago."

Aggie sighed. "I lost my parents when I was little, and my adoptive father earlier this year. There isn't a day that goes by that I don't think about them. I was hoping it got easier."

He met her gaze. "It does not."

The rich aroma of fresh, hot coffee filled the air around them. Aggie went to pour their cups. "Do you like sugar in yours?"

"Yes." His answer was immediate—and far nearer to her than she'd expected. She hadn't heard him move from the back of the cabin. She poured the coffee, then brought the cake over. He stood beside the table, giving no indication that he knew what was expected of him.

Aggie smiled and gestured toward the chair opposite her own. "Please, have a seat." She knew how thoroughly indecent it was for her to entertain in her state of undress, but he seemed to take no notice of it, and if she made anything of it now, she might make him aware of just how little she'd been wearing. And, a bigger concern, he might leave before she had a chance to convince him to sit for her.

"Shall I serve you?" she asked, remembering his dining customs and hers were different. He was politely deferring to her lead. When he nodded, she cut a large square of the coffee cake with its heavy streusel topping and set it on a plate for him, then pushed the butter and jam his way. She cut a smaller piece for herself. When he hadn't made any attempt to add condiments to his serving, she added them to hers, then cut into it with her fork.

"Do you like it?" she asked. He'd nearly consumed the whole piece in three bites. She pushed the cake dish toward him when he nodded. "Have some more." While he ate, she studied his attire. He was bare-chested today, wearing his choker, breastplate, and necklaces. His hair was parted on the side and worn in two ponytails, both of which had been wrapped in a red fabric and lay in front of his shoulders. He had the lean and powerful build of a man of action. Her gaze traveled down his arm to his hands, which had ceased moving. She glanced at him, curious about his stillness.

"You eye me as if you will eat me."

Aggie laughed. "You are so pretty—"

"And you insult me?"

She smiled at his reaction. "You are pretty *and* fearsome. I'm curious how both can exist in one person."

"I am *Lakȟóta*. I am a warrior."

"I've seen many warriors among my people. They don't look as you do." She studied him another moment. "Will you sit for me?" He frowned at her. She clarified: "Let me paint your portrait."

"No." He took the last bite of his second piece.

"I'll cook for you."

"You cannot create art and cook."

"I cook for me." Sometimes. When she thought of it—when eating was an absolute necessity. The look he gave her refuted that. Just how closely had he been watching her? "Please?"

"Why do you want to paint me?"

"To tell your story."

"You don't know my story."

"Your story is in your eyes, in your face, in your clothing, in your posture. You are your story, and I would very much like to help others to see it."

Chayton sipped the last of his coffee. He looked at the coffee cake. Aggie wrapped it up in a tea towel and gave it to him. "I will think on your request," he told her.

"Thank you." She followed him outside and around the house to where he'd left his horse. The yellow afternoon sun caught him standing next to his horse as he lifted his horse's reins. "Chayton. Wait. Don't move." Though he paused out of curiosity and not compliance, he'd stilled long enough for the image of him standing with his horse to set in her mind. She shut her eyes, locking that sight away for a moment, giving her brain a chance to remember what she'd just seen.

When she opened her eyes, he was gone. She hurried to her tent, searching for her sketchpad so that she could rough out the subject of her next painting.

CHAPTER EIGHT

Several days later, she had a new four-foot-wide by three-foot-tall painting of Chayton standing in front of his horse. The colors weren't ones she usually favored; they were the washed-out afternoon tones of ochre, tan, and beige with the brilliant spots of cobalt, green, and white in Chayton's beadwork cuffs, and the white coat with black splashes of his horse. She'd changed out the background, setting the tree-lined creek behind him. She'd captured the mood of the afternoon sun, the way it hit Chayton and his horse. The earth tones made the brilliant blue sky, with its white clouds, stand in sharp contrast.

Tired from long days on her feet, she indulged in a soaking bath that evening, then ate a small bowl of the stew she'd started earlier. She was preparing for bed when she heard a horse in front of the house.

"Agkhee Hamilton. I would speak with you."

Chayton! She grabbed a shawl and hurried to open the front door.

He lifted something from the bench and handed it to her. "I didn't mean to wake you."

"You didn't wake me." She took the soft bundle from him. It was a folded and rolled deerskin. "What's this?"

"You wanted my story." He nodded to the bundle.

Aggie opened the door wider. "Won't you come in?"

He stepped inside, lingering by the door.

"Are you hungry? The stew is still hot."

"I am hungry."

"Sit down. I'll get you a bowl. I was making tea for myself. Would you like a cup?"

"Yes."

He sat at the table. She dished out a big bowl of the stew she'd made for supper. She was keeping it warm so that she could have it for breakfast. Besides, even though the days were brutally hot, the nights still became quite cool. The warmth from the stove would be welcome through the night. She set a cup of tea and a jar of honey on the table for him. Then she moved a lamp to the table so that she could see what he'd given her.

She unrolled the bundle carefully and saw the pictograph it held—an oval path that wound clockwise in widening rotations, filling the entire skin one figure at a time. Some of the pictures were people, some were tipis, some were horses or other animals, some were warriors, some were soldiers.

She looked in awe at Chayton. "You did this?"

He nodded. "I am not an artist, like you or my wife. Or the historian in my band who counts the winters. And it is not an annual record. It shows the significant things in my life, three or four of them a year."

Doing a quick calculation, she guessed Chayton was somewhere in his mid-thirties. Aggie sat down and leaned close to the light. Starting with the first image, which was of a hawk, she studied each image. "Why a hawk?"

"I was named after the hawk. My full name is Hawk That Watches."

She traveled along the path of his life. Some pictures she understood, some she didn't. "You remember all of these events?"

"Not all of them. The early ones were told to me."

Aggie studied the pictograph, touching some of the images, trying to understand them. "Will you read it to me?"

"Not tonight. Tonight, you will consider it so that when we speak about it, you will know what questions you have."

Aggie looked up, a smile slowly working its way across her face. "I'd like that." It was nice having Chayton visit with her, she realized. He didn't know enough about white people's customs to know she was an utter disgrace in her world. No respectable woman would receive a male visitor in her perpetual state of undress, much less at night and alone. Especially not a renegade Lakota warrior. And no respectable woman would try to make a life out of her art. As much as people admired her work and paid good prices for it, she hadn't been able to sign her paintings with her full name while she'd been apprenticed to Theo—even when the works were ones she'd completed for herself and not for his clients. It was a simple truth that works by a woman artist carried less value.

She studied the man sitting at her table. The light from the kerosene lanterns, even with two of them on the table, was dim, casting a soft, warm glow over everything in the room. Chayton's features were harsh. Dark eyes, straight, low brows, high cheekbones. His lips were wide and rounded, indented at the corners. Creases lined the sides of his mouth, others feathered out from his eyes and others made furrows in his forehead. He was always neatly groomed when she'd seen him. No late-night shadow hid his pronounced chin or the rigid line of his jaw. His nose was straight, thin but triangular and masculine. His dark hair was thick and long. He took care that it was combed and styled in different ways that fascinated her.

Her gaze returned to his eyes. They were the most eloquent eyes she'd ever seen. She looked for such things in her subjects. It was what Theo had loved most about her work—the personality and humanity she revealed in the people she painted.

"Will you let me paint you?" she asked, still watching him.

"Yes."

She smiled. "Thank you."

"How do I do it?"

"Come here tomorrow morning. Early. I will make breakfast for you, then we'll get started."

She followed him when he walked to the door. She touched his arm, then pulled her hand away quickly. She was painfully aware of his masculinity—all the differences between their bodies. His height. The coiled strength in his lean body. The warm glow of his tanned skin. The wild scent of him, a mix of dust and leather, sunshine and sage. He was too much for her senses. And tomorrow, she would get to paint him.

"Thank you for the pictograph. I look forward to the time we can discuss it."

He nodded, studying her as he stood at the threshold. He murmured something in Lakota, which she didn't understand and he didn't translate, then he stepped outside to his waiting pony.

* * *

While Chayton ate the breakfast she made for him the next morning, Aggie went out to arrange things in the tent for the sitting. She put a stool against a section of the north tent wall. She wanted him to face east so that the light would be the most favorable during the morning. She'd set up the easel, prepared a canvas, and laid out her brushes, paints, and other supplies.

The white canvas of the tent diffused the day's

bright light, casting a soft glow over Chayton's features when he came out to sit for her. She stood next to her easel, considering him. "Could you turn toward me a bit more?" He inched around. Still, he wasn't set up quite right. She went to adjust him. He wore his hair parted in the middle, loose except for two thin braids at the front. Two eagle feathers decorated the back of his hair. Both had thin strips of hair tied to their tips. She moved his hair so that it split over his shoulder, with the long braid nearest her visible. She closed her mind to its silky texture. She tapped his right thigh. "Raise this leg and lower the other." His leggings had an intricate panel of beadwork along the seam that she wanted focus on.

She lifted his arm, adjusting where his wrist rested against his leg. The warmth of his bare skin and the weight of his arm made her aware of him in an uncomfortably intimate way. She glanced up at him, wondering what it was about him that was causing such a reaction within her. She'd painted men before, but hadn't been aware of them except in the context of a composition—the colors that would be needed to express their image, how light played on their skin, hair, and clothes.

With Chayton, it was something different entirely. He didn't avoid her eyes. He had an unusual intensity about him, like a tree that was still when all the others around it fluttered in the breeze. She pulled her hands away from his arm and backed away, seeking the safety and distance her easel provided.

With the way she worked, she didn't need him to pose for long. It was nice, however, to have the luxury of a formal sitting so that she didn't have to go through the exercise of rigorously committing her observations to memory. And with his consent to let her paint him, she hoped to have several sittings with him, each in different apparel so that she could paint him in a wide range of gear.

She focused on her work, separating herself from the strange sense of connection she felt with him. She sketched out on the canvas a rough, quick study of him. Then, on the hard board of her palette, she mixed the pigments that would give her his flesh tone, along with the colors she would need to create shadow and highlights, giving his body depth on the flat surface of her canvas.

She had the odd sense that Chayton was being created anew as she painted him. Seeing his body take shape on the canvas, it was as if he was pushing through the fabric to stand before her. Each stroke began to feel as if she were touching him. She looked over at him, wondering if he felt the feathery touch of her brush.

His eyes held no emotion, and yet, somehow, every emotion. He was beautiful, powerful, knowledgeable. He was a force of nature that no one would ever know existed without her capturing him on canvas.

Aggie refocused on her work, but it only intensified the strange feelings that were swirling around inside of her. Each brush stroke on the canvas felt as if she were learning him, tracing the curves of the lean strength in his arms with her fingers. After a time, the tent began to feel terribly warm. She'd worn a light muslin dress out of a sense of propriety, knowing she'd be spending the day in his company and the tent would likely be too warm. And even though the day's heat hadn't set in yet, she was already uncomfortable.

She switched her brush to her left hand, freeing her right hand to loosen the buttons at the base of her throat. She moved behind the canvas, hoping he wouldn't see the adjustment she made to her clothes.

This was ridiculous. She'd painted men before, even nude men. Theo had had her paint nude men and women over and over until she lost her shyness around them and began to see them with artist's eyes first and always. When she could objectify them, she could see them as representations of color, emotion, life.

Why was her training failing her now?

Theo had taught her that every painting had its own story. Perhaps the sensuality that she was experiencing had nothing to do with her and everything to do with Chayton. Perhaps that was the story of this painting. That realization let her distance herself from Chayton and focus on her representation of him. Which she did, with such intensity that when she next looked over at him, she found his stool was empty. The sun was high overhead, the bluish light of morning giving way to the yellowish glare of afternoon, even muted as it was by the heavy fabric of the tent.

She stretched, then went outside, wondering when he'd left his perch. She was still in something of a daze when she stepped into the sunlight. He was nowhere to be seen. She looked toward her corral. His horse was there, outside the corral, calmly munching on grass. Her horse was missing, however.

Just as she made that discovery, the ground began to rumble with the sound of a rider fast approaching her little spread. She looked around, uncertain which direction the rider was coming from. As she looked toward the hill that was east of her house, Chayton rode over it on her gelding, his brightly colored saddle pad a stark contrast to her horse's sorrel coat. Chayton's dark hair flew behind him. His feathers danced and jumped. He wasn't using the bit she used for riding, but his halter made from braided leather.

Chayton stopped in front of her. He grinned and called out something in Lakota, directing the horse to dance in a tight circle. He rode off again at a fast pace, calling for his horse. When it caught up to them, Chayton leapt from her horse to his, then back again—while moving at a full gallop. He had complete control of both horses. They came back around her tent and over the hill, easing to a stop outside her corral.

Aggie couldn't help but smile at him, amazed at his skill—and the fact that he'd obviously been training her horse. When he stilled, he smiled down at her and once more said something she didn't understand. She shook her head. "I'm sorry, Chayton. I don't understand. Could you say that in English?"

The joy in his eyes slowly died. He did not repeat what he'd said. Instead, he turned her horse out in the corral, retrieved his tack, put it on his horse and rode away. Aggie rubbed her horse down. He'd been exercised hard. She sent a look toward the tent, wondering how long she'd been focused on her work. She brought fresh feed and water for him, then took a break herself before resuming her work.

She wondered if Chayton would return in the morning. How wonderful it had been to see him smile, see his joy this afternoon. She wished she understood what he'd been happy about.

CHAPTER NINE

Chayton did not show up the next morning. Or for the next several days. Aggie finished his painting, then did a study of him smiling down at her from atop her horse. When a week went by without any sight of him, she began to fear, once more, he would never return. In the quiet of her cabin that night, she retrieved the pictograph he'd given her. She sat on her bed and spread the fine deerskin out over her knees so she could study the images that represented his life. One hundred and eighteen images were drawn in an oval wheel moving clockwise around the first four images. If he'd used four images to represent each year, then he was in his early thirties.

She touched the pictures, wondering at the image choices he'd made and their significance for him. Some were cryptic pictures of animals, others were miniature battles and scenes of terrible bloodshed. She considered what her wheel of life would look like and what images she would use to depict it. Her parents were long gone; she had no one left who could tell her about her earliest years she no longer remembered.

A breeze came into her cabin from the open door, swirling about the small space before leaving the same way it entered. She took a deep breath of the cool night air and wished Chayton was with her so that she could ask him to tell her the meaning of the symbols on his pictograph.

No sooner had she made that wish, she looked up to see him standing in the open front door. Aggie smiled. "Hi."

He didn't answer her, didn't attempt to enter, didn't appear happy to see her, but his eyes belied his stoicism—they were heated and intense and entirely focused on her. She indicated the pictograph on her lap. "I was hoping you'd come by. I don't understand many of the events you show here."

She rearranged the pillows, then scooted over on the bed so that he could sit next to her. It wasn't inappropriate; the bed was the only place to sit. She'd moved some of her paintings over from the tent so that she could consider their compositions and decide if they were finished enough to be signed. Those pieces were stacked on the table and chairs, hung on the walls. The only other place to sit was the floor. Besides, she was fully dressed—not in her usual state of dishabille.

He crossed the room and watched her as he settled on her bed. His shoulder touched hers. He didn't avoid touching her as he stretched out. His long legs were crossed at the ankles. The buckskin leggings had molded to the shape of his legs, leaving little to the imagination about the musculature beneath them.

The breeze in the cabin had been cool a few minutes earlier, but now she was feeling quite a bit warmer. Aggie looked up at him, then felt a furious flush of color warm her neck and cheeks. He returned her gaze, his eyes steady.

She smiled and turned her attention to the deerskin spread over her knees. "Tell me what these symbols mean."

"When my mother was giving birth to me, a hawk was flying over our village. He hunted in the prairie the entire time she was in labor, crying as he circled. She had a vision that I was that hawk. She saw, in that vision, that I would have the ability to see with the great perspective of a hawk. It is why she gave me my name, Hawk That Watches. Logan shortened it to 'Hawk' or Chayton."

Aggie looked over at Chayton. "Can you? See with a hawk's eye?"

He considered his words. "It isn't just being able to see clearly, it is also being able to see with the perspective of a bird high in the air. No, I cannot see what she hoped I would. Not yet."

"When I paint a landscape, I find it is much more difficult to face the sun and try to see the land than it is if my back is to the sun. Perhaps you won't see things the way she hoped you would until you are older."

Chayton frowned. "Yes. Perhaps." He pointed to some marks next to the hawk, two vertical bars and one short horizontal bar. "I was the fourth child born to my parents. I had two older brothers and a sister."

Aggie imagined the young family he was born into. "I wish I had not been an only child. What happened to your family?"

Chayton gave her a frustrated look. "I have written it in the pictures. You will soon learn." The next image was of a wooden stand with strips of something hanging down it. "That year was a good one for buffalo. No one in the village went hungry."

Over the next hour, in his calm, melodic voice, Chayton told the story of his boyhood: when he learned to swim as an infant; the year of the terrible snows when his father had buried each of them inside a snowdrift to wait out a blizzard; the night a bear had come into their camp to give them his body for food and his fur for warmth; when he began his history lessons with various wise men who knew the important legends of his people.

The summer that he was fostered to a master horse trainer was also the year that his wife was born in a different band. She was represented by an image of water rapidly moving. "Her name was Laughs-Like-Water. Like you, she was a great artist."

"Were your families friendly with each other?"

"Yes. Our mothers were quite close. Often our bands camped together. I played with her brothers. It is said that I was the first person her infant eyes focused upon, but I cared nothing for that honor. To me, she was just another infant in a cradleboard." He pointed to the next image, one of a snake. "In this year, my oldest brother was bitten by a rattlesnake and died soon after."

"Oh, how terrible. What became of your sister and other brother?"

"Agkhee, I cannot tell a story backwards. You must take the journey with me so that you understand the man that I am. Otherwise, you will not know what I know and will judge me in error."

Aggie kept the smile from her face. "Of course. Please continue." They had only covered the first third of his life, and she very much wanted to hear about the rest of it. There were battles with the Shoshone and Crow, treaties that were hotly debated among his people, raids against stage stations.

He marked the summer he met Logan—they fought, and he almost killed the man who was to become his friend. Instead, they spent the summer together, capturing wild horses and training them so that Chayton could pay the bride price for Laughs-Like-Water.

"I wish I could have known her. I imagine she was extraordinary."

"She was. Full of kindness and joy. Her skill in working bead art was such that several important warriors and chiefs commissioned work from her. She had begun training apprentices to help with the work. And she was expecting our third child when she was killed." He frowned at her. "But again, you wish to rush to the end. There is much traveling to do before the story is over."

The symbols he was covering were on the far side of the deerskin, so Aggie moved closer to Chayton, slipping into his arms so that he could more easily point out where they were in his timeline. A quick scan of the remaining images showed far too many that were battles or deaths. She leaned against him with her back to his chest, her temple against his chin.

Strange how comfortable she felt in his arms when she considered how terrifying he'd been when they first met.

"This year, my parents were killed. I had formed my own small group separate from my father's band. We were traveling to meet with traders to sell my wife's goods. While we were away, my parents had moved with their village to an area by a fort where the soldiers told them they would be safe. After being there three days, the camp was raided by soldiers and my parents killed. My sister and two of her children were also killed in that massacre. Her husband survived and now lives at the Agency."

Aggie desperately wanted to ask questions about why soldiers would do something so insidious, but she could feel the tension building in Chayton's body and did not want him to stop telling her the story of him. Instead, she reached up to touch his hair, holding it in her fingers as she drew them down its long length.

More battles now. The warriors among his people

needed the horses he was training as fast as he could train them. His other brother died in one of the battles. His daughter was born. The carcasses of buffalo, so wastefully slaughtered for their skins and heads, were scattered across an entire prairie, feeding no one. Even the scavengers could not eat them all.

The very last image was of a white man holding a string of long hair. "One day, a group of white men who were scalp hunters came to my village while I was out hunting with the men. Logan had warned me they were in the area. I thought because we were in the lands protected by treaty that we would be safe. They killed dozens of my people—women, children, and elders. They took the scalps of the women and children. Laughs-Like-Water had been raped and beaten and shot. My son had been shot lying over her body."

Aggie couldn't hold back her tears. She turned in Chayton's arms and wept. At first, he didn't hold her but he didn't push her away. After a minute, she felt his arms wrap around her shoulders, holding her tighter and tighter. How could one person—how could an entire people—survive what he and his people had survived?

When her tears had stopped, Aggie pushed herself up to look at Chayton. "The story on the deerskin ends with that terrible day, but that was a few years ago. Why isn't there anything else in the timeline?"

"Because I ended that day."

Aggie dug a handkerchief out of her pocket. She

wiped her eyes and blew her nose. She turned and looked back at Chayton. "Why did you leave the reservation?"

His lips thinned. His nostrils flared. His jaw shifted from side to side as if he fought the first words into his mouth. "My white grandmother made it impossible for me to stay."

Aggie frowned. "White grandmother? I thought your parents were Lakota."

"They were. My mother was adopted into the tribe when she was about White Bird's age."

"She was a captive." Aggie was shocked.

"She was one of us. She had her freedom. She could have left at any time. But she loved my father and their life together. It was from her, and later Logan, that I learned English."

"You speak it very well. I didn't think you could at first."

"I do not like to speak your language."

"Tell me why are you here and not with your people at the Agency?"

"I was asked to leave by my chief."

"Why? Did you do something wrong?"

He shook his head. "It is because I was born of a white mother. After my family was murdered, I went with my village to live at the Agency. It was there that my mother's people found me. They attempted to ransom me from my people. I told them they could not ransom me because I was *Lakȟóta*. My mother's people have more money than sense. They kept increasing their offer until the Agency managers agreed to sell me to them."

Aggie threaded her fingers through his, offering her strength to him.

"Still, I did not want to go. The white men from my mother's people decided they would take me. I fought with them. Others joined the fight. A great *Lakȟóta* man was killed. And a child. Their deaths were my fault. My mother's people were banned from the Agency. And I was as well."

Chayton sat up and began folding the pictograph, then rolled and tied it. She reached over and took his hand. "What happens now, Chayton?"

He looked at their twined fingers. His thumb brushed against hers. "It is up to you."

She studied him. "I think you should go meet your grandmother."

"No." He stood and walked to the table to set the pictograph down.

"Why not?"

"Because if I see her, I will kill her. She has interfered in my life, made it impossible for me to be with my people. I am a man of my tribe, Agkhee. I cannot live without my people."

"You have your daughter, still."

"She is where she needs to be. Logan and Sarah are teaching her how to live in the white world. Any interaction from me will distract her from the path she must follow."

Aggie stood up. "Then I will be your people,

Chayton." He stared at her. After a long minute, he came toward her, crossing the room in three long strides. He grasped her face in his hands and bent down to kiss her.

Aggie closed her eyes, savoring everything about the moment: the way his body felt against hers, the sweet, wild smell of him, the way his hair curtained them, the calluses on his palms, and the pressure of his fingers against her face. And, most wondrous of all, the way his lips felt on hers.

She was twenty-five years old, and she'd never been romantically kissed. She'd spent more than half her life in Theo's household, but for much of that time, they were isolated from the rest of the world by his work and her studies. When his artist friends visited, he was careful to keep her chaperoned. One time, she'd asked Theo about whether he'd ever been in love. He'd given her a long look, then left the room without answering her. In fact, it wasn't until he lay in his bed, dying, that he answered her.

"You asked once if I ever loved anyone," he whispered. *Aggie nodded, moving to sit on the bed so that he wouldn't have to make an effort to speak. How she would miss talking with him, the wisdom he imparted.* *"I was in love."*

"What happened?"

He shrugged. *"I loved my art more. I couldn't tolerate any interference or separation from it. And now, what have I to show for my life? I'm alone and about to leave my art anyway when I die. I wish like hell I'd not been alone in my life."*

"You aren't alone, Theo. You've had me for thirteen years. I've tried to be like a daughter to you."

"You are my daughter. And how lucky I was to have you when I refused to let anyone else in my life." He reached up and patted her cheek, his hand stiff and cold, knotted with rheumatism. "Don't make the same mistake. Go out there, girl. Find your art. And find your heart. And keep both as close as you possibly can. I've kept you from the world for far too long."

Aggie reached around Chayton's waist. It was strange standing so close to someone else, having another body next to hers. Ever since her childhood, there'd been no one in her life who'd hugged her, held her. This was nice. Chayton's mouth moved against hers, opening. She followed his lead. He touched his tongue inside her mouth. Startled, she pulled back and looked up at him.

He smiled down at her, then frowned. "Agkhee, have you never been with a man?"

"No."

He sighed. She felt the tension in his body tighten. He wrapped his arms around her and held her closely with her face tucked against his neck. "It is time for me to go."

"What do you mean 'go'?"

He ran his fingers over her cheek. "I cannot stay with you. You are not my wife."

"But I'll see you again, right? You'll be back?"

He nodded. "It is hard to stay away from you." He

started toward the door. Aggie followed him. He looked back at her.

She smiled. "Are you glad you didn't kill me that first night?"

Chayton grinned. "Time will tell."

"Well, I'm glad you didn't kill me. And I'm glad you didn't let that mountain lion get me."

"That lion guards my cave. I raised her from a cub. She warns me when the men from town come for me."

"Oh, Chayton. How can you stand to be so alone?"

"I cannot." He kissed her forehead. "Have a good sleep tonight."

She waved to him as he slipped into the darkness outside. "Good night to you as well."

CHAPTER TEN

Chayton stood in front of Agkhee's house once again. Two more nights had passed since he was last here. If he could have kept away, even tonight, he would have.

"I will be your people," she'd said to him. "I will be your people," he repeated to himself, longing for what she offered. He stared into the shadowy interior of the woman's house from the window. A fire flickered and danced in the hearth. He yearned to enter, yearned to be welcomed to someone's fire once again. He knew, were he to announce himself, she would invite him in. She always had, except for that first night he'd broken in. She couldn't know what it meant for a lone woman to welcome a man to join her. She'd admitted her innocence, and still she opened her home to him. *Wašíču* customs were different from those of his people. Such a thing probably meant nothing to her. Nothing of any importance meant anything to a *wašíču*.

In the end, because he was weak, because he ached for any amount of time not spent alone, he opened her door and stepped across the threshold into her house. She looked up quickly, then hurried toward him.

"Chayton! You're soaking." She drew him forward, close to the fire's warmth. Her touch sent a shiver through him. "And freezing." She put another log on the fire. "How long were you out there?"

So very long, he answered silently.

"You should remove your wet clothes. I'll get you a towel. And a blanket."

She returned as he was removing his tunic. Her gaze slipped across his chest before lowering to the bundle she carried. He could feel himself thickening. He told himself it was because of his cold body being so close to the fire, but even he didn't believe that lie.

He wanted this woman. The fire illuminated her hair as it lay about her face in tawny streams of red, gold, and brown—the colors of river rocks. Her eyes were like the sky on a bright summer day. Tiny spots of color sprinkled across her nose on a background of white skin. He was a head taller than her, and half again as wide—he liked the differences in their sizes.

He hadn't hungered for a woman since Laughs-Like-Water was murdered. Not for any of the women, widowed or maiden, at the Agency. Not for the *wašíču* women he'd seen in town the few times he went there. When his people kicked him out of the Agency, he'd accepted that he would walk alone for the rest of his life. And yet here he was, aching for this woman, the one named Agkhee. Without his tunic, it was impossible to hide his reaction, so he didn't try. He untied his leggings from the thong about his waist, then sat to remove them and his moccasins.

When he looked up at the woman, she was preparing something by the stove, her back to him. "Are you hungry?" she asked without turning around.

"Yes."

The small room was filled with a rich scent coming from the big iron stove Agkhee was working over. His stomach growled. She'd fed him several times now. She was a good cook. Tomorrow he would bring her another rabbit. Maybe he would cook it for her while she worked on her paintings. The first rabbit didn't count toward a courtship because she'd been deep in a vision and hadn't been aware of being provided with food. The second one didn't count either, since he'd exchanged it for the pie she'd made.

But now, if she accepted fresh meat from him— consciously and without an exchange of any sort—he would know she was interested in him.

He wondered if white women were courted differently than *Lakȟóta* women. If he and Agkhee were still among his people, he would have an elder female relative of his speak to an elder female relative of hers to gauge her interest in a courtship. But they were alone, each of them, in this middle place between his world and hers.

Unless Logan represented her. Perhaps his friend was thinking of taking a second wife, despite his words to the contrary. What else would explain the gifts and provisions he brought her? Chayton thought about bringing Agkhee a deer haunch tomorrow instead of a rabbit so there would be no doubt about his suit. And he would speak to Logan about her.

Agkhee carried a plate to the table. She returned a moment later with two steaming mugs of coffee.

"Are you not hungry?" he asked.

"I've already eaten. I'm glad you came by. I made far too much food for just myself."

He laid his things out by the fire, then tied the blanket about his waist for warmth. He sat at the table, but didn't dig in. She had a knit shawl tied about her shoulders and was sitting with her legs folded before her within the drape of her big cotton dress. She looked entirely at ease.

He, on the other hand, was not. He crossed his legs, then uncrossed them. He didn't like sitting on chairs. They were too bony. It was impossible to settle in them. Why whites liked them, he didn't know. He set his feet on the floor, then sat straight in the uncomfortable chair to keep himself from squirming like a boy who hadn't yet counted coup.

"Agkhee." He looked at the woman. "Is there someone who speaks for you?"

She frowned. "'Speaks for me'?" She shook her head. "I don't need anyone to speak for me. I speak for myself."

"No parents, brothers, uncles?"

"No."

"Does Logan speak for you, then?"

"Chayton, if there's something you need to say, say it. I'm all there is."

He stared at her, glad for the cover of the blanket. It was a poor bargaining stance to show too much interest in what he most wanted. "Is Logan courting you?"

Agkhee's eyes widened. He'd shocked her. "Logan's married."

"Perhaps he seeks a second wife."

"He can't. By law. And by custom. We have only one spouse each. In our world."

Her world was the only one that mattered anymore, and he understood so little of it. "Do you desire him?"

Her eyebrows lifted. "No. Why would I?"

"He has given you a place to live. He brings you gifts."

She lowered her gaze. Even in the dim light of the evening, he couldn't miss the flush that rose across her neck and face. "He's my patron. That means he's helping me succeed in my work so that he can have first selection of my paintings. Does that make sense? He is happily married to a wonderful woman."

"So he is trading with you."

"Yes. He's trading with me."

"He is a tough negotiator. He traded with my wife." It hurt to think of Laughs-Like-Water, at this moment, when he was courting another woman—something he'd had no intention of ever doing. But even now, he was hard for the white woman sitting with him. "Is any man courting you now?"

"No. Why do you ask this?"

He didn't answer her. It wasn't something that needed an answer. It was obvious what he was seeking. He dug into his food, deciding instead to show her that he enjoyed her cooking. She'd made him a biscuit like the ones Logan used to make for the two of them when they were young boys, tracking horses. It was covered in a white sauce that had bits of dried beef in it. It was hot and salty and satisfying. The coffee she made to go with it was rich and sweet. He finished his cup and pushed it toward her for a refill.

"Why did you come by tonight, Chayton?"

He came every night, unless he was checking on his horses in the Valley of Painted Walls. "I wanted to be sure you were safe."

"Why wouldn't I be safe?" She frowned as she contemplated his words.

He didn't answer her. His statement was not meant to indicate she wasn't safe, only that he wished to see for himself that she was. English was a cumbersome language. When he finished eating, she took his dishes and set them on another piece of furniture, in a bucket with other dishes. She refilled their coffees.

He took his cup and went to the door, which he'd opened. The storm still raged. It would be a long, rainy night. Agkhee came to stand next to him. She sipped her coffee as she stared out into the storm. The wind blew erratically, blustering from the north, then the west, breaking into the house in cold bursts. It was nice to be dry and watch the storm.

Agkhee shivered beside him. He set his coffee down, then spread his arms wide, opening his blanket to her. "Agkhee, will you stand with me in my blanket?" His voice was oddly raspy. He hoped he didn't frighten her away.

She looked up at him as she considered his invitation. "If you wouldn't mind. I'd like that. Or I can get my own blanket…"

"Mine is already warm."

"All right, then." She took a hesitant step toward him. He wrapped his arms around her, turning her toward the door, her back against his front. The blanket covered all but their feet. She was like ice, but he was fire. Soon she was warm in his embrace. She handed him her coffee and asked him to set it by his on the table. Then she leaned back, resting her slight weight against him. He closed his eyes, focusing less on the storm outside and more on the one raging within himself.

How long had it been since he'd shared his body's heat with a woman? Many, many summers. A lifetime. His arms tightened around her. He wondered if she understood the significance of standing with him inside his blanket. Even with no others to witness her acceptance of him, it mattered that she'd come to him.

The fabric of her white dress was thin. There was little barrier separating her body from his. Her bottom rested below his breechcloth. She wasn't even as tall as Laughs-Like-Water. She was thinner, narrower. Different. She smelled of a sweet scent. A white woman's flower. It wasn't a scent he recognized. He breathed again of the sweetness in her hair.

He longed to let his hands wander over her body, exploring her beneath the shield of his blanket. It was an indulgence allowed him now that she'd accepted him. But white women reacted differently to such things than the women of his people. He remembered how rigid Logan's wife had been about any affection from her husband where people could see them. But they were alone now. And Agkhee was relaxed, leaning softly against him.

He ran his hand up her arm, over her shoulder, to the base of her neck. Everywhere he touched the cotton of her gown. He wanted to feel the velvet of her skin. He drew his palm up her neck to cup her jaw and leaned his face against the side of her head as he bent to whisper, "This is nice, standing with you this way."

He could feel the slight nod of her head. "I don't understand what it is that I feel for you, Chayton. I crave the sight of you. I want to paint you in all the different ways that I see you. I want to keep you in a canvas so that I never forget you. You make me feel wild, like this storm. Like this land."

Chayton's arms tightened around her slight body. It was a very bad idea that had taken root within him. He was not a good marriage prospect for her. A man without a people could never provide his wife true security. Her people would never accept him. He had no rights in her world. If they ever had children, they would be taken away from them, as all native children were. He didn't know enough about the white world to raise them as white. And he wouldn't even if he did. He could teach them what they needed to survive, to understand their world. It was better than the way white children were raised, by strangers in school buildings, learning nothing of the world around them.

Light speared across the sky, illuminating the gray clouds on either side of its zigzag path. Agkhee tensed, then jumped when the thunder followed the light.

"Are you warm enough?" he asked. "We could go stand by the fire." Agkhee's little cabin was much more snug in the storm than the tipis his people had. The wind was only getting in through the open door where they stood, though it whined and howled all around the outside walls.

She shook her head. "The storm's right over us. I want to watch it a little longer. Are you too cold?"

"No." His feet were like ice, exposed to the wet, stormy air as they were, but the rest of him was hot. He wondered if Agkhee knew he was aroused, standing as close as they were now, her back against his front. Soon she would be his. Soon he would discover the mysteries of her body. Soon he would sleep an entire night in the warm arms of a wife.

Tomorrow, he would hunt. When he brought her a

deer, she would know what a good provider he was. When she accepted his gift of food, he would know she was ready to be his wife.

Aggie felt safe in the cocoon of Chayton's blanket, with his strength all around her. She wasn't unaware of the bulge pressing against the small of her back— she knew it wasn't entirely attributable to the breechcloth he wore. As she watched the storm fight the darkness of the night, she had to admit she was pleased with Chayton's reaction to her. His stoicism and utter lack of conversational skills made it difficult to read him, but no translation was needed for what his body said.

Perhaps his reaction was just that he was near a woman after being alone so long. Perhaps any woman would trigger the same response in him. She'd no sooner thought that than she rejected it. No man who could live alone in this rugged land for as long as he had would be someone ruled by the needs of his body. Which meant he wanted her for her. She leaned her head against his shoulder, reveling in that realization. The lightning grew softer, more distant. The wind continued, but the rain was easing up as well. Perhaps the worst of the storm had passed.

For now, for this moment, she was safe. Protected. Wanted. She sighed, enjoying the euphoria of the moment. "Thank you."

"Why do you thank me?" he whispered inches from her ear.

"I'm enjoying being here with you."

"As am I."

"I think the storm's passed. For now."

He loosened his hold on her. "Then I will leave."

She turned inside the cover of the blanket, facing him. Perhaps it was very forward of her, but she took hold of his lean, bare waist. His skin was warm and soft, but the muscles beneath were hard. "I hope I will see you again. Soon. I'd like to do some paintings of you on your horse."

He took the blanket from his back and spread it around her shoulders. His eyes were solemn as he gazed down at her. He touched two fingers to her cheek, drawing them downward from her cheekbone to her chin. "Tomorrow, I hunt. When I return, we will have much to discuss."

Aggie smiled. He was an unusually silent man. She wondered what having "much to discuss" meant to him. "I'll be here."

He crossed the room to his drying leathers. He watched her as he stepped into his leggings. Aggie didn't move. His gaze held her immobile, filling her with a liquid heat that spilled through her veins. He pulled his moccasins on, drew his tunic over his head, draped his necklaces over his neck, then took up his horse blanket and saddle pad.

He walked to the door. Oh, how very badly she wished he would stay, wanted it as she'd never wanted anything else. He was a madness within her, a need as imperative as that for water or air. He paused at the door and looked back at her. Her heart was hammering in her throat. She couldn't speak. He grasped the saddle and blanket in one hand and came toward her, closing the distance between them in one fast stride. He lifted his free hand and cupped the curve of her chin and neck. His nostrils flared. His black eyes raged. The lines on either side of his mouth deepened as he bent down to kiss her.

Aggie shut her eyes, losing herself in the swirl of sensations. The scent of him in his leathers, the damp smell of rain outside, the feel of his callused hand below her ear. He lifted her face with his thumb beneath her chin. Then his lips were there, against hers. She reached over and grabbed fistfuls of suede at his sides, holding on as his mouth twisted against hers.

His mouth opened, forcing hers to do the same. He thrust his tongue into her mouth. She groaned in response, consumed by her desire for him. He dropped his saddle and blanket and used his freed hand to pull her in tightly against him. He smashed his nose against hers as he turned to kiss her from a different angle. She ran her hands up his heavy tunic to his shoulders, tightening her hold around his neck as she dug her hands into his hair.

The room started moving. She was dimly aware that he was pushing her back against the wall. When he had her pinned there, he ground his hips against hers. With her nightgown on, she couldn't open to him more than just a little. She made a little mewl of frustration. At the sound, he yielded. He pulled his hands free and braced himself against the wall as he glared down at her.

"Agkhee. Agkhee," he hissed as he fisted her hair, his mouth open against her cheek. She still clutched his back. She wanted to weep, so badly did she need him to hold her, love her.

"Stay with me, Chayton."

He pulled back enough that he could look at her. His hand slipped from her hair as he said something she didn't understand; he'd fallen back into Lakota. Aggie was glad she was leaning against the cabin wall when he fully released her and dipped down to pick up his saddle and blanket.

He paused at the door. He said something first in Lakota, then in English. "I will be back. And I will make you mine."

His words jumped around in a jumbled mess in her head. It wasn't until he was gone that she made sense of them. When his meaning clicked, she sucked in a sharp breath. Chayton's pronouncement, however, caused her to think her life might take an unexpected turn—one not entirely unwelcome, though fraught with its own dangers and troubles.

Taking a Lakota warrior as a lover may not be the smartest thing she'd ever done, but it would certainly be a chapter in her life that she'd never forget. And after everything they'd each been through, weren't they due a little joy?

CHAPTER ELEVEN

Chayton waited in the shadows beneath the big cottonwood in front of Logan's house a couple of days later. He'd taken two bucks. One for Agkhee, one for his daughter. He'd deposited his daughter's where he left his food offering every month or two. A woman in Logan's household would discover the meat he provided. Shortly afterward, his friend would come outside, searching the surroundings for him. Every time, when he couldn't find Chayton, he would make the gesture that indicated gratitude, then turn away.

This month, Chayton stood in the open, watching as his friend strode toward him. Logan reached forward, gripped his forearm, then clapped him on the shoulder as he stared into his eyes. "It's good to see you, my friend."

"You as well." Chayton held himself in an erect posture. It was good to see his friend. He owed his life, and that of his daughter, to Logan. But the discussion he'd come to have was potentially a bloody one that could end life as they knew it.

Chayton knew the instant that Logan became aware of his reticence. His friend put some space between them. "I'm grateful for your successful hunts."

"I'm grateful for the care you've given my daughter."

"We have a fresh pot of coffee on the stove. Will you come in and join us?"

"Yes."

Some of Logan's men had come for the deer he'd left on the front porch. They set the deer down and eyed Chayton suspiciously. Logan set a hand on Chayton's shoulder and walked with him past the men.

"Sarah! Come see our visitor!" he called as they stepped inside the house. Chayton tensed as they walked through the entrance hall. Walls always made him nervous. It was hard to breathe inside *wašíču* dwellings.

Logan's wife greeted them in the entranceway. She smiled when she saw him and came forward with her hands extended. She held his hands as if he were a cherished member of her family and leaned up to kiss his cheek. She was even more beautiful now than when he'd first met her, years ago, when Laughs-Like-Water was still alive. It hurt to look at her, because he couldn't do so without remembering how much his wife had enjoyed her visit to their camp that summer.

When he still had a family—and his people, his

freedom, his world.

He fought back the wave of emotion that flooded him, listening to the humming in his ears instead of the words Logan's wife said. But his flagging attention cost him, because another young woman stepped forward. Sarah put an arm around her. White Bird. His very own, very precious daughter.

Emotion danced about her face. Joy. Anger. Fear. Worry. Joy again. Then anger. She didn't come forward until Sarah gave her a gentle push toward him. She looked hauntingly like her mother, with her narrow, oval face. Black brows that arched gracefully over almond-shaped eyes. So much strength and courage in her face. From that alone, he knew he'd chosen the right foster family for her. She'd been spared the nightmare at the Agency and the further tragedy of forced separation when the children were taken away to boarding school.

He reached forward to touch her. How he ached to hold her. And then she opened her mouth and let out a whirlwind of scolding for his prolonged absence. All of it said in *Lakȟóta*. It was the most beautiful thing he'd ever heard.

He smiled and took hold of her face in both of his hands. He looked over at Logan. "You let her keep her language." Rarely did he state something so obvious, but he was awed by the discovery.

"Of course we did," Logan answered in their language. "Not only had she lost her family and her way of life, but we couldn't take her language and her culture, too. We can't teach her as much as you could, but we share what we are able. She's also learning Shoshone from my brother and his sons."

Chayton blinked away the moisture that gathered in his eyes as he pulled his daughter into a tight embrace. "You are right. I have stayed away too long. It is good that you scold me." He looked down at his daughter. "You look just like your mother. Have they told you that?"

"Yes," White Bird answered. "Sarah-*m'amá*"—she switched to English as she looked at her foster mother—"must I go upstairs to read? I'd like to stay and visit."

"No," Chayton answered. "What I have to discuss with Logan is not a matter for women. You must do as Sarah asks."

White Bird lifted angry eyes to him. It cut at his heart to see his beloved wife's angry face in her features. "Will you be here when I'm finished?" she asked.

"No."

"Will you come back soon?"

"Yes."

His daughter studied him, assessing the truth of his statement. "Then I will go."

He called after her, stopping her before she left the hall. "White Bird, you have made me proud."

She smiled, then ran back to give him a brief, tight hug.

Sarah wrapped an arm around her shoulders and

led her away. "Why don't you take Chayton to the den?" she said to Logan. "I'll see White Bird started with her reading, then bring you some coffee."

"Right." Logan led him toward the office. "My father, Sid, is visiting my brother, Sager. I would have liked for him to meet you. You've been out this way for close to a year now, and never visited. I've spoken to you more in the last month than in all of the last year." He indicated a chair in front of the big desk. "Please, have a seat." Logan sat in the companion chair, facing him.

"All is well for you here?" Chayton asked, remembering the long years Logan had been separated from his own family. For many years, Chayton's band had become Logan's surrogate family.

"Very well. I was angry and confused when I left here, way back when. I built the problem up in my mind until I thought it was unresolvable. Because of Sarah, I found my way home, and my family set things straight for me—much as your daughter just did for you." Logan smiled.

Chayton wondered if he would still be smiling once he heard what Chayton had come to tell him. "Where are your children, my brother? Your house is silent."

"We haven't been able to have any yet. Sarah was damaged from her time with Swift Elk. It's taken a long time to heal her emotional scars, but her physical ones are permanent. We will not have children of our own."

A tension deepened within Chayton. It was no

137

wonder Logan wished to take another wife. He was not going to like what Chayton was going to ask. "It saddens me to hear that news."

"I'm just happy to have Sarah in life, whole and healthy. She loves White Bird. We both do."

"I can see that. And I am grateful for the care you've given her."

"So tell me, why have you come here today? I've sought you out many times, and you rarely came forward."

Chayton thought back to all the times he'd hidden from his friend, listened to the news he reported without ever responding or greeting him. And still Logan brought him news, traded goods with him when asked, and cared for his daughter.

"I have been no friend to you at all, Logan. I'm surprised you accept me into your home."

"Chayton, if I was only a friend when the sun shines, I'd be no friend at all. You are always welcome in my home."

Sarah entered then with a tray of cups and a pot of coffee. The rich scent of it filled the room. He considered starting a pipe for the two of them to smoke, but he wasn't sure about the white customs for such things and preferred to follow Logan's lead. He looked at Sarah, waiting for her to finish serving them and leave. Logan looked at him expectantly, ignoring his wife's presence. Sarah was pouring their coffee. Chayton loved that drink. It was a special treat for him.

"I would like to make a trade with you," he began, deciding to ignore Logan's wife, too. Logan had long been a welcome trader among the people. He made fair bargains and always kept his word.

"What kind of trade did you have in mind?"

Sarah handed him a cup of the dark liquid. She'd added sugar and milk to it so that it was a murky brown color. He sipped the hot drink. "I would like to buy your second wife."

Logan's wife made a loud clattering with the dishes on the tray. Chayton glared at her.

Logan frowned. "I don't understand. I don't have a second wife."

"The woman who lives in your cabin and makes the paintings. Your guest."

"Miss Hamilton? She's not my wife."

"You provide her with food. You've given her a home and a tent."

Logan smiled, genuine humor in his eyes. Chayton narrowed his eyes as he watched the trader, waiting for the trick. The man was fair, true, but he was also savvy. Why would he pretend the woman didn't belong to him if he weren't up to something?

"She's a tenant. She paid me for the use of that cabin. I am sending her food and supplies so that I can have my pick of the work she is doing." He smiled up at Sarah, who had not left the room. Logan reached for her hand and threaded his fingers with hers. "I'm trading with her. The supplies and tent for first choice of her work. She's not my wife."

Chayton looked from Logan to Sarah. While it was common among Chayton's people for a man to have multiple wives, he knew white men rarely practiced the same—something Agkhee herself had confirmed. Still, he couldn't account for Agkhee's situation in any other way than that she'd been Logan's second wife.

"So you have no claim to Agkhee?"

"None to the woman, but to her work, I do."

"Her paintings."

"Yes."

"Then you will agree to stop sending her food and supplies?"

"No. I have made an agreement with her that I cannot undo for you."

"When she becomes my wife, I will see to her needs."

"Chayton," Sarah interrupted, "are you courting Aggie?"

"I have decided to take her as my wife."

Sarah's face grew even more pale than usual. She blinked, then looked over at Logan. She leaned against the edge of the desk and gave him a solemn look. "I hope you know that I am your friend, and I don't mean to offend you with what I am about to say. It's difficult for people of two different ethnicities to marry. It makes life very hard. Being your wife would limit her choices in her white world. And being white, she would not fit in your world."

Chayton knew that Sarah spoke the truth. Before

Logan, Sarah had been the wife of a *Lakȟóta* chief—not by choice, and not for long, but it had not been a good experience for her. Had Chayton's world not collapsed, his choice of Agkhee for a wife would have meant he'd have to leave his little band. Now that he had no people, he was free to go with his heart. But she was not. She still belonged in a bigger world that he wanted no part of and in which there was no place for him.

"Sarah," Logan countered, "there is more at stake here than the fabric of society. There are two hearts calling to each other. Let them explore their options and make their own decisions." To Chayton, he said, "The world is open to you, Chayton, in ways you don't yet even know. If Aggie has taken your heart, then there is no reason, none at all, that you should not be married. Sarah and I will stand beside you, whatever your decision."

He looked at Logan. "I am not certain what is expected of a man when courting white women."

Logan grinned. "Whatever you try, it won't be sufficient. They're impossible."

Sarah swatted her husband's shoulder. "Nonsense. If we don't make you work for our hearts, how will we know you truly value us?" Sarah grumbled. "Perhaps if you brought her a gift?"

"I have brought her small game. I have drawn for her the story of my life in the manner of a winter count. I have stood with her in my blanket." He pressed his lips shut in a thin line. "It is not enough.

She does not understand my intentions."

"Remember that it wasn't even two months ago that you tried to kill her," Sarah said. "She may need time to become comfortable with you. In our world, usually"—she smiled at Logan—"men and women decide on marriage after an extended period of courting."

Chayton looked at Logan. "You did not court Sarah for a long time."

"No, but there were extenuating circumstances. She was in danger and needed my protection."

"Agkhee needs my protection. When she paints, she becomes lost in a vision. She cannot exist alone. Someone must care for her."

"She mentioned her father recently passed away in her correspondence with us," Logan told him. "She may not be used to being alone and may not realize the dangers."

"It is not safe for her."

"Then give her the gift of time and your attention," Sarah suggested.

"Take her to the Valley of Painted Walls. Show her your herd, your world. Let her get to know you," Logan said. "But don't mention marriage too soon or you will frighten her away."

Sarah frowned at Logan. Did she disagree with his suggestion? "It is disrespectful for a man to travel alone with a woman who is not his wife," he said, voicing what she did not.

"True," Logan conceded. "It is so in your world

and in ours. But we know you will not disrespect her. And who will judge? Not Sarah and I. We only want to see you happy."

Chayton looked between Logan and Sarah. "I will consider making the trip with her."

"Consider this as well," Logan said. "If you meet your grandmother and accept her into your life, you will have a far greater chance of being able to have a full and joyful life with Aggie in her world. Doing so will give you options you don't have in your present circumstances."

* * *

Logan watched Chayton ride away a short while later. He became aware of Sarah standing silently next to him. He leaned against a porch support and drew her into his arms. "You seem worried. I thought Chayton looked good," he said.

"Do you think he and Aggie are a good match?" she asked as she looked up at him.

Logan nodded. "Yes. They are both so alone. She's an artist, like Laughs-Like-Water; he understands the creative mind. I think she's perfect for him. Especially with what we know he's going to have to face soon."

"True. Why didn't you tell him you'd invited his grandmother out to see us?"

Logan frowned. He'd learned about Chayton's grandmother from the officers at the reservation. When he hadn't been able to find Chayton for their annual summer trade last year, he'd found out his friend had been kicked out after some trouble brought on by a visit from his grandmother's men. Logan had been corresponding with her since then. Finally, she'd decided to come up to Defiance from Denver, where she lived. Her husband, who had passed away a few years back, had founded a wholesale business by supplying goods to forts, trading posts, and grocery stores in the ever-expanding west. That business had grown into a dynasty, making Chayton's family American nobility. There was no way the Agency could have allowed Chayton to stay once such powerful people wanted him out.

The woman was in a fever to meet her grandson; she'd made it clear that at her advanced age of seventy-four, she wasn't looking at a limitless future, and demanded that the man passing himself off as her grandson present himself immediately.

Logan hadn't yet responded to her latest missive. It was yet another order for him to produce the impostor who called himself her grandson. He hadn't given her any details about Chayton because he didn't want to corner his friend—he had no doubt she would send up her own men. In fact, he was surprised she hadn't done that yet. Something of this magnitude needed to be eased into with a man like Chayton, whose entire identity was rooted in his Lakota foundation.

Sighing, Logan eased a wisp of his wife's hair from her cheek. "I couldn't tell him yet. He has only now decided to rejoin the living. I will, though—soon. He has enough on his mind courting Aggie."

"Did you send him off to his valley so that he wouldn't be here when she arrived?"

Logan couldn't hold back a sheepish grin. "Maybe…"

Sarah sighed. "You know he's going to be furious, absolutely raging mad. And Chayton mad is not a fun sight."

"I know. It's true, and you're right, but better ask for forgiveness than permission, no?"

"Not with him." Sarah watched the horizon. "Do you think" —she paused— "if he and Aggie do get married that they'll take White Bird from us?"

Logan tightened his arms around her. "I think that if they want White Bird to go live with them, we have to let her go. And if she wants to live with them, we have to let her go. But if she wants to stay here, we'll make that happen." He waited a minute, then added, "I spoke to Audrey when we were last down at her and Julian's place, about adopting."

"She used to run Defiance's orphanage, didn't she?"

"Nothing so organized as an orphanage, no. She took in strays and foundlings during and after the war. But as soon as she did, the little waifs became hers. She's still active with orphanages, however, and knows of several children who need a home. She could help us select a child or two, or however many you'd like, if you're interested."

Sarah looked up at him. "Are you?"

He smiled. "I am if you are. All I've ever wanted was your happiness. In my heart, White Bird is our daughter. But if you want a larger family, we can make it happen."

"I want a larger family."

"Then that's what we'll do." He stroked her cheek. "Do you mind if we let the dust settle around Chayton and Aggie first? I don't want White Bird to have too many changes to deal with at once. And I don't want her to think any changes we're making in our family have anything to do with the changes happening with Chayton and Aggie."

"I don't mind. Families take time. And White Bird is our first priority. I hope she decides to stay with us. And I hope they let us keep her, Logan."

"I do, too, but we have to let that play out as it will."

Logan thought of all the trouble that had come about when his stepbrother, Sager, was taken from the Shoshone family that had raised him and was brought home to live with them. All the misplaced anger and hatred and lost years that followed. He didn't want the same thing to happen to White Bird and Chayton.

CHAPTER TWELVE

Aggie took several breaks several days later, hoping to see Chayton waiting for her somewhere around her cabin. He wasn't there at noon. He wasn't there mid-afternoon. He wasn't there in the evening.

He'd said he was going to hunt, so perhaps his efforts had taken him farther than he'd expected. Maybe hunting wasn't as easy as he made it sound. Maybe he'd hurt himself and was stranded someplace. She stepped to her door, looked west toward the mountains. If he didn't come back in a few days, she would ride over to Logan's. He could send someone out after Chayton.

She forced him from her mind, determined not to worry about him. He was as much a part of the land as the land itself was. He knew how to survive.

She looked for him again the next morning while doing her chores. There was only wind. And land. And sun as far as she could see. She remembered Logan saying that Chayton, like the wind, was often there but never seen. He would make himself known when it suited him, not a minute before.

In a dudgeon, she took out her frustration on her work. She built a new canvas, cutting stretchers to fit a large portrait. The story she wanted to create came to her in brilliant flashes of images. Chayton, upon his horse, a storm looming behind him, wind fighting him, frightening his horse, which rose up on his hind legs and pawed the air. All she could see were the colors, the storm, the wind.

She arranged her paints and brushes, linseed oil, and turpentine so that it was all near at hand. The canvas she'd prepared was longer than it was wide, six feet by four. She stared at it vertically, seeing in the tall and narrow canvas the finished work, then decided to turn it sideways. She adjusted her easel and looked at it again, deciding that sideways was the correct orientation. She squeezed a thick coil of white paint and another of black and another of blue, then set to work on the sky.

* * *

The first thing Aggie became aware of was that her tongue felt swollen. The next was how bright her room was. Sun was beating down against her eyelids. She went to rub her eyes and felt something thick and crusty covering her fingertips. Paint. Caked on and dried. She sighed, realizing she was waking from another painting binge. This time, she woke on the bed Logan and Sarah had sent for her use in the tent. She sighed and relaxed against the pillows. How they'd known she'd need the bed, she'd probably never know.

There was a movement near the bed. Cautiously, Aggie opened her eyes again and turned toward the sound. Chayton sat on a chair in front of the screen, watching her. He was bare-chested, his arms crossed. He looked exceedingly angry and—worried.

She sighed again and sat up, wishing, wishing with all of her might, that she could be normal. Her painting was a madness, a sickness that stole her mind and owned her soul. It had been the same with Theo, or perhaps she'd learned it from him. Either way, she could see why he'd shied away from a relationship with anyone.

Aggie climbed out of the bed. She still had her painting smock on. She needed a bath. She needed food. And she was thirsty enough to drain a small lake. She said nothing to Chayton as she walked around the screen and went to her easel and paints, intent on finding the turpentine to get the paint off her fingers.

She did not get that far.

The painting she'd been working on confronted her, stole her breath, stopped her in her tracks. Mother of God. It was exquisite. Her best work yet. The emotion on Chayton's face and the terror in his horse's expression mirrored the violence of the sky. She could almost feel the storm they were in: the wind, the wet splash of rain.

She wiped the sudden wash of tears from her face. Each work took a piece of her soul. Perhaps she voluntarily gave each a bit of her soul. She looked back at real-life Chayton, who'd come around the screen to watch her. He would be the death of her, she had no doubt, because she'd only just started producing the body of work he inspired.

She poured a bit of turpentine on a rag and scrubbed at her fingers. When she left the painting tent, Chayton followed. Still they didn't speak. A scent curled around Aggie when she stepped outside—rich, like meat cooking. Her eyes searched for the source.

Over on the south side of the house was a four-sided rack made of long branches. Thin strips of meat were draped over each branch. A fire smoked in the center of the rack. On another fire, one of her large pots simmered with a thick stew.

Good heavens, she was hungry.

She made a quick circuit of her yard to check the horse in the corral. She had a vague memory of tending to him when she'd taken potty breaks, but those breaks had been few and far between over the last few days. How many days had she been out of her mind?

She grabbed a pitcher then went to the pump. She drew the water, collecting it in her hands to wash her face, then filled the pitcher. She drank half of what she'd drawn. She filled the pitcher again and took it inside the cabin. After firing up the stove, she set several pots on top to heat water for a bath. It would take several trips to the pump to fill them all. On her third trip, Chayton stopped her, handing her a bowl full of a stew.

"Eat," he ordered.

She set her water pail down. Her hand shook as she took the bowl. Chayton gripped her arm and led her to the bench in front of her house. She didn't need prompting to collapse upon it. The stew he'd prepared was different from the ones she usually made. Sweet and savory, with spices she couldn't identify. It was delicious. She emptied the bowl in record time.

Chayton filled the water in the pots on the stove while she ate. When she was finished, he took her bowl from her. "Do what you are going to do with the water, then we will talk."

It was a directive he didn't leave open to discussion. He walked away from her, going around the side of the house. Aggie leaned her head back against the wall. She could hear the water on the stove from the open front door. It wasn't boiling yet. She didn't have the strength to move yet, so she sat and contemplated Chayton.

He'd been there the first time she'd awakened from one of her painting binges, crouched by the door, watching her. He'd given her water—she remembered the tin cup sitting on the floor. She wondered what he thought of her. He probably considered her too strange and too much of a burden to stay around for long. And she was. She knew it. No wonder Theo had made the choices he'd made.

After a while, she could hear the water heating up. It sizzled as it splashed out of the pots onto the hot stove. She hoisted herself up and went inside to fetch the things she would need for a full bath: the tub, linens, fresh clothes, soap, lotion.

She drew several more buckets of water for the tub, then tempered them with the hot water from the stove. She shut and locked the front door, then barred the windows. In the darkened quiet of her front room, she peeled off her stale clothes and slipped down into the welcome heat of the tub. So soothing it almost put her to sleep again. The soap she used was sweet smelling, made from eastern honeysuckle flowers. When the water started to cool, she washed her hair and scrubbed herself clean.

An hour later, she'd dressed, brushed her teeth, and straightened her cottage. Ready to face Chayton, she stepped outside to find him. He looked up, saw her, looked her over, then made a face as if he were holding back words he'd rather not say.

"I'm ready to talk now," she said, standing by the poles of the drying cage he'd built. She watched him warily, seeing she hadn't misinterpreted his anger. He straightened from the task of turning the curing meat.

"You are a danger to yourself."

Aggie lifted her head, holding her hands behind her back as she steeled herself for the vitriol that was coming.

"You live alone, unguarded, uncared for, a woman without defenses. I have never seen someone take so many soul journeys, except for a few medicine men— and one medicine woman."

Aggie shut her eyes, hoping the tears she felt wouldn't make a full appearance. It wasn't by her choice that she was alone. But given who and what she was, she was not a choice fit for any marriage-minded men.

"I think you should become my wife."

It took a minute for his words to sink in. She blinked, setting a few tears free to roll down her cheek. "What?"

"I no longer wish to live alone. And you cannot survive alone."

"Chayton, that's a bad idea, for so many reasons."

"Explain them to me."

"We come from different worlds. I-I never meant to stay here. Eventually, I will return to my people."

"You could choose to stay. Logan has many trading posts. He could sell your artwork as he did my wife's."

"I don't know that I could survive a winter here."

"I will show you how. I will help you."

Oh, it was so tempting to accept what he offered. To relax and be what she was. "Chayton, I'm not normal. I will disappoint you in every way a wife could disappoint a husband."

He made a face. She could almost hear him gathering the words he would say next. "You are an

Other. Others are sacred. It is an honor to care for an Other, and an even greater honor to be married to one."

"What do you mean I'm an 'other'?"

"Others walk between this life and *Wakȟáŋ Tȟáŋka,* the Great Spirit. They talk more to the Great Spirit than to their own people, but they share the Great Spirit's purpose with those of us who cannot otherwise know it."

Aggie bowed her head, humbled by his assessment of her madness. How nice it would be to not be alone. To be loved and cared for by someone who understood her. "We barely know each other," she said, choosing instead to go with an argument he couldn't refute.

"I have watched you for one cycle of the moon. I have spoken and visited with you for another cycle. You are not unknown to me. I have seen your work. I am not unknown to you."

When she looked up again, she realized he'd moved to the drying rack he'd set up, with thin strips of meat hanging on it. He reworked the fire. The smoky heat rose up through the ladder of branches, flavoring and drying the meat. She could see that the strips of venison were nearly done; they'd shrunken and dried until they were stiff to the touch.

"How long was I gone?"

"Three days, working but not aware, one day sleeping."

She wondered how long before he'd returned that

she'd been absorbed by her work.

"Your current painting had only part of the sky done when I arrived," he answered, as if reading her mind. "You were not alone long." He looked at her. "I tried to talk to you, but soon realized you were not you. Do you remember that I brought you water and food?"

"No."

"You did not eat, and only drank a little. It is as if you were taken over by a vision. A waking dream. For me, it is like seeing a turtle walk out of her shell— something that should not happen, but is somehow sacred. I watched over you. I have watched over you before. Many times."

She smiled. "Maybe that's why I miss you when you're not here."

"I have always been with you. Since the first night you arrived."

"Why?"

"Because the wind gave you to me."

Aggie's heart tore a little bit at the thought that she would get Chayton mixed up in her odd life. She wasn't normal. She would never be normal. And the worst of it was that she didn't want to be normal. She loved her creative life. But, God help her, how she yearned to be loved by a man.

No—not just any man. This man, who stood before her, bare-chested, wearing some of his necklaces, his breechcloth and leggings, his long, black hair braided and wrapped in strips of hide. He'd survived the worst that life had to offer and stood unbent by the weight of his losses.

She stepped forward and he stepped forward. In seconds, they were body to body. She lifted her hands to the bare skin of his sides. She was afraid of looking up, of lifting her face to his, so she stared at his throat, breathed his scent, felt the rumble of her heartbeat in her ears. When he reached for her waist, a shiver rippled through her. He leaned down and nuzzled the side of her hair, her temple, her cheek, moving ever so carefully to kiss her.

She lifted her face, a little, then a little more until their faces were against each other. His breath was warm against her chin and neck. She was breathing fast, too fast, but she wanted—wanted *something*. Her lips parted. Her gaze lifted to his. She saw his nostrils flare, his expression harden. Then he took her face in his hands and held her for his kiss, rough and hungry. She opened herself to him, meeting his tongue with hers across the boundary of their teeth. He tilted his head sideways, melding his mouth to hers. She stood on her tiptoes to leverage their connection.

One of his hands moved to her hair, fisting it, pinning her for another plundering kiss as his arm pulled her tighter against himself. She reached up his back and hooked her hands over his shoulders. She could feel the strength in the play of his muscles beneath her hands. She looked up at him, saw the shadows that filtered through his eyes. The lines bracketing his mouth tightened.

He abruptly released her and stepped back, then turned and walked away around the cabin. It took her several long moments before she followed him. When she did, he was nowhere to be seen.

CHAPTER THIRTEEN

Aggie stood in her tent early the next morning, looking over her paintings with a critical eye. She'd been unable to sleep, fretting over Chayton's decision that they should marry. Her heart rejected every objection she came up with. She was tired of being alone, too. If he meant what he'd said, then she knew she would go down that road with him. And he'd proven he would take care of her. Not only did he understand her madness, he thought it sacred. She could look the world over and never find that in another man.

Still, it was such a big decision—not one to be made casually. How she wished she had someone to talk to about it.

She glanced around her again at her paintings, seeking to distract herself with busywork while her mind resolved the matter of her future. A few of the pieces needed to be retouched. Most were ready to go. If she stopped now, by the time the storm painting dried, she'd have plenty of time to get the pieces down to Denver so that she could work out the frames for them. Framing them would deplete the last of her reserves. Maybe she could sell a few pieces to Logan before she left. Or perhaps his patronage would cover her framing expenses. The two large works could be the show's anchor. In total, she had over twenty pieces of varying sizes and compositions. She set up her palette with the colors she needed, then moved about the tent, doing the touch-ups, signing the works "A. Hamilton" and marking the year on them.

It was late afternoon when she emerged from the tent to wash her brushes. Chayton was taking the jerky down from the drying ladder. He straightened when he saw her. She drew a sharp breath, struck by his appearance, his very primal nature. The way his hair moved as he moved, the look in his dark, serious eyes.

"The meat is dry. I am packing it away for this winter."

Winter. Aggie wouldn't be here, unless she accepted him as her husband. The thought of never seeing him again caused her physical pain. She went inside the cabin and started preparing their supper. No matter what happened, she would never forget him. Or this time. Not just because he was the focus of so many of her paintings, but because he had etched himself on her heart.

* * *

Aggie took two cups of tea outside that evening. Chayton sat on the bench beside the front door. She paused at the threshold. The wood of the cabin behind him shone in warm orange and brown. He was watching the setting sun. The ridges of the mountains were darker shades of lavender, blue, and purple that contrasted with the pastel pinks and oranges filling the sky. Chayton looked over at her, giving her a small smile in greeting. Nothing was untouched by the sunset, not even him. He wore his buckskin tunic and necklaces. His black hair was loose and long over his shoulders. The lowering sun brought out red and blue highlights in it. It warmed his skin and cast blue shadows beneath his necklaces.

She handed him one of the mugs she carried. He took it, lifting his free hand for her to sit next to him. She did, snuggling close, touching him from hip to knee. He was warm, and the evening was cool despite the warm glow of the setting sun.

She looked up at him, and he down at her. She felt as if she was all that he saw—incredible when she thought of the show the sky was putting on.

"When you look at me, what do you see?" he asked, his voice quiet.

She glanced at his face, his hair, his body. "Many things simultaneously. I see colors. Beautiful colors that should clash, but instead they complement each other. But it isn't only colors that I see. There is a mood about you. An energy. It's powerful, generous, controlled. I feel as if I could survive on your energy without ever needing food."

His smile became wistful. He looked west, toward the mountains. Aggie bent her legs, resting her head on his shoulder and her knees over his thighs. She curled into him, holding her mug in the cup of her hands. He wrapped his arm around her and leaned his face against her hair.

"I think Father Sky sees in colors, too, when he gazes down at Mother Earth. He does not judge but simply basks in what he observes. It is a good feeling."

Aggie sat in the quiet glow that came from Chayton. He could be so still, like wind caught in the act of being. It was one of the big differences between them. She was always racing ahead, looking at the future, becoming something. But he was always being.

"Chayton, was your wife an Other?"

"Yes. She could weave energy. Not everyone can do that, but all can feel the result of that. The great warriors of our people would commission her work for their warshirts and ceremonial clothes. Maidens would bring their dance dresses and shoes to her so that she could weave the correct energies in with the beadwork she applied. She taught Logan to sense those energies. She was highly revered among our people. Many maidens were apprenticed to her so that she could teach them how to do what she did. Her death was a great loss to my people."

Aggie smiled and lifted a hand to touch his chin.

"Logan said you had the gentlest soul of anyone he'd ever met. I didn't believe it that first night."

He pressed his lips together as he considered her words. He said nothing for a long time. Aggie set her cup down and shifted against him, leaning her back against his chest as she watched the setting sun. She threaded her fingers through his where his hand rested on her shoulder.

At last, he broke the silence. "I will be a gift to you, Agkhee."

She shifted around to hug him. "You already have been."

His arm tightened around her. He smelled like wood smoke from the fire he'd been tending and well-worn leather, heated by his body and the last rays of the setting sun. He captured her cheek with his free hand and kissed her forehead, her temple, her cheek. Aggie turned slightly, touching her lips to his. Their noses pressed against each other. She was practically sitting on his lap now. She leaned forward to hug him, enjoying the feel of a solid man in her arms and not the empty weight of an imagined lover.

"Agkhee, I would like to take a journey with you."

She smiled. "All right."

"Tomorrow, we will travel into the Valley of Painted Walls."

"That sounds beautiful."

He nodded. "It is. It is a secret and sacred place. Logan is the only white man who knows about it." He looked down at her. "It is there I will make you mine."

She frowned. This was why she had a knot in her stomach. "Do you mean wife or lover?"

"Wife and lover."

"Forever?"

"For as long as I breathe."

She studied him a long moment. His statement earlier hadn't been random. He meant a real marriage. Each bonded to the other. Once married, she could stay here and paint him until the need had run its course. And when she turned her focus to another subject, he would be with her, guarding her, feeding her, seeing her safely back to her shell after her work binges.

The next morning, they rode east for a few hours, keeping the sandstone bluffs on their left. After a while, Chayton turned them toward the pine forest that was thickening around the base of the mountain. They climbed up, following a trail that was uncomfortably steep. Aggie was leaning forward, almost against the horse's neck. Now and then, her mount would stumble, leaving her with terrible thoughts about tumbling down the mountain, crushed by the horse and rocks below them. She decided that on the homeward trip, she'd go down on foot. This ride, in reverse, had to be ten times worse.

Eventually, their path leveled out…into a narrow trail navigable only by mountain goats. Her eyes locked in an unfocused way on the ground at the bottom of the ravine, far, far below. Her breathing grew increasingly shallow. If she didn't ask for help now, she soon wouldn't be able to communicate. Or move. Or breathe.

"Chay—" her first attempt to call his name was softer than a half-exhalation. "Chayton. Please. I can't do this."

He made a sound that caused his horse to stop, a reaction that slipped through the packhorse and back to her horse. She slammed her eyes shut. The only thing worse than walking this narrow ledge was not walking it. The wind alone would blow them off this peak.

Warm, firm hands freed her reins from her frozen grip. Her thighs tightened on the horse's sides, making it shift its weight side to side. It couldn't go forward with the others stopped. Chayton set a hand to its neck and spoke to it in a calming voice.

"Lean into me," he directed, a hand behind her back and another under her knees. "I have you." She made her stiff body shift toward him, wondering as she did so who had him. Behind him was the bottomless ravine.

She squeezed his shoulders and buried her face in his neck. He walked a nonexistent path next to the horses and hoisted her up on his horse, then swung up behind her. He leaned forward and picked up the reins. She felt his thighs squeeze his mount, then they started forward again. She faced away from the wide valley to their right, keeping her eyes shut and her face against his throat.

"I never meant for my Other to be scared." His voice was a low rumble against the side of her head. "I will not let you fall. There is nothing you need to fear here. Breathe. Breathe in the air that is so cool and the sun that is so hot. Agkhee, open your eyes." Every time he said her name, he drew out the last syllable in a long sigh. *Ag-khee.* "We are high, like eagles flying. Open your eyes and feed your soul."

How could she not when he made their cliff-side perch sound like a blessing and not a death sentence? He held the reins of his pony in his left hand. His right arm was wrapped over hers, his hand spread wide over hers. She felt his strength, his utter lack of fear. She opened her eyes and watched the craggy wall they slowly passed. Still facing away from the deep ravine below her, she drew a long breath, then slowly released it. She held her body perfectly still, but turned her face into the sun.

"Did you know you could fly?" he whispered.

She couldn't answer. No words were equal to the majesty of the natural beauty spread out as a feast for her senses. She was glad Chayton's hold on her was still firm, because she did feel as if she were flying.

"Will you paint this for me, Agkhee?"

She nodded but didn't speak, didn't want to break the spell of what she was seeing. In too short a time, they began their descent into the valley below, following a switchback trail that led them down into a pine and aspen forest. Her mind was buzzing with possible compositions.

Chayton let her ride with him until they reached their destination—a shallow cave in a granite outcropping about twenty feet deep. A flat ledge of the same rock provided a natural overhang that extended over a bare campsite, hidden by the boulders and trees.

Chayton dismounted, then lifted her down but didn't immediately release her. She eased her hands up his arms to his shoulders, then into his hair. He wore it braided in the front and loose in the back. She slipped her hands through his black mane.

"Thank you for bringing me here," she said. He smiled and leaned forward to kiss her. Their lips just touched when Aggie pulled back to frown at him. "Though I already fear the return trip."

"I will hold you going back. I won't let my Other fall down the side of a mountain." He gripped the back of her head, holding her in place as he bent over and kissed her. Aggie tightened her arm around his neck and held him while he deepened the kiss. His hand moved from her cheek, down her side. She wondered if he would make love to her here, now.

"Agkhee…" He straightened his hold on her, letting her stand upright without releasing her. He leaned his face against hers. "This is another place I frequently stay. Let us get your painting items arranged so that you have everything as you need it when you are ready to step out of your shell."

She laughed. "It's called painting."

"It is not painting. I have painted before. You are

taken by visions. It is the *Wakȟáŋ Tȟáŋka* talking to you."

Aggie smiled up at him and set her hand over his heart. "I love you, Chayton." The words spilled out without any forethought on her part, startling both of them.

He caught her hand and kissed her fingers. "I am yours, Agkhee, as you are mine. I did not think I would love again, but you have shown me the way to feel my heart once more."

A round fire pit sat at the mouth of the cave. Inside the narrow dwelling area, a heavy skin strung across a low wooden frame made a narrow cot. A shelf that was dug out of the cave wall held a few different vessels and baskets. Clusters of spices hung upside down over one end of the shelf. A thick buffalo robe was folded on one end of the shelf.

She helped him unload her easel, rolls of canvas, sketchpads, pencils, wooden stretchers, tools, paints, oils, varnishes, jars, and brushes. Touching her equipment made her itchy to get started, though something whispered she hadn't seen yet what she most needed to paint.

Chayton went to hunt some small game for their supper. She swept out the cave floor using a rough broom that was propped near the shelf, and shook out the big buffalo fur, then set it on the cot along with the other blankets she'd packed. She put the food she'd brought nearer to the fire pit, then stowed the satchel of her clothes under the cot.

When she'd made the space as tidy and organized as possible, she went out to collect firewood. With all the cottonwoods in the area, it was plentiful. She brought several armloads into the cave. She'd only packed a few kitchenware items: a pot for stew, the tin pot and cups for coffee, and a bucket, which she grabbed before leaving to get water.

The valley was protected from the wind that sometimes blistered the high ridges above, leaving the woods still and quiet. And green. Aggie had seen the narrow river when she went for firewood, and she headed in that direction now. Somewhere near her, a twig snapped. She stopped and listened. Deciding it must have been a squirrel or some small forest creature, she resumed her walk toward the river. Again she heard something, someone, walking near her. She remembered being confronted with the mountain lion up by Chayton's other cave. Was it a big animal that followed her through the woods? A bear?

She checked the woods behind her as she asked, "Chayton? Is that you?" No answer came back to her from the green quiet of the forest. She held herself still for a long moment, searching the space around her. Maybe she should bring up extra firewood when she was done with the water. She certainly didn't want to have to fetch more in the dark of the night. She continued on toward the river. She heard an animal sound off to her side, a strange, deep snuffling. Her heart began to pound. What was that?

She could hear the river ahead. She would be out of these woods in a few more steps. She hurried her pace, but even as she did, a rumble shook the ground, a deep, thundering bass that she heard and felt. She leaned back against the base of a wide cottonwood as the sound swelled around her. Something moved to her left, then to her right as large animals ran through the woods. Horses. She straightened, no longer frightened—now she was stunned. When the herd had moved beyond her area, she followed them down to the water.

She stopped for a minute to watch them, keeping within the cover of the woods. She'd never been this close to a herd of wild horses. It was a large group, maybe three dozen. And colorful—a strange mix of roans, buckskins, paints, sorrels. They looked smaller than quarter horses, more short-legged, like mustangs. She was surprised they tolerated her presence. She edged past them, following the line of woods, hoping to move upstream without exciting their interest or alarming them.

She was not so lucky. A roan came over to her, no larger than the rest, but a whole lot bigger than she was. Aggie stayed close to a tree, thinking it was the only cover available if the horse decided to charge her. She held perfectly still, careful to not stare at the animal. She didn't know enough about horses to know if that mattered with them as it did with dogs, but she was desperate.

The horse wasn't having any of her reticence. He

came right up to her and nudged her hand. Surprised, she reached up and scratched his cheek and chin, then patted his muscular neck. He looked healthy, lean but not skinny. Another horse snuffled off to her left. She looked up to see Chayton sitting bareback on a paint.

He grinned at her. He wore his long-sleeved buckskin shirt, with its tattered fringe, his colorful necklaces, his hair loose except for those two front braids he'd threaded through with ribbons of hide. While she watched, he stepped out of the woods. Sunlight poured over him, brightening the front half of his horse.

She couldn't respond to his greeting. Couldn't do anything but shut her eyes and preserve the image of him she'd just seen. The shadow of the woods behind him. The way light made the green aspen leaves a vibrant, verdant color. The herd of horses in front of Chayton, clustered around the rocky riverbank.

She opened her eyes after a moment. Saying nothing to Chayton, she moved upstream, filled her bucket, then walked through the forest, keeping her mind numb to other observations as she made her way back to their camp.

Once there, she set the water down near the fire pit and started preparing a canvas. She was aware of Chayton following her up to the camp. He didn't speak, didn't make any requests of her. His nearness was a comfort. He was no doubt guarding her shell, because she was pretty certain she'd just walked out of it.

* * *

It was dark when she set her brush down and stepped back to look at her work. The fog had cleared from her mind. She became aware of the fire dancing in the pit off to her left, casting a bright light that reflected against the cave walls. She looked around her, wondering where Chayton was. He sat on the cot with this back propped against the wall. The buffalo robe was wrapped around his bare legs and waist.

He met her gaze, maintaining his silence. She smiled at him.

"Will you eat now?" he asked.

At the mention of food, her stomach growled. "Yes. Let me clean up. Did you eat already?"

He nodded. "Hours ago."

Aggie took care of her brushes and removed the paint from her fingers and hands. She never really understood how she ended up with so much on her hands after completing a canvas. There was something about touching the painting to make small adjustments that only her fingers could navigate—it tightened her connection with the work.

When she came back to the cave, Chayton held a bowl and spoon out to her, both carved of wood. He wore only his breechcloth. She watched the muscles of his legs and flanks flex. Raw strength. Her gaze moved up his body. It was here he would make her his wife. The thought heated her blood, sent it thrumming in her ears. She sat next to the fire, barely able to breathe as he returned to the cot and the buffalo robe. She watched him look at her painting.

"Come, sit with me. Bring your stew." He sat straighter against the wall, giving her room to sit in front of him. He held the robe open to her. She crossed the space to him. He turned her and drew her down between his legs so that she leaned back against him. She rested her head against his shoulder. They sat on the buffalo blanket. He wrapped his arms and the robe around her waist.

"Am I hurting you?" she asked as she settled against him.

"No." He kissed the side of her head. "It is beautiful, what you created today. I watched as you built a world on your canvas. The horses look as if they are standing nearby, as if they would move at any time and step out of your painting. You would not eat or drink. I was not sure how long you'd be gone. I like the smaller paintings because you are not away from me too long." One of his hands covered hers, holding the spoon with her as he dipped it into the bowl and lifted it to her mouth. "Eat."

Aggie chewed and swallowed. "The horses are beautiful. And friendly. Are they yours?"

He repeated the motion with the spoon. "Yes. I have worked with this herd for many years."

She took the spoon from him. Those first few tastes of his delicious stew helped her realize how hungry she was. "Worked with them? How so?"

"When my people lived free, I trained horses for the warriors and the women, as you know. It was here that I would train them. I was well known for my work, and beloved."

"Don't they still need horses?"

"I have no people now. I cannot return to the Agency."

Aggie finished her stew in silence. She went to the fire and set her bowl down. She looked back at Chayton sitting on the narrow cot, lounging back against the cave wall. She heard Theo's words filter through her mind: *"Go out and find your art, find your heart, and hold them both close."*

There would never be another man who understood her as well as Chayton. She had no doubt that she would be safe and fed and adored should they take the next step in their lives. In a solemn mood, she went over and knelt beside him on the cot.

She took hold of his hand in hers. "There are things we must discuss before we really do marry."

He said nothing, but watched her.

"Things about reality. Differences in our worlds. How we'll live."

Chayton's face grew shuttered. "Sarah has said that a marriage between us will never be accepted by your people."

"Would she and Logan object to it? They're your friends. And they're raising your daughter. I care more about them than the world of people we don't know."

"I have spoken with them about it. They would not object."

Aggie bit her bottom lip, then smiled at the implications of Chayton's statement. They could make this work, out here at least, in this remote corner of the world. "I have a floor in a warehouse in Denver where I lived with my father. It's where he painted, but if Logan and Sarah would continue to rent the cabin to us, I would prefer it. I know I'll make enough from my exhibition to pay for it."

"Agkhee, you saw how your people react to me in town. It would be the same—or worse—in Denver."

"Maybe. But I don't live in the circle of society, Chayton." She sighed. "Though sometimes I wish I could be normal, I'm not. I'm an artist. I can't document a world I'm a part of—I have to stand outside of it to have any true observations of it. I don't think that would change."

He watched her with a steady regard.

"I'm saying I don't care what my people think of us."

He reached up and tucked a strand of hair behind her ear. "I care. If we are to live among your people, because we cannot live among mine, then you will never be safe if they do not accept our relationship. They would find ways to punish you. And if we ever had children, they would be at risk as well. It is this, and only this, that keeps me from making you my wife now."

Tears welled in Aggie's eyes. She lowered her gaze

to his hand, which now clasped hers. She didn't want to even think about a future that didn't include Chayton.

He leaned over and kissed her forehead. "You are tired. Sleep now. We will find your shell in the morning." He moved so that he lay on his side. She stretched out beside him, comforted by the feel of his arms around her. "Until we wake, I will be your shell. Tomorrow, we will decide together what our future will be."

CHAPTER FOURTEEN

Chayton draped the strap of her work satchel over her head and smiled as he lifted her hair free. A smiling Chayton was hypnotic; Aggie couldn't help but smile back at him. They'd been together the entire night. She couldn't remember when she'd last been snuggled near another human through the dark of the night; certainly not since she left the orphanage. Theo had been kind to her but never demonstrative. Chayton made her feel safe, revered, and best of all, understood.

"I have someplace special to show you today," he said as he stood before her at the entrance to his cave.

"Someplace special to sketch?"

"Among other things." He smiled cryptically. "Can you swim, Agkhee?"

She frowned. "No."

"No? How can white parents not teach their young to swim?"

"Mine died when I was too young. And Theo was

too busy."

"Ours learn when they are infants."

"Is it safe where we're going?"

"With me it is."

He took her hand and led her into the forest. They climbed up a steep hill, then went higher over a treeless, rocky bluff, moving deeper and deeper into a primeval land governed only by the laws of nature, populated only by wild creatures. Like Chayton.

They moved around a bend in the rocky ledge. A distant roaring sound filled Aggie's ears. Chayton looked back at her and grinned. Another hundred feet brought them around into a deep canyon.

He took her hand. "Keep up, Agkhee. It is steep here."

Heights. Again. "I'm not a mountain goat, Chayton. You know I don't like these cliffs."

He paused, drawing her up against his body. "Close your eyes."

She did as he asked.

"Do you hear the water?"

She did. It was roaring now. The falls echoed off the canyon walls. She looked at him. Seeing the joy in his eyes, she took a calming breath. If he said they were safe on this steep ridge, then they were safe. And she would have risked any danger to see his eyes light up as they were now. "Carry on. I'll be fine."

They spent the next twenty minutes traveling downward via a scant path that wound around boulders and brush. The narrow canyon was much cooler than the rocky ledge up top—it stayed in the shade except during the noon hour, when the sun was directly overhead. The shadows the cliff walls cast were blue, spilling across the striated layers of different colored rock.

When they finally reached level ground, they stood at the banks of a swiftly flowing river maybe ten yards wide. The river was deep, the water green. Here and there it spilled over short ledges of worn boulders, churning into dangerous white water.

Chayton led her forward to the waterfall, which dropped several hundred feet over stepped ledges higher up the cliff. As they rounded a bend in the canyon wall, a wide lake spread out before them—deep, dark, and surprisingly calm for the violent waters that churned at either end.

Aggie looked up at the huge, nearly smooth cliff face bordering the lake and saw the enormous pictographs painted on the wall. A hunting scene with horses, hunters, and buffalo. The cliff face was slightly inverted and concave—perhaps that was what had protected the ancient art from the elements for so long.

"When you said this was the Valley of Painted Walls, I assumed it was because of the colorful rock formations. This is extraordinary."

"This is a sacred place of my people. Many young braves would come here for their vision quests. Others came to hunt or recover from wounds. Game is plentiful here. And the waters heal. This is where I met Logan many years ago."

Chayton walked over to a sandy bank and set down the pack he'd brought, dropping the blanket over top of it. He began to remove his various necklaces, untied the feathers in his hair. He removed his moccasins, slipped out of his leggings, and took off his tunic. In very short order, he stood before her wearing only his breechcloth.

Her heart began a loud noise when he reached for her satchel and set it down next to his belongings. He led her to a low boulder and had her sit down. He lifted one of her legs and rested her foot against his bare thigh, then began untying her boots.

"What are you doing?"

"It is time you shared your body with me."

Aggie's eyes widened. She let her gaze dip down Chayton's torso to his breechcloth. "I-I'm not sure that's wise."

He set her boots aside, then pushed her skirt up higher and found the tie binding her stocking, below the hem of her drawers. "I have decided that we will find a way to make a life together. I already speak your language. I will step into your world when necessary. And we will live in my world all other times."

"But Chayton, we've only been discussing marriage. We haven't actually become married."

"I hunted for you, and you accepted the meat I brought you. You have stood with me in my blanket. You have cooked for me and I have eaten your food.

We have been alone together in your home and in my cave here. You are already my wife." He lifted her to her feet. She didn't resist as he pulled her shirt from the waistband of her skirt.

"But I didn't know that's what those things meant."

"I did." He made a face as he set about unbuttoning the many tiny buttons of her blouse. He spread the sides of her shirt and looked at her chest hungrily.

Aggie's skin instantly heated, the flush rising from below her collarbone to her throat. She knew she should protest the giant leap he'd made, but couldn't calm her jumping nerves long enough to form a coherent argument.

Chayton leaned forward and kissed her neck. "Your skin is pink."

She leaned her face into his. "I don't know how to do this."

"I will show you."

"What if I'm no good at it?"

He laughed, his breath a hot puff of air on her neck. "Others are always good at making love. Do you know why?" She shook her head. "Because they savor all the feelings it gives them." He released the buttons at her wrists, then tugged at each sleeve. "Take it off. And your skirt."

Aggie pulled her shirt off and stepped out of her skirt and petticoat. She hadn't worn the proper ensemble of underclothes since she came out to this remote land, and now had very few layers between herself and the impending consummation of their decision to marry. The wind caressed her bare skin. Though she still wore her chemise and pantalettes, she felt utterly exposed. He smiled and reached for her, his hands a warm mocha on her pale skin. He rubbed them up and down, sending little shivers over her spine. She flattened her hands against his chest, white skin against dark. His black hair hung freely about his shoulders. She reached up and held a fistful of it. He smiled at her. She opened her hand and let it sift through her fingers.

Chayton spread one of the two blankets he'd brought over the sand and pebbles at the side of the wide lake. When he turned back, he caught Aggie as she was unbuttoning her camisole. His intense gaze locked on her hands. Aggie stopped moving. His gaze lifted to her face. He didn't speak or move, but she knew he wanted her to continue. She unfastened the remaining buttons. His gaze stroked the column of white skin revealed by the slightly open panels of flimsy cotton.

When he started walking toward her, her heartbeat sped up. He touched her collarbone, then drew his fingers downward in a light caress until he came level with her breasts. He looked into her eyes. She locked on to his gaze, feeling heat swirl in strange places inside her body. He pushed one panel of her chemise aside. Aggie's breathing became shallow as his fingertips moved over the swell of her breast, navigating to her now-erect nipple. Her lips parted. He stroked her sensitive peak with his fingertips, then rubbed his open palm over the tight nipple.

His gaze lifted to meet hers. His eyes were intense, hungry. He moved his hand to her other breast, cupping her as he drew her against himself. "I want to see you. All of you. With your hair down. I want to feel your body against mine."

"Someone will see us—"

"No one knows of this hidden place. We will not be disturbed."

Aggie hesitated, then pulled her chemise off.

The tension deepened in his face as he looked at her bare torso. "And those." He nodded at her bloomers. "What do you call them?"

"Bloomers. Pantalettes. Underwear. Many things, I guess."

"Take them off."

Aggie did as he asked. He sucked in a sharp pull of air when at last she stood before him fully nude. Feeling the air on her stomach and thighs was a decadent sensation. "And you? Are you going to stay clothed?"

"No." He unfastened the wide leather strap about his hips that held his breechcloth in place and pushed it off. When he straightened, she could not take her eyes off his fully aroused member. The nude men Theo had had her paint had not been erect; they'd looked nothing like Chayton did at this moment. He was heavy and rigid, his penis pointing forward at an angle.

He reached for her and pulled her up against his

body. She stretched her arms up around his shoulders. His hands were on her back, moving up and down, feeling her shoulders, spine, and bottom. He kissed her neck, her shoulder, her chin. "Release your hair. I want to feel that, too."

Aggie pulled her hairpins free and dropped them by her chemise. She forked her fingers through her hair, smoothing it out for him. He reached up and took handfuls of it, wrapping it about his fists as he lifted one, then the other, to his face.

"Agkhee," he whispered as he bent his forehead to hers, "Agkhee, I cannot wait longer." He kissed her as he walked them backward to the blanket, kissed her as they knelt down, kissed her as he leaned her back on the blanket. He pressed his body down on hers, firing off powerful sensations she'd never before experienced. He smiled at her, but his eyes looked sad.

He kneed her legs apart and settled himself against her most secret flesh, rocking against her in a slow, easy motion that made her hunger for more, for a deeper contact. She knew he would eventually enter her, a thought that filled her with fear and excitement. How she craved a complete connection with him. She spread her legs wider.

He held his weight on his elbows, giving himself room to kiss and taste her skin. His mouth was gentle as he made his way from the center of her throat down to the valley between her breasts. She gasped when he took hold of her breast. Pointing her nipple upwards, he sucked her sensitive peak. Aggie cried out and arched beneath him. She gripped his shoulders as he repeated that ministration with her other breast.

His long hair spilled over his shoulders to trail over her sensitized skin. He looked up at her, then reached up to touch her cheek. God, she loved his eyes. So intense, as eloquent and changeable as the moody plains. She lifted herself up on her elbows to watch as he took hold of himself, stroking between her legs with his hardened penis. He rubbed himself at the apex of her core, over an area so sensitive she cried out again. He looked up at her and grinned. She didn't return his joy. She wanted more of what he'd just done.

Reading her body's cues, he did just that, stroking forward and back. Her body started to move as if with a mind of its own, pressing back against his thrusts. As a strange feeling started to overtake her, he pushed himself into her. He was thick and hard, stretching her. Aggie groaned, her body registering dozens of new sensations.

"Oh, Chayton. Oh."

He answered her in Lakota. She didn't understand his words, but his teeth were clenched, his nostrils flared. Sweat made a fine sheen on his chest. He was inching forward, holding a fist around himself as if he feared going too deep too fast. She arched her hips, pushing herself up to meet him.

"Chayton, let me feel you. Please."

"Agkhee—it has been so long. I will not be able to

go slowly."

"I don't want slow. Please, Chayton."

He moved his hand away, plunging himself into her slick body. She cried out. He rocked over her, watching her, his gaze locked on her eyes. He was solemn. Intense. She could feel every movement he made, in and out, his hips rolling against hers. He slipped his hands between their bodies and touched that wonderful spot he'd stroked with his penis. Aggie dug her heels into the blanket as a force she never knew existed within her exploded to life. She bucked against his body, lifting her legs to wrap around his, holding him in place while her body throbbed and writhed beneath his.

His thrusts began in earnest. He pounded into her despite the tight hold of her legs. The sensation that had started to abate roared to life again. She groaned as she felt him stiffen at the same time, his sex pulsing inside of her. He stayed joined with her as her tremors slowly calmed, watching as her eyes regained focus. She reached up and brought his face down to hers. She kissed him, her mouth closed, then open. Their tongues met and stroked each other.

"*Čhéye šni yo*. Don't cry, Agkhee," he translated, swiping away a tear from the corner of her eye.

"I've missed you all of my life, even before I knew it was you I was missing. I can't believe I found you."

He kissed her forehead, then took hold of her hand and brought it to his heart. "Your light fills my dark heart."

She stroked his hair. "I love you, Chayton."

"*Thečhíȟila*." He smiled at her frown. "It means 'I love you.' I will teach you my language now that you are my wife." He eased himself from her body, then sat up and reached a hand for her. "Let us go into the water."

"I can't swim."

"We will stay on the edge of the fall, but I will teach you to swim while we are here, too." He led her along a wide path that rose over steps of neatly placed rocks, up to the side of the waterfall. She laughed at the feel of the sun and breeze on her nude body. They were playing outside, naked. It was such a freeing feeling that she thought she might never put her clothes back on.

The water there splashed gently down as it spilled side to side down polished granite boulders. The water was cold, but the day was hot. Chayton wrapped an arm around her waist, then turned with her so that they faced the valley. He propped her hands on either side of the little alcove. Water washed down over them. The midday sun lit the red canyon walls like fire and turned the green lake into a living emerald. The beauty of the vista before them overwhelmed her. She went to her knees. Chayton sat down with her, keeping a hand around her waist. He didn't speak, didn't shift his hold on her, didn't in any way interfere with her concentration.

After a long while, she leaned back against him and wrapped her arms over his, which still banded her waist. "I don't want to ever leave."

"We have no need to hurry our visit."

"What about our horses?"

"They are pastured with the herd. They have no need of us."

"Can we live here?"

"No." He kissed the side of her hair. "It is a sacred place that cannot belong to anyone because it belongs to everyone already. But we can come here as often as you like."

"I can't wait to sketch this."

He nodded. "I will catch fish for supper."

CHAPTER FIFTEEN

Sarah sat in the shade of the front porch, which was perfectly situated to receive the afternoon breeze. Unfortunately, today that breeze was as hot as an oven, shade or no shade. White Bird paced with an excess of nervous energy. They'd come outside to read while they awaited the arrival of Chayton's grandmother, Ester Burkholder.

The household had been in an uproar since yesterday when they received her telegram that she'd arrived in Defiance and would set out for the Circle Bar the next morning. They'd laundered all the bed linens, swept the entire house, beat the carpets, and washed the windows. And then Sarah and White Bird had set about baking fresh bread, pies, and cookies so that they'd have something delicious to offer Mrs. Burkholder.

"White Bird, do you think you could try to sit quietly? It's far too hot to be so agitated."

Her foster daughter turned from the railing and

gave her such a soulful look that Sarah opened her arms. "Come here, child." At nine years old, she was too big to sit on Sarah's lap, but still small enough to slip onto the seat next to her. "What has you so distraught this afternoon?"

She looked up at Sarah with her big brown eyes. "What if my great-grandmother doesn't like me?"

Sarah felt a little frisson unsettle her nerves. Her worry was not if Mrs. Burkholder wouldn't like White Bird—for who could resist the little girl's kind eyes or sweet temperament? Her greater concern was whether Chayton's grandmother would insist on taking over fostering her.

She gave White Bird a little hug. "If she doesn't like you, or your dad, or anyone, then we will politely ask her to leave. We don't need to give hospitality to anyone who comes here merely to judge us. But consider this situation from her shoes. She spent long years looking for her daughter—your grandmother—only to learn that her child passed away. And her daughter's only surviving child—your father—wants nothing to do with her. I don't think she even knows about you. I know you're nervous to meet her, but she must be equally worried about what she'll be met with here. How brave she is to face this head on."

"Do you think my *até* is truly her grandson, Sarah-*m'amá*?"

"I don't know if your father's her grandson. I'm not sure it could be proven one way or the other. Perhaps it's something they'll know when they meet each other. Perhaps he'll remember some detail about your grandmother that could only be if she was Mrs. Burkholder's daughter."

"Look!" White Bird pointed toward a dust cloud rising on the hill above the house. "She's here!"

Sarah tensed, then forced herself to appear calm. "Go get Logan. Ask him and Sid to wait for us in the living room. Then stay with Maria until I call for you."

Logan stepped out to the porch about the same time the carriage pulled to a stop in front of the house. He wrapped an arm around Sarah's shoulders and gave her a reassuring smile. The shotgun rider jumped down and opened the passenger door to give Mrs. Burkholder a hand down. Logan's foreman came out from the side of the house and directed the driver to pull the carriage around back to the stable, where they could see to the horses and get the men some grub.

Sarah studied the woman coming up the porch stairs. She looked to be in her early seventies. Her face was paper white, and her hair—what little Sarah could see beneath her bonnet—was a mixture of blond and gray. She was slim, her posture straight, her shoulders square. Though she carried a cane, she had only the slightest hitch in her walk. *Vim and vigor*, Sarah's father would have said.

She wore a linen traveling suit in a lovely shade of lavender. Yards of crisp lace spilled from her jacket's neckline, colored beige from the fine dust of the trail. Sarah wondered if she weren't desperately hot given the day's terrible heat.

"Mrs. Burkholder, I'm Logan Taggert. And my wife, Sarah. Welcome."

Sarah stepped forward to greet her.

"Good day, Mr. Taggert, Mrs. Taggert." The woman leaned slightly on her ebony cane.

"Was the trip terrible?" Sarah asked.

Mrs. Burkholder's brow lifted. She eyed Sarah as if she'd been asked a flippant question. "It was as you might expect. Long, dirty, rough, and hot, but mercifully direct."

Sarah gestured toward the front door. "Perhaps you would like to refresh yourself before our visit? I have refreshments waiting for us in the living room." She showed the woman inside. Maria hurried forward to take her suit jacket, gloves, and hat, then led her down the hall to the washroom. Her driver brought her luggage down to Sid's room, which he'd vacated for her use.

Sarah went ahead to the parlor. Logan watched her come into the room. They exchanged a look full of worry and unspoken words. He needed no further urging to hurry to her side and wrap his arms around her. "It is for the best that we have this meeting, sweetheart. None of us can move forward with this hanging over our heads, including Chayton and Aggie."

Sarah fought the tears welling in her eyes. "I will lose my heart if they take White Bird."

Logan hugged her. "No one's taking anyone.

Everything will be all right. You'll see."

Sarah leaned her forehead against his shoulder. "I know. I know. We've been in worse situations and lived to tell."

He smiled. "That's my girl. God knows we have." He handed her his handkerchief. "Now don't let her see you cry. She'll eat you alive and chew your bones for dessert."

"That's terrible." She laughed and gave him a little shove. The break in her mood helped. She had herself composed by the time Logan's stepfather, Sid, came into the room. The two men exchanged a hard glance. Sid had been in this situation before when Logan's stepbrother, Sager, had first come home from his life with the Shoshone.

When Mrs. Burkholder joined them, she'd changed from her traveling ensemble to another lavender outfit—this one of cool muslin with collar and cuffs of lace. Her graying hair was impeccably pinned. She looked as fresh as any proper lady visiting for tea.

They all stood to greet her. "Mrs. Burkholder, this is my father, Sid Taggert," Logan said.

Sid took her hand and offered an elegant half-bow over it. "Mrs. Burkholder. I'm happy we can meet finally."

"How do you do?"

Sarah gestured toward the sofa. "You must be parched and famished after your journey. I have cold lemonade, iced tea, and sandwiches. If you prefer hot tea, I'd be happy to have some made."

"Not at all. The lemonade would be wonderful." She took the glass goblet that Sarah handed her. "An iced beverage. Such a refreshing surprise for these wild lands."

"We have an ice house," Sarah explained. "Every winter we store ice cut from a nearby lake. We're running low now that it's so late in the season, but this seemed a good opportunity to splurge." Sarah served everyone a beverage, then offered the tray of tea sandwiches to their guest.

They made small talk for a few minutes while they enjoyed the refreshments. After a while, Mrs. Burkholder set her dishes down on the side table, then focused on Logan. "Would you please tell me about the man you feel may be my grandson?"

Logan gazed at the older woman, measuring her. "I will tell you about my friend, but as yet I cannot be certain he is your grandson. Perhaps you could give us some background for your interest, first?"

Mrs. Burkholder sent a look at the three Taggerts. Her lips were pursed, her chin high. "My husband, God rest his soul, and I had four children. Our daughter, Lucy, was the next to the eldest. One summer, nearly forty years ago now, it was time for a shipment of goods to be delivered." She paused as the impact of that fact filtered through her own mind. "It was our custom to accompany different our supply trains to various forts and trading posts. Relations with the aborigines along those routes were fairly calm, usually pleasant, often lucrative. Lucy was nine years old that summer. Her brothers were eleven, seven, and three. My husband felt it was important that our children learn the business early so that it would be deeply integrated with their lives.

"Anyway, that summer, I was not able to accompany them on their supply run because of my youngest's health—he had scarlet fever. They were traveling into settled lands in Iowa. I had no cause to be worried about them."

Sarah closed her eyes. She knew what was coming. She'd lived it herself. Strange how the room grew cold. She folded her arms tightly about herself. Logan was watching her with concerned eyes.

"Well, they weren't safe. They were set upon by a Sioux war party. My oldest son was killed and scalped. My husband and middle son were shot with multiple arrows. Even with several wounds, my husband managed to fight them off, protecting our children." Mrs. Burkholder paused. "Those murdering heathens left them to die. They took my daughter and most of the goods my husband was transporting." She retrieved a lace handkerchief and dabbed at her eyes.

"Eventually, my husband and son were discovered by a nearby farmer. They were taken in by him and nursed back to health. They were weeks late getting home. I knew—I just knew—something terrible had happened." Her face hardened as she collected her composure. "Our youngest succumbed to the fever while they were gone."

She pulled a golden locket out of her pocket. For a

minute, she was lost in time and memories. "My daughter had desperately wanted to go with her father and brothers on that trip, but she also worried about being away from me. I gave her this locket to comfort her on the journey." She opened it, then handed it to Sarah. "My mother gave it to me. It contains miniature portraits of my mother and me when I was a young girl.

"Over the years, my husband and I never stopped looking for Lucy, our only surviving child. There were sightings reported, here and there, now and then—a little blond girl among a band of Natives. Those reports took weeks coming to us, and by the time we could follow up on them, the heathens had moved to new locations. One of the last reports came to me a few years ago. My husband and I had offered a reward for any information leading to her recovery. A man recently out of the Army came forward with a report that my grandson had moved to the Great Sioux Reservation."

She paused, looking around at them. "It was from that man I learned Lucy had passed away years earlier. That news drained my husband's last will to live. He died only a few months later. But I was not ready to give up. My daughter had had a son. My grandson. I determined then that I would find him and bring him home."

Sid, who'd sat unmoving through Mrs. Burkholder's lengthy tale, blew a loud breath of air, then got up and went to a sideboard where a decanter of brandy sat on a tray with glasses. He poured himself a glass, swallowed it fast, then poured another before he turned and faced the room.

"Mrs. Burkholder, may I offer you a glass? Or perhaps you'd prefer a cordial?"

"Brandy will be fine."

Sarah could not find any words, either as a hostess or as a survivor of Indian depredations herself.

"Logan, would you like a glass?" Sid asked.

He was watching her and did not look away. "No thanks, Dad." He crossed the room and held a hand out to her. "Sarah, I think I heard White Bird call for you. Why don't you go see what she needs?"

Sarah took hold of his warm hand and let him draw her to her feet. She looked at Mrs. Burkholder, but words still failed her. All she could do was nod at her, hand Logan the locket, then take herself from the room before her self-control dissolved.

Logan watched Sarah leave. He knew that White Bird was listening from inside the dining room and didn't need Sarah at all, but his wife had desperately needed a bit of space to breathe. There was nothing he was going to say to Mrs. Burkholder that he hadn't already said to his foster daughter when she'd asked him about her family history.

He gazed down at the little oval windows and the tiny faces that looked back at him. He didn't recognize the young Mrs. Burkholder on the right half of the locket. But her mother was the spitting image of the adult Lucy he had known. He closed the locket. Any doubts he had that Chayton was this woman's grandson vanished.

"Logan may have informed you of the similar experiences that have touched our lives," Sid said, breaking the silence. "No one who settles these lands has done so unscathed. The Sioux took my wife while she was carrying my son. Like you, I spent years searching for them only to learn that my wife died shortly after giving birth. Many more years passed before I learned my boy had been traded to the Shoshone as an infant, that I'd wasted years looking for him among the wrong people. The Shoshone were not allies of the Sioux. It never occurred to me to look for him in their villages." He looked at Logan, letting him take up the conversation.

"Sarah herself was a captive. She's still recovering from that experience. I don't think one ever recovers from the things she went through." Logan leaned forward, bracing his arms on his knees as he looked at Mrs. Burkholder. "I don't know if what I am about to say will help or not. I met your daughter. She was known as 'Spotted Horse Woman.' She was a much-beloved member of the tribe. She maintained her language by acting as a translator for the tribe and speaking with any English-speaking visitors they had. She taught her children to speak English."

"Children? I have more grandchildren?"

"I'm sorry." He shook his head. "None living other than Chayton. In every way that mattered, Lucy was fully Lakota. But when I met her, you couldn't mistake her coloring for anything but a white woman. I asked her once if she remembered her first family. She had only very vague memories of her time with you. She'd been told her family had died in a terrible event that led to her being rescued by the Lakota. It wasn't something she questioned or was curious about. She loved her husband. Loved her children."

"So that's why she never tried to find us." Mrs. Burkholder was quiet for a time. "What became of her? And her children? Do you know?"

Logan sighed. There was no good side to the story. "After the '68 treaty at Fort Laramie, some of the Lakota began to camp in areas designated for that purpose. They'd been decimated by the years of war on their people and lands. They were starving and broken. She and her husband were in such a camp when soldiers attacked it. It was a massacre. She was killed outright, but her husband lingered for days before passing. At that point, her children were grown, but Chayton's sister, who was also in that camp, died with them. One of Chayton's brothers died as a child. His other brother died in a different battle a few years ago."

"Where is my grandson now?"

Logan exchanged a look with Sid. "He's nearby."

"Does he know I've come for him?"

"No. And, if I may offer a word of advice, don't tell him that. He's an adult. A Lakota warrior. He won't do anything a white person tells him. He not only lost his parents to white men, he lost his first wife and son to a raid by a group of white men seeking bounties from Indian scalps."

Mrs. Burkholder closed her eyes. "So much death." Then, as a thought struck her, she flashed a glance at Logan. "*First* wife?"

Logan had to fight the urge to smile. The woman was a generation older than his father, but still sharp as a whip. "I believe he may have married again."

"No!" Mrs. Burkholder banged her cane on the wood floor. "No. That is not acceptable. I need him separated from his Indian life. I have plans for him that don't include any heathen wife of his. I'm an old woman, Mr. Taggert. I don't have time or patience for such shenanigans. He must leave his former life behind."

Logan's temper heated up. "You cannot separate a man from his soul and expect him to survive. Tread lightly. If you want any type of future with him, you'd best find a way to take him as he is—married or not, wild or not. The Lakota people were his life." He and Mrs. Burkholder exchanged heated glares. "You opened an artery in him when you forced him from the reservation. He is only now regaining a will to live." Breaking eye contact with her, he barked an order, summoning Chayton's daughter.

"Yes, Logan-*p'apá*?" she asked as she came from the dining room.

Logan lifted his hand and beckoned her near. Though he tried to calm himself, she read the emotion on his face and looked from him to Mrs. Burkholder with some trepidation. "I would like you to meet your great-grandmother."

White Bird faced Mrs. Burkholder and gave a quick curtsey. "It's nice to meet you, *kȟúŋši*."

Mrs. Burkholder's face was pale. She looked at Logan. "What does 'khoonshi' mean?"

"It is a Lakota title of respect for a paternal grandmother."

"You will speak only in English to me, girl."

White Bird did not blink, did not acknowledge that command. Logan silently commended her courage and resistance. He and Sarah had spent the last few years reinforcing how important it would be for her to maintain her knowledge of and pride in her native culture. They often spoke in a mixture of English and Lakota among the three of them, selecting the word that best fit the situation. English was sorely lacking in rich words that blended emotional and physical realities.

"Come closer. I'm old and I cannot see you so far away."

White Bird moved around the coffee table to stand before her great-grandmother. Mrs. Burkholder put a pair of spectacles on, then opened her locket and compared the faces inside it to that of her great-granddaughter. "You don't resemble my daughter."

"How do you have my grandmother's locket?"

"You remember this?"

"Of course. It was part of her medicine. She kept it

with her always."

Mrs. Burkholder looked to Logan for a translation. "The Lakota keep a small pouch of little items that impart a spiritual meaning to them. It provides them with guidance, wisdom, protection. Lucy kept your locket in her medicine pouch."

"Did she tell you who these people were?" Mrs. Burkholder asked White Bird.

"Her mother—you—and her grandmother."

"So, she never forgot us."

"We are *Lakȟóta*. We never forget family."

"She remembered us, but never tried to find us."

"We believed her white family was dead."

Mrs. Burkholder frowned. "It is a shame that you have such strong ethnic features. And brown skin."

"My father says I have the beauty of a running brook, as my mother did. She was called Laughs-Like-Water. Perhaps such beauty is not seen by white eyes?"

Her great-grandmother drew herself up, catching the insult. "Do you challenge me, girl?"

"I cannot answer that question for you, Grandmother."

Mrs. Burkholder's eyes narrowed.

Logan called White Bird over to him. "Why don't you go see if you can help Maria with supper?"

"Yes, Logan-*p'apá*." She turned back to her great-grandmother and did another brief curtsey. "It was nice meeting you. I hope your visit is a pleasant one, Grandmother."

They watched her leave the room. "You've done a good job with her. For all of her impertinence, she is rather civilized. Tell me, is she very much like my grandson?"

Logan smiled. "There are many ways to describe Chayton. 'Civilized' is not one of them."

CHAPTER SIXTEEN

The fire sent an orange glow over the painted walls arching above the cove where they nestled. Aggie lay close to Chayton, between the blankets he'd set out on the wide, sandy bank. Her head was on his shoulder. His head rested on their clothes—which they had not worn the entire day, yet again. Her fingers were threaded through his, their joined hands resting on her ribs.

She closed her eyes and listened to the falling water and the snap and crackle of the fire.

"Agkhee, look at the sky." She did as he asked, seeing sparkling lights spread like fairy dust across the sky. "Do the stars look the same in your world?"

"Chayton, your world and mine share the same sky and the same earth."

"No. Your world builds towns like crusted scabs upon the earth. My world lives with the earth, in the way that it lives."

"Perhaps you're right. I've never seen so many

stars as I do out here."

He kissed her temple. "I do not want to be right. I want everything to be as it was before."

"Before, you and I did not exist. Would you undo us?"

Chayton sighed. "It is wrong to live in any time but the present. And right now, you are everything to me. But it is difficult to not think of everything that no longer is."

"I know. I don't have my parents anymore. And I don't have Theo. Loss is never easy. It takes a piece of us, I think."

His arms tightened around her. "Agkhee, I am glad you are my wife. With you, my life will be one worth living."

Aggie smiled. She would have answered, but his hands distracted her as one moved to cup a breast and the other stroked down her belly to slip between her legs. She didn't open her legs to his caress, but enjoyed the sensations of his wide finger easing between her soft feminine folds. He kissed her neck. His hot, moist tongue stroked her skin, sucking it, tasting it. His palm moved from one breast to the other, and he caught her nipple between his thumb and forefinger.

"Oh," she groaned, unable to articulate a coherent comment. His hands and mouth were everywhere. She could feel his growing erection against her bottom. Somehow, he'd lifted her over his body. His thumb was massaging that spot that was so terribly, wonderfully sensitive. She spread her legs over his, aching for more of his touch, for his body to join hers. They'd been intimate several times over the last few days. She couldn't seem to get enough of him.

He sat up, holding her on his lap, working her body until sensations flooded her, forcing cries from her as she writhed, empty of him, yearning for him to take her. As the first throes of passion ebbed, he lifted her and slipped her down over his erect penis. She folded her legs by his thighs and took over the movements, slipping up and down him as his hands gripped her hips, managing her angle and speed, slowing her strokes despite her attempts to go faster. His pace was maddening. She groaned a complaint. "Chayton, please!"

He leaned over her, pushing her forward onto her hands and knees. She could feel so much of him. He braced his hands beside hers on the blanket as he pumped into her. Every thrust jostled her breasts, stroked her body in intimate places. He kissed her back, grazing her with his teeth. He leaned on one hand, freeing his other hand to capture her breasts, holding her as he pumped into her. When he eased that hand lower down her body, touching the place above where he entered her, she couldn't hold back her response. She bucked against his hips, drawing him deeper, deeper inside of her, crying out with the extraordinary pleasure he was giving her.

The sounds of her pleasure echoed against the canyon walls. Her reaction triggered his release. He straightened on his knees, gripped her hips, banging himself against her body with a fury he'd not yet shown in their couplings, thrusting, thrusting, then holding their bodies tightly clenched as his release pulsed inside of her.

When the waves eased between them, she was spent, utterly without strength to support herself. She collapsed beside him. He drew the cover over them, then leaned on his side and grinned down at her as she fought for breath. She smiled up at him. He set a hand on her abdomen, spreading his fingers out over the soft skin between her hips. He looked at her, then swept a glance around the painted walls hanging over them. "This is an auspicious place to create a baby."

She looked down at his hand, then covered it with both of hers. "Do you think we did?"

"It would give me joy to be a father again."

She smiled at him, reaching a hand up to touch his serious face. "I love you."

His gaze was solemn as he looked at her. "I will protect you, Agkhee. You and our children. I love you." He leaned over to kiss her forehead, her nose, her mouth. His hair slipped forward, stroking her skin in its warm, silky length.

* * *

White Bird heard a floorboard creek in the hallway outside her room, followed by the audible step of a cane. She had enough time to slip her father's portrait down behind her dresser before her great-grandmother stepped into her room. Of course, the painting landed with a loud thud. She faced the door and pretended as if the noise hadn't come from her room.

A cane pushed the door wider. Her grandmother stood in the doorway, eyeing her. "What have you there, girl?"

White Bird held her hands up. "Nothing."

Her great-grandmother, who was as formidable as any of the elders among the Lakota, was unconvinced. "I saw the painting before you dropped it behind the dresser. I'd like to see it again."

There was no point pretending she hadn't done the very thing her great-grandmother accused her of—that would be dishonest. She reached behind the dresser and retrieved Miss Hamilton's work. After propping it up against some trinket boxes on her dresser, she stepped back to look at it. She wasn't supposed to have it, but she knew that Logan-*p'apá* was going to get some of the artist's paintings, and since they were just sitting there in the tent down at the hunting cabin, with no one to guard them or even look at and enjoy them, she thought it wouldn't be bad if she brought one home early.

She looked at her great-grandmother out of the corner of her eye. They'd been waiting for more than a week for her father and Miss Hamilton to return from the Valley of Painted Walls. Tension was running high in the house as they all tried to keep her elder distracted from her father's absence.

"That's my grandson, isn't it?"

"It is. He's fierce and handsome, isn't he?"

Mrs. Burkholder didn't respond. "Where did you get this?"

"From Miss Hamilton. She's been painting him. There are several more of him. Would you like to see them?"

"Yes."

White Bird took her grandmother's hand. "I will show them to you. I will saddle horses for us."

"Not horses. Haven't you a surrey? If you don't, we'll take my carriage. We'll make the journey in comfort. How far is it?"

"Not far. Only an hour south of here."

"Very well. I will change. Perhaps you could tell Mrs. Taggert to join us. I think a picnic lunch would be a lovely idea."

A half-hour later, the three of them were on their way down to Miss Hamilton's cabin. Ester had to hide her smile at White Bird's excitement over the excursion. She liked her great-granddaughter, despite her unfortunate skin color. She was as vivacious and charming as her own Lucy had been. The ride down to the cabin was shorter than she expected. She caught herself leaning forward as a cabin and a large white tent came into sight. They stopped in front of the cabin. The surrey shifted as Mrs. Taggert climbed down, then helped her down.

"Miss Hamilton has been very busy painting this entire summer," Mrs. Taggert said as they crossed the grounds to the big tent. "She's preparing for a grand show in Denver this autumn."

"Have you seen her work?" Ester asked her hostess.

"Only a little of it. She's very talented."

"Hurry! Her work is in the tent!" White Bird called, running ahead to stand at the tent's entrance.

"White Bird, you haven't been down here bothering Miss Hamilton, have you?" Mrs. Taggert asked the girl.

"No—I was curious. She has a tent full of paintings. My *até's* in all of them, Sarah-*m'amá*."

Ester followed the girl into the tent. The art that met her stopped her in her tracks. All of it was museum quality, exquisitely detailed. The works were expert compositions with depth and rich colors. She moved a few steps deeper into the tent. White Bird hadn't exaggerated. She stepped around a couple of tall screens on which were hung various landscapes, some of which included an Indian. Looking up, she saw two tall portraits of a warrior, the same man in the small painting White Bird kept hidden in her room.

Ester didn't believe in the "noble savage" mythology. The indigenous people she'd met were simply savages—brutal killers by nature who deserved to be eliminated from the land they roamed like wild animals. They'd destroyed her family and were a scourge to noble settlers everywhere. Her beliefs were empirical, learned over a lifetime through numerous encounters of her own and through those experiences of her friends, colleagues, and acquaintances.

Yet here she was, confronted with the truth of her grandson's life: he was far more Indian than white man. Even she didn't miss the irony that he was the only future she had, and he gave no indication her legacy held any value to him. She felt the weight of her years as she stood in that tent, studying the image of a descendant she didn't know but upon whom so much rested, including the peace of his ancestors. His *white* ancestors.

She moved closer, searching the painted image of her grandson. His face was a stoic mask, but his eyes were full of life, sharp and intelligent. They looked out at her from the flat canvas as if judging her and finding her lacking. She squared her shoulders, refusing the implications of the standoff she sensed was coming.

She wasn't going to live forever. He had no choice but to come into her world and pick up the reins of his mother's heritage.

CHAPTER SEVENTEEN

Aggie followed Chayton as they made the return hike through the woods back to their base camp in the cave. She couldn't wait to dive into a few canvases covering the painted canyon they'd visited and the ravine that Chayton wanted her to paint. Her sketchbook was filled with vistas awaiting their birth in canvas and paint; she had several weeks of work ready to start. Perhaps she should take the works she'd finished down to Denver, then return to paint the sketches she'd made.

She sighed, unable to decide. She didn't want to take the time away from her work. It would interrupt her momentum. But she had to get down to Denver to see if she could secure show space with Theo's friends who owned a gallery.

Her gaze sought out Chayton as he moved over the rough ground of the aspen and evergreen forest. There wasn't very much brush or undergrowth to climb over—the deer and elk kept it trimmed. Chayton was as much at home on these rocky slopes as any of its native wildlife. She loved watching his legs move with their innate grace as he navigated the terrain. His bow was slung over a shoulder, his pack of quivers slanted across his back.

He wore his hair parted in the middle and brought forward in twin braids covered in a wrap of red fabric. She'd learned his intricate toilet during their days together—how he liked to wear his hair, how meticulous he was in plucking his facial and body hair. She understood now why he was always so well groomed. She wore far less ornamentation than he did, preferring to braid her hair or twist it into a simple bun at the base of her neck. He liked to adorn his hair with feathers, beads, and wraps. Everything he wore held a meaning and conveyed protection, strength, or memories. He was a graceful and kind man who honored the land and his ancestors in everything he did. She couldn't believe how lucky she was that their paths had crossed.

"Chayton," she called out to him. He paused and looked back at her as he stood above her on the slope. "I love you."

"Why?"

"Because you make me realize how wondrous life is."

He nodded, then started forward again. "It is a good reason."

As they reached the wider path that led down to the cave, Chayton paused and reached a hand back toward her. She smiled as she put her hand in his. His dark eyes grew somber as he looked down at her. Heat spread over her body. She thought about their leisurely morning by the falls, when he'd sat calmly in front of her, waiting patiently while she wove his long hair into twin braids. She felt as if she'd cast some spell over a large and violent predator, causing him to behave in a gentle manner only with her.

She'd styled his hair several different ways, waiting to see when his patience would break. At last, he'd twisted around, grabbed her by the waist, and thrust her beneath him. "Enough, woman!" he'd growled. "I am not a doll." With a small adjustment of their clothes, he'd entered her. She'd laughed at the sight of his frown, until his fervor stirred her desire and she met his thrusts with her own.

And now he frowned at her all over again. Was it terrible that she wanted to be in his arms again?

"Agkhee, we should return to the cabin. If you step out of your shell here, it will be difficult to transport so many paintings."

Aggie linked her arms up around his neck. She loved touching him, hated when they were far apart. "I've been thinking the same thing. I'll get our things ready while you fetch our horses. When we return, will you stay with me at the cabin?"

"You are my wife, *mahasani*. Our lives are one now. I will always be with you."

She stood on tiptoes to kiss his mouth, then moaned when he tightened his arms around her and fisted her hair, deepening their kiss. When the kiss ended, his reluctance to let her go was written in the rigid features of his face.

"I will get the horses," he said.

* * *

Logan walked outside to watch the horizon for the incoming riders that had been spotted heading onto the property. He leaned against a support post of his front porch as he watched them come down the lane. When they were closer, he saw the afternoon sun glint off the sheriff stars they wore. He went down the porch steps, preparing himself for whatever bad news they brought. Cal Declan was a good man and an honest sheriff, but wasn't known for making friendly social calls—leastwise, not this far north of town.

Sheriff Declan let his reins rest against his thigh as touched his hat. "Logan. You know my deputy, Brody Rogers."

"Good day, sheriff, deputy. What brings you so far north?" Logan asked.

Sheriff Declan handed him a wanted poster. Logan unfolded it. A cold sweat chilled his skin, even in the heat of the hot summer day. The grisly face staring back at him was bearded. The flattened nose sat at an odd angle. The man's hair had thinned since Logan last saw him. Hugh Landry, goddamn his soul. He was wanted, dead or alive, for a bank robbery in Santa Fe. The poster offered a hefty reward not only for his capture but also for the return of the stolen money. There were several other names listed as his known associates; some of them, Logan recognized as men who'd run with him during his scalp hunter days.

The bastard still went by the alias of Skinner, as he had when he'd hit Chayton's small village four years ago, killing and raping Laughs-Like-Water, killing his little son, leaving their scalped bodies—and those of so many others—to rot in the sun.

"You think he's in the area?"

The sheriff nodded. "Had a couple teams of bounty hunters come into Defiance. They'd been tracking him and his gang into these hills. I'd like to get him and his boys locked up before those who're after him make any trouble, 'cause they ain't much better than the ones they're chasing. Thought you'd know some likely places where he might like to lay low hereabouts. And I was hoping we could get fresh horses."

Logan felt a shaft of foreboding slip through him. The Valley of Painted Walls was the perfect hidey-hole for Skinner. "I do know a place. The pass into it is tricky—I think I'd best lead you. Chayton's taken Miss Hamilton there to paint." Logan set his hands on his hips and stared at the ground, fighting to calm the rage rising inside him. "I gotta tell you, sheriff—if that bastard's on my property, he ain't leaving it alive. I've got an ax to grind with him."

Sheriff Declan looked at Logan from beneath the shade of his wide-brimmed hat. "If you're gonna try to do my job for me, then you can stay here. Him and his boys, they ain't gonna fight fair. If we find them, Deputy Rogers and I'll be the ones takin' the risks."

"How many men is he running with?" Logan asked.

"Seven, including him."

Logan and the sheriff exchanged a long look. "Go swap out your horses, and have one readied for me. I'll meet you out at the stable in ten minutes. Go on in to the kitchen if you change your mind about the sandwiches."

"Trouble, *señor*?" Maria asked when Logan came back into the house.

"Yes. Trouble. When did the ladies say they'd be back from their visit to the cabin?"

"I packed a lunch for them. I do not know when they will be back. What is the trouble?"

"There are some outlaws passing through the area. I don't want you to be alarmed, but you're to stay in the house. I'm going to send a few men after the ladies, and then I'm going to escort the sheriff into Chayton's valley. I want you women to stay in the house and be safe, do you understand, Maria?"

"*Si, señor.*"

* * *

Chayton went down to the river to find the herd. They usually stayed near the cave when he was in the valley. The herd wasn't where he expected it to be. He jogged along the riverbank for a mile, following their tracks. There were no horses. He went up a steep hill, heading for a high point so he could see where they'd gone.

The scent of the woods changed as he neared the ridge. Fire. He looked skyward, but could not see a plume indicating a widespread forest fire. That could only mean one thing: someone was in his valley.

Chayton moved stealthily forward until he found the camp. Three men were sitting around a campfire. A pot of coffee was steaming, and a couple of fish were sizzling in a pan over the fire. He stayed hidden and watched them, waiting to see if there were more of them away from camp. Why were they in his valley? They were agitated about something. Their grumbled words were hard to make sense of at first. Chayton edged closer. One man was pacing angrily, looking off into the woods near where Chayton hid. He tossed his coffee onto the fire, shooting hissing steam up around the pan.

"What are you doin'?" the man by the fire said.

"He ain't coming back. Jesus, how stupid could we be?"

"We sent Corbin with him as a witness for the stash location. You sayin' you don't trust my twin?"

The angry man stopped pacing and turned to glare at the lone twin. "No, idiot. I'm saying I don't trust Landry. He's got the gold. He's got his old crew with him from his scalping days. The only thing standin' between him and freedom is your idiot brother. And we let him go." He waved a hand toward the woods. "We just let him walk right outta here." He kicked dirt into the fire, spilling the coffee pot over.

The other men cursed and jumped out of the way of flying debris and hot liquid. "He said there's no way out of the valley in the direction he went," one of them pointed out. "He should know. He climbed all over this hell pit country taking scalps."

"Of course, he'd say that!" The first man began breaking camp.

The hackles lifted on Chayton's neck. *Landry* was a name he'd never forget. The murdering rapist had returned to his valley. Terror sheared through him as he remembered he'd left Agkhee alone at the cave.

He ducked behind a copse of low-growth evergreens as the men mounted and rode off in the direction of his cave. What was the monster doing back in this area? Chayton's people were mostly gone, reduced to lives on the reservation. There was nothing for a scalp hunter like him here.

Chayton gave a loud whistle, summoning his horse. He could tell from the hoof prints he'd followed that the herd was near. His faithful paint came over the hill. Chayton leapt to the pony's back and turned him, without bridle or saddle, to the cave where Agkhee was preparing for their return trip.

* * *

Aggie was humming a cheerful tune when she

heard Chayton return with the horses. She'd left the bedding as the last thing to pack up and store away; she was hoping to convince him to delay leaving for a little longer. A warm flush colored her cheeks at the direction her thoughts were taking as she stepped out of the cave.

The smile on her lips slowly died as she looked at the four mounted men. She frowned. No one was supposed to know about this valley. Who were they? And why were they there? None of them were well groomed. Their shirts were greasy and sweat stained. They looked like they'd been traveling hard for some time. She was glad Chayton was not here. Men like these would pick a fight with him just for the amusement of it.

"Skinner, you rat bastard," one of the men sneered, winning a dark look from the others. "You've been holding out on us."

"Good afternoon, ma'am." The man who seemed to be in charge tipped his hat toward her. The shifting light on his face showed a flattened nose. "We're traveling up to Casper. A friend said this valley cut a day off the route, but I don't agree with him. We've been round and round and can't see any way out of the canyon except by the way we came in."

Aggie had never been to the other end of the valley, so she didn't know how to direct them back that way. It was best if she told them how to get out via the high pass she and Chayton had come in by. Maybe they would follow her directions and be long gone before he returned.

"There is another way. It's difficult, however. You might be more comfortable returning the way you came."

"No." The man leaned forward in his saddle. The tension around his eyes gave him an edge that made her nervous. She took a step back. "Where's the other way out?" he asked.

"Ride over to that ridge. Climb to the top of it, then follow the deer trail that leads west."

The leader gave her a skeptical look. "That ain't no way out."

"It is. I've come over that trail myself."

"Can you show us the way?"

Aggie looked from one man to the other. She shook her head. "No. I can't."

"That's 'cause it ain't a trail, boss. She's lying."

The man with the flat nose looked at her. He slanted his head, as if to take her measure. His eyes narrowed. "You wouldn't lie to us now, would you?"

"Why would I?" Aggie's heart was beating far too fast. These men were dangerous. God, if they lingered much longer, Chayton would return and find them. "You'd best head on your way. My husband will be returning shortly."

Flat-nose smiled. "You are a font of information." He slipped his gun from its holster.

Aggie's eyes widened. She backed up a step. He arced the gun from her to one of his friends and pulled the trigger. Aggie screamed as the man's body landed on the ground with a heavy thud.

The flat-nosed man pointed the gun at her. "Get on his horse. You're leading us out of here. And remember, I shot him—I'll kill you as easily."

Aggie hurried to the horse and mounted up. She was so nervous that she gave the horse all the wrong cues, squeezing too tightly with her knees and pulling the reins too hard. Agitated, it reared up. Again she cried out. The man behind her moved forward, into the hip of her horse, urging it forward. They went as fast as she dared through the woods, over hills, across a creek, moving ever closer to the ridge and its terrible, narrow path. All the while she knew, with an otherworldly certainty, that she was not going to get out of this alive.

CHAPTER EIGHTEEN

Aggie entered the woods with them. She didn't know exactly where the path came down from the ridge. The man in front was heading in the right direction. God, what would happen when they figured out she didn't know where it was? She looked around, desperately trying to find the trailhead. They moved over the rough terrain, the men going ahead and circling back.

"She's lying, Skinner. There ain't no way out at this end of the canyon," one of them growled.

The leader, the one the others called "Skinner," shifted in his seat to look at her. He took his six-shooter from his holster. Aggie felt a tear spill over her cheek. What would her death do to Chayton? He was only beginning to recover from his first wife and son's death and everything else that had happened to him.

Skinner opened the cylinder to replace the spent bullet. He pointed the gun at her and cocked it. "Truth, woman. Is there a path?"

Aggie nodded. "I have only traveled through here one time. I know we came down from the ridge somewhere around here. Once we find that trail, we can take it all the way out of here."

He uncocked his gun and holstered it again.

"Shoot her, Skinner," one of the men urged. "We don't need a witness. We'll find the path ourselves."

"True enough. We don't need a witness, but we sure could use a woman." He grinned back at his compatriots. "Besides, if she's lying, I gotta teach her a lesson. Move quickly. The kid's brother coulda heard that gunshot. If you don't want to share the gold, we gotta get outta here before the others catch up to us."

"What about her husband?"

"What about him? I got plenty of bullets left."

They spread out to find the trail. Skinner forced her to go with him. They moved up and up toward where the switchback opened into the canyon, and it was there they picked up the narrow path. Aggie looked ahead to the narrows, already shaking at the thought of having to travel that way without Chayton's help.

She had no choice but to go forward. If she couldn't lead the men out of the valley, Chayton would catch up to them. And if he did, he was a dead man.

* * *

Chayton lay low on his horse's back as he charged through the woods to catch up with the three men. They were riding hard in a direction that would take them right to the cave. Clinging to his pony with his legs, he notched an arrow and waited for the right moment to let it fly. Trees kept getting in the way. The men were hot on the trail of Landry, which worked in Chayton's favor; Landry was going to meet his fate today, in as bloody and brutal a way as Chayton could make it. The scalp taker was not going to harm another person he loved.

The last man in the group moved into a clear space. Chayton shot an arrow into the base of his neck, dropping him from his horse. His mount slowed up and moved out of the way of Chayton's charging horse. He was closing in on the others when they pulled to a stop. One was pointing up toward the ridge and the pass that led out of the canyon.

"Hey—where'd Rick go? He was right behind me."

"Who cares? Landry's getting away. Look there! I knew he'd try to get out of the canyon."

Both men looked up to the ridge where he was pointing. Chayton did as well, and what he saw was chilling. Aggie was riding point, heading into the switchbacks. She was on a stranger's horse, leading cruel men, riding into terrain that terrified her. He shut his eyes and prayed for his ancestors to protect and guide her through the journey she faced without him.

"I don't see nothing. The only way out's the way we came in."

"He was up there. I saw him. I'm tellin' you, he was on that ridge."

"If he was, then he's ridin' into a dead end."

"Yeah? Well, that'll work in our favor. Let's go."

Chayton let them start forward, holding back to keep a little distance between himself and the men. They were all that separated him from Landry now, two men moving with the grace and intent of typical white-eyes. They weren't seeing the little signs that would lead them to the pass. They fumbled about, moving forward and backward, searching for the way to get up to the place where they'd spotted Landry. Unfortunately, there was too much cover for him to hit them here. If they didn't find the path soon, he was going to have to move around them and go after Landry and Agkhee. Every second he lost put her deeper in danger. He knew how afraid she was of the switchbacks. And the fact that she was riding a strange horse meant there had been another man in the gang who was no longer riding with them. What had happened to him, Chayton could only guess.

The men finally found the start of the path that led into the pass. They took it fast—too fast for riders unfamiliar with its dangers. The second horse slid off the path and stumbled down the steep side of the ridge before the rider fell off. The leader moved forward, determined nothing would stop them from catching up with Landry.

"Watch out! Don't push through too fast," the first one called to the other as he got back in line behind him. "I told you I saw Landry on this ridge. We'll catch up to him and get our share of the bank money from wherever he stashed it. It ain't gonna do you any good if you kill yourself first."

At last, the two were on the trail and moving forward. Chayton stayed in the cover of the woods until they'd rounded the corner of the first switchback. When they were out of sight, he moved onto the path, keeping back far enough that they wouldn't see him if they looked this way from the opposite side of the winding path. The echoes of their conversation filtered back to him. He didn't need to worry; they were so focused on moving forward, neither of them were checking their back trail.

When they reached the next turn, he waited for the first to step around, then the second. He'd decided to let the two go ahead all the way out of the canyon. Let them scare out any ambush that might be waiting. Landry and his men expected their other fellows to follow them, but no one was watching for him. He'd catch up to these two by the hill where Agkhee liked to paint, then he'd go for Landry.

He trailed them through the narrows. When they went into the boulder fields, then moved down over the ridge that led by his caves, Chayton moved up, above his caves, riding ahead to get in position so he could pick them off as they descended toward Agkhee's hill. He looked as far into the distance as he could see, but found no sign of Agkhee and the men she was with, other than a slowly dissipating cloud of dust that led in the direction of her cabin.

As the two came into sight below him, he let loose a warrior's cry. It bounced off the canyon walls, echoing and magnifying until it sounded like a hundred warriors shouting. Perhaps it was. Perhaps it was the voices of his ancestors come to help him. Chayton urged his horse forward and screamed his cry again. This time, the man ahead of him withdrew his six-shooter and began to fire haphazardly back at Chayton as he twisted in his saddle to face him. Chayton laughed at the outlaw's desperate attempts to end his forward progress. He notched an arrow and let it fly. The man's back arched as the blade entered his shoulder. Chayton notched another and sent it into the man's other shoulder. The outlaw still tried to shoot at him. Chayton's next arrow went through the wrist of his gun hand.

The outlaw faced forward and put all of his energy into outriding Chayton—an impossible feat. Chayton and his pony moved like one being in separate skins. So thorough was his paint's training that he knew exactly what was needed of him even before Chayton gave him a cue. It was what Chayton had been known for among his people. The great warriors of his tribe made profitable trades with him in order to receive a warhorse he'd trained. It allowed him to care for the many people in his extended family, even when the brutal times had increased the quantity of his dependents in such terrible numbers.

Most of those warriors were dead now, but they'd

run the narrows with him today, and the wind of their spirits guided his arrows to their precise targets. Emboldened, Chayton squeezed his mount to greater speed. He came even with the man he'd wounded. Leaping from his horse, he jumped into him, dropping both of them to the ground. Chayton pulled his knife, slit his throat, removed his scalp, and returned to his pony and his pursuit of the next man in mere seconds.

The man was headed in the direction of Agkhee's cabin. Chayton's horse ran with a speed that seemed supernatural. Wind pulled at Chayton's hair, and the grit kicked up by the man he was chasing made Chayton's eyes tear. Chayton shot an arrow into the center of the man's back. He arched his back, flinging his hands wide as he dropped the reins, then fell from his horse.

Chayton slowed his mount, checking for signs that Landry had come this way. Sure enough, he found several distinct sets of fresh hoof prints leading west, which correlated with the dust cloud he'd seen from high up on the ridge. From this point, Agkhee would be closer to her cabin than to Logan's ranch. The only thing playing in her favor now was the fact that Landry loved to torment those weaker than himself. He wouldn't kill Agkhee outright. It was far more likely he would taunt and torture her until he tired of the sport. Chayton didn't have long to save her from Landry's deadly game.

* * *

Logan rode neck and neck with the sheriff and his deputy up to the short pass that led to Chayton's side of the sandstone ridge. As soon as they started their descent on the other side, he took the lead. They'd topped the hill and were about to start their climb toward Chayton's cave when they encountered two saddled but rider-less horses.

And one dead body. Riddled with arrows and scalped.

"Shit," Deputy Rogers growled. "You tellin' me we're also dealing with renegade Indians?"

"No. That's Chayton. He's gone after them. Stay here," Logan ordered as he dismounted and started searching for tracks. He wasn't the natural tracker that his brother or Chayton were, but if several horses had ridden through here recently, it shouldn't be too hard to see what direction they took. The soft dirt of the sloping hill made it easy to spot the tracks of an unshod horse—Chayton's mount. Near it were the tracks of several other shod horses. He hurried back to his mount and swung up into the saddle.

"They're heading toward Miss Hamilton's cabin."

CHAPTER NINETEEN

Aggie heard a sharp clap behind her. Dirt exploded off to one side of her. The mad man was shooting at her! She leaned lower over her saddle, stretching as far forward as the saddle horn would allow. By intent or poor skill, the outlaw's shots were striking the ground either side of her. If he hit her or her mount, her horse would down, and she'd break her neck. She had none of Chayton's athletic skill when it came to leaping from a moving horse or responding to the falls it might take.

When she saw the hill by her house, she dared to hope she could get around to the front door and slam it shut before the outlaws behind her could reach her. She topped the hill, then spun to the left around the corral, heading for the front door. As she came in front of the house, she saw a surrey parked there.

No! Someone was here! No, no, no. She pulled up, quickly dismounted, and ran inside the house, hoping that was where her visitors were. It was empty. She hurried to her painting tent. The men who'd abducted her were at the top of the hill. If she could get to the visitors quickly, they might be able to get inside the house.

Or not. There were three women in the tent: White Bird, Sarah, and another older lady she hadn't yet met.

"Quick!" she shouted to them. "Hide!" The trio, who were dispersed about the space of the tent, looked at her with startled faces.

The older woman drew herself up over her cane, which she stamped against the hard ground. "Now see here, young lady—"

Aggie exchanged a panicked look with Sarah, who needed no further prodding. She rushed over to grab White Bird, but still they were not quick enough. The men who had been chasing her reached the tent, their horses snorting and breathing hard. Sarah and White Bird had just enough time to duck behind one of the painting screens as Skinner forced open the tent flap and stepped inside.

"What is the meaning of this intrusion? And who are you, sir?" the older woman demanded of the stranger. Her forthright attitude was wonderfully reassuring to Aggie. If anyone could set the topsy-turvy world back to rights, Aggie had no doubt the older woman could.

She turned to face the man who'd taken her from Chayton's valley. How many bullets had he fired? She looked at his gun belt, trying to determine if he'd reloaded after shooting at her. It would have been hard to do at the pace he'd kept while chasing her, but Chayton could have done it.

The man turned from her, blocking her line of sight to his gun belt. He ignored the older woman as his gaze settled on Aggie, and he smiled, the expression ghastly on his gaunt face. "Well, well, well. Isn't this a nice social gathering?" He looked around them. "And at a gallery, no less. Out here, in the middle of nowhere." He strolled around the place, looking at her paintings.

Aggie was frozen in place, afraid to move lest her actions draw attention to Sarah and White Bird's hiding spot. The man spoke so reasonably, but looked and acted crazed; she couldn't reconcile the dichotomy. He still had his six-shooter in his hand. He slowly worked his way over to her. She couldn't control her shaking when he lifted the pistol's long muzzle up to her face, bringing it against her cheek. She felt its cold metal stroke her skin.

"What do you want?" she asked him.

He smiled. "I have many wants, my dear." He lifted the gun away and pointed it toward the older woman. "Who is she?"

Aggie shook her head. "I don't know."

"What is this place?"

Again, Aggie shook her head. "It was the first dwelling I came upon. I was hoping there'd be a man here who could help me."

"Ah. Such a pretty hope. A pretty—and unmet— hope." He stroked the gun down her neck, down the opening V of her shirt. "What will you do to save yourself, I wonder?"

She batted the gun aside. He grabbed the hair she'd knotted at the base of her neck, jerking her body up to his, holding her immobile while his hot breath puffed over her cheek.

Aggie barely heard the whimper of fear. She thought it had come from her, but she saw a small, dark-haired person dash out of the tent, immediately followed by Sarah. The man thrust her away from him and gave chase.

"No!" Aggie grabbed the man's arm, hoping to stop him from going after the Taggert women. He shoved her aside without a second thought. The older woman came over and bent down to lend her a hand.

"Are you hurt?" she asked Aggie.

"No." She was dazed. And she'd bitten her cheek when she hit the ground. She took the older woman's arm and led her to the other tent entrance. "Go to the house. Lock yourself in." She had no doubt that Chayton had by now discovered her absence; she didn't know if she could keep things from escalating for the length of time needed for him to make his way here.

"Not so fast, you two." A man met them outside the tent, his gun pointed at them.

Aggie saw that Sarah and White Bird hadn't gotten far. Skinner had caught them and was now stroking Sarah with his gun. Rage filled Aggie with courage. She moved toward them and shoved the outlaw away

233

from Sarah. Her bravado won her a clap on the side of her face. Sarah reached for her, exposing White Bird to him.

"Oh! What have we here?" he purred in an unctuous voice. White Bird didn't duck or hide, didn't shrink beneath his disturbing gaze. He reached out his left hand to finger her thick black hair, like an interested buyer pawing a pelt. "Pity it is so hard to market Indian scalps anymore. Yours would fetch a fine sum." He smiled as he spoke. "It's thick enough I could sell it as a warrior's, which would fetch the best price."

The other men were standing by, grinning and laughing at the terror Skinner was causing the women. She could tell that Sarah was beyond frightened—her pallor warned she was only inches from all-out shock. Aggie inserted herself between the two of them and faced Skinner. "What do you want with us?"

"Brave little thing, aren't you?" His gaze slipped over her. "What do I want?" He shrugged. "What any man wants who's been too long without female company. And food." His eyes narrowed. "And no witnesses." He reached around Aggie and yanked Sarah free, shoving her back toward one of his men. "Take that one."

"No!" Aggie shouted as the man grabbed for Sarah and pushed her toward the cabin. Her friend went without hesitation. Aggie would have followed, but Skinner grabbed hold of White Bird and started to walk away with her.

"And Manny, you can have that one." He nodded toward Aggie. "Set fire to the tent," he ordered over his shoulder. "I saw the homage being paid to the 'noble Indian.' That trash needs to be destroyed."

Aggie stood frozen in place, left with the older woman and the third man. He tucked his gun into his shirt, then took out a box of matches. He struck one with his nail, then dropped it on the loose tent flap. She immediately set about trying to put the fire out while still keeping an eye on White Bird. In quick succession, he lit two other areas at the base of the tent.

The older woman came to her assistance, using her cane to fight the man back. Aggie almost had one of the burning areas put out when she noticed that Skinner and White Bird had disappeared around the corner of the tent. She started to go after them, but heard the older woman cry out.

"Go! Help my great-granddaughter!" she ordered Aggie as she bludgeoned the man with her cane.

Aggie hurried around the corner, running up behind Skinner. She shoved her fists into his back, pushing him down, then grabbed Chayton's daughter. A scream unlike any she'd ever heard erupted into the air. Fierce and unholy, it tore into her ears. She shoved White Bird behind her, backing away from the man as she searched for the source of the sound. Had it come from Sarah or the older woman? What on earth made that kind of noise?

A gunshot went off. Aggie pressed White Bird to

the ground as a screaming blur rode by. Skinner shrieked. Aggie looked back at him and saw an arrow protruding from his right hand. His gun had fallen to the ground. She scrambled to grab it, then hurried back to provide shelter to White Bird. The little girl cowered behind her, her head buried in Aggie's back.

She looked up in time to see the crazed rider come around again. *Chayton*. Skinner saw him as well. He began to beg and whimper, holding out his uninjured hand as he pleaded, "No! Please, please—"

Chayton shot another arrow into his neck—not giving him the release of an instant death, but a slow ending as his heart pulsed blood from the wound. The next arrow hit him in the crotch. Skinner screamed.

Chayton spared not a glance at her as he threw a leg over his horse's back, drawing his knife before his feet hit the ground. Skinner was still alive, still crying and pleading as Chayton knelt and caught a fistful of his hair.

Aggie turned away, clasping White Bird to her chest, fearing what Chayton would do next. She'd never seen such rage in his face, not even on that first night when he'd broken into her cabin. She remembered the way Skinner had fingered White Bird's hair, and a sickening thought took root in her mind.

Had this been the man who'd attacked Chayton's family, the one who'd scalped them? If so, then God have mercy on Skinner's soul, for she knew Chayton wouldn't.

Chayton came to them, shoving a wide strip of bloody flesh into his pouch as he knelt beside them. Skinner was whining and gurgling on the ground. Aggie resisted the urge to look at him. She forced herself to look at Chayton's eyes. Only his eyes. These were the eyes of the man she loved, a man who would fight to the death to protect her and his daughter and anyone in his world that he loved.

"There are two other men." She pointed around the corner of the tent. "One around the front of the tent, one with Sarah at the cabin. Hurry."

Aggie ordered White Bird to stay where she was with her face against her knees. "Do not look up. Listen for me to call you." She crept forward to peek around the corner of the tent. The older woman had managed to put the fires out. The man who'd tried to set them now lay bleeding on the ground, dead and scalped. Chayton was running toward the house, silent and fast.

Aggie went back for White Bird, then rushed to the old woman, who was sobbing.

"Grandmother!" White Bird grabbed her and wrapped her arms around the older woman. "Are you hurt, Grandmother?"

The woman sat up and hugged White Bird tightly. Her hysterical sobs stopped immediately. After a few seconds of deep breaths, the older woman answered, "No. I am not harmed. And you, child?" She touched White Bird's face. "Are you hurt?"

"No. Aggie helped me, then my father saved us."

237

All three of them looked over to the cabin. A man was backing out of it in a stumbling gait, one of Aggie's knives in his hand, dripping blood. "Oh no," Aggie whispered. As they watched, Chayton reached him. He grabbed the man from behind with a hand over his forehead and sliced his throat.

A terrible thundering slipped into Aggie's consciousness. She worried more of Skinner's men were coming to the aid of their friends. Instead, she saw Logan riding in hard with men wearing sheriff badges. She looked around, wondering where she could take White Bird and her grandmother so that they could be shielded from the dead and bleeding men scattered about the cabin's property. Out of the corner of her eye, she saw movement and turned to see Sarah step to the threshold of her house. Relief poured through her veins. She gathered the others and moved them toward the cabin.

As Aggie watched, Logan leapt from his horse and rushed toward Sarah. Her eyes never left the corpse before her. She was pale and so quiet.

"Sarah," Logan said as he lifted her face. "Honey, look at me. Tell me what happened. Are you hurt?"

"I killed him. He was going to rape me. And probably kill me. But I killed him first." She looked at Logan. "Never again," she ground out through clenched teeth. "I killed him."

Logan smiled. "Yes, you did. You took care of him. You did what you needed to do—you protected yourself."

As if waking from a dream, Sarah gave a startled look around her. "Where's White Bird?"

"She's safe." Logan nodded toward the three of them.

Aggie looked at Chayton's grandmother, who stood on the other side of White Bird. Her head was held high, her shoulders back, one hand grasping her cane. Her clothes were torn; blood marred her white lawn blouse in small blotches. Her skirt was stained with black soot from putting out the flames. She had not come out of the skirmish unscathed, nor had it dimmed her spirit. She held one arm around White Bird, who still had an arm around her waist. Aggie wondered who was supporting whom.

As she looked at Chayton, he sheathed his knife, then came to her. Though his hands were damp with blood and stuck to her sleeves, she'd never been so glad to see anyone. She reached up and wrapped her arms around his shoulders. For a long moment, they simply held each other, then he pulled back and held an arm out for his daughter to join them.

"*Até, khúŋši* is here," White Bird told him.

Chayton lifted his gaze to the woman. The chill in his eyes sent ice down Aggie's spine. "She was brave, Chayton. She put out the fires they tried to start and fought one of the men herself."

He did not speak to the older woman. Instead, he shifted his gaze to his daughter and said something in Lakota that made her weep and bow her head. He touched his daughter's face, her hair, her shoulders, keeping her at arm's length so that he could check her over, before pulling her close to hold her tight. Chayton's face as he examined his daughter etched itself in Aggie's artist's mind. His nostrils were flared, his eyes watered; his cheeks and jaw were rigid.

He looked at Aggie, then repeated himself, this time in English: "I have killed the men who killed White Bird's mother and brother. I have given them peace so that they no longer have to walk the earth. They can now rejoin our ancestors."

"You did more than that, Chayton." The sheriff joined them. "You took out an entire gang of bank robbers. There'll be a large reward for you to collect from my office in the next week."

Chayton studied the sheriff. Aggie wondered if he was deciding whether to believe the promised reward would be there when he arrived—and perhaps if the trip to fetch it would be worth the experience he'd have coming into town.

"I'll bring him down to collect it," Logan said as he joined them, an arm around Sarah.

White Bird hurried to hug her foster mother. They murmured soft words to each other, Sarah's hands quickly doing a pass over the little girl's head and shoulders. More riders came in, men she recognized from Logan's ranch. Logan went to speak to them.

"Ladies," Chayton's grandmother addressed the group, both hands stacked over the top of her cane, "let us adjourn to the tent while the men clean up this mess. I don't think it would be wise for us to leave without their escort."

Aggie looked at Sarah, who nodded her agreement. "Aggie, I don't think you've been introduced to Chayton's grandmother yet," she said as they entered the tent. "This is Mrs. Burkholder." Sarah gestured toward Aggie. "And this is my friend, Agnes Hamilton."

The two women nodded at each other, then Mrs. Burkholder wandered among the paintings. Aggie reached for Sarah's hand. "Were you hurt?" she asked her friend in a quiet voice.

"No. I wasn't going to let any man corner me again," Sarah told her. Aggie wondered what had happened in Sarah's past that she would make such a comment. "I went straight into your cabin and found a knife." Sarah looked at White Bird. "What happened after I lost sight of you? Were you hurt?"

"No. Aggie came after me, kept that man from me, then my *até* showed up. And Logan-*p'apá*. It was scary, though. My *até* said the man who took me was the one who killed my *iná* and brother. It was a good day for us. I'm glad it happened."

Sarah shook her head and hugged White Bird tightly. "You are so strong."

"Stronger than she should have to be." Mrs. Burkholder stood before them. She sent a look over the three of them, judgment and determination in her eyes. "How is it that you know my grandson, Miss Hamilton? And why is he featured so prominently in your work?"

Aggie looked around the tent, seeing so many iterations of Chayton. "I'm his wife."

CHAPTER TWENTY

"Agkhee, ride with me." Chayton stood next to the surrey. Sarah, White Bird, and Mrs. Burkholder were already inside. The sheriff, his deputy, and Logan's men were gathering the outlaws' horses and would bring their bodies up to Logan's ranch later.

Aggie wanted more than anything to be close to him. The day's violence left her feeling achy and cold, despite the heat of the waning sun. Chayton lifted her into the saddle of one of the outlaws' horses, then swung up behind her and took up the reins. They followed behind the carriage, and his pony followed them.

"How are you, *mahasani?*" *My other skin.* Aggie smiled as she leaned against Chayton. English had no equivalent for that Lakota endearment. Perhaps the closest translation was "the other half of me."

"I'm tired. And sad. I'm sorry your daughter had to see all that happened today. Those men were bad, through and through. I'm afraid to think of what would have happened if you hadn't come when you did."

His arm tightened around her. "It was a good day for my daughter. She has seen now the thing that haunted her is no more. Now she can just be a child."

"And you? Can you be more at peace now?"

Chayton leaned his face against her forehead. "I am trying. The spirits of my wife and son can find rest now, but much still lies ahead of us. My grandmother is here. I think nothing will be as it was."

"She was brave today. Fearless. She fought one of the men and kept my tent from burning."

He gave a quick nod. "It is good a day. For many reasons."

* * *

A knock sounded on the door of the room she and Chayton had been given upstairs at Sarah and Logan's house. She pulled the sides of her borrowed dressing gown tight and opened the door to find Maria standing there with an armload of clothes and grooming items. Aggie had left most of her things at the cave, and, in the mayhem that followed the fight at the cabin, she'd forgotten to collect an extra outfit.

"Thank you, Maria."

"Of course, *señora. Señor* Chayton is bathing in the men's barracks. He has been given a change of clothes as well. You will need help with your hair, *si*?"

"No, thank you. I'll dry it with the linen."

"*Bueno*. You need me, you summon me." She

pointed to a bell pull near the door. "*La familia* has gathered below. *Señor* Logan's brother, *Señor* Sager, is here. He is no happy at the excitement today. *La señora* asks you to join when you are ready, *si*?"

"Yes. Of course. Thank you, Maria."

Chayton entered their room a short while later. He was dressed in an interesting blend of fancy and common clothes. He wore a stiff pair of new indigo denims, a white cotton shirt, and a red silk vest. His borrowed clothes fit his lean, broad-shouldered body in a way that heated her own body. She smiled at him. He glared at her.

"My body wants to run, lose these white man's clothes. My mind fights for control over my body. I am at war with myself."

Aggie's smile widened. She crossed the room and took his face in her hands. "You look very handsome."

"Do I? Logan let me pick the vest."

"You have good taste."

Chayton started to open the buttons of his fly. "I have bloomers, too." He tugged at his white shorts.

Aggie bit her lip, suddenly terribly aware that she stood before him in only her borrowed underclothes. Very little fabric separated their bodies. "There's something missing from your fine new outfit."

He frowned. "What would that be?"

"Your necklaces. Your cuffs." She picked up his necklaces, then led him to the bed and had him sit down. Standing in front of him, she took a small beaded pouch and draped it over his head. He looked up at her, watching her, trying to catch her gaze. When her eyes met his, she forgot everything in the world but him.

He reached up and caught the side of her face. "*Thečhíȟila, mahasani.* I love you, my heart."

Aggie's eyes watered. Life had never felt more right than it did at the moment. She climbed over his lap, straddling him so she could be close to him when he kissed her. He pulled her face down to his, his great, dark eyes watching hers until their lips touched. The kiss was gentle at first. She felt his restraint, the power he held in check.

She smiled against his mouth. "Chayton, it is all right to let your body run now."

He groaned, caught her face in both of his hands. His mouth opened against hers. She touched her tongue to his, welcoming his lunges into her mouth as she bent her head slightly. He broke the kiss, pressing his mouth to the side of hers. His breath was hot on her cheek. He pulled her hips tighter over his. He arched against her spread thighs, his arms wound tightly around her ribs and waist.

Aggie could feel her body heating up, craving his. He fisted her braid and bent her head back as he kissed her throat, kissing the long arch of her neck up to her chin. He switched his focus to her breasts, cupping them while his hot mouth sucked her nipples through the thin fabric. Her response came as a hissed sigh. His dark eyes had gone fully black as he looked up at her. Catching the fabric at the top of her chemise in his fists, she just managed to stop him before he ripped the two sides apart.

"Wait! I don't own this. I will unbutton it." She pushed his hands away, then began slowly easing each button free. His eyes never left her hands. His nostrils flared at her progress.

She ground her hips against his lap. He gave her a warning look. She smiled and repeated her motion, grinding with each freed button. When all the tiny buttons were released, Chayton spread the two flaps aside and palmed her breasts. Holding each to his mouth, he tongued her nipples, then sucked them. After a few minutes of torture, he reached down and stroked between her legs. Aggie bucked hard against his hand. He found the opening in her drawers and slipped his fingers inside her. She gasped at the sensation on her heated flesh.

"Your bloomers open." He smiled up at her. He freed himself with his other hand. His penis was thick and rigid. "So do mine." He stroked himself even as he worked her with his fingers and thumb.

Unable to stand any more stimulation, Aggie lifted on her knees and slipped down over him, lowering herself slowly, slowly, until he groaned. He grabbed her hips and scated himself completely within her, then lifted her and repeated the feverish motion. He bared clenched teeth as their gazes were locked on each other. Their breaths came out hot and rapid.

He watched her as he stroked the engorged flesh

just above her opening with his thumb. She cried out, surrendering to the waves that owned her body. He let her ride him until her passion crested, then he began bucking beneath her, pumping into her, thrusting and retreating. He wrapped his arms around her tightly as he pressed his face against her chest. Lifting her slightly, he held her immobile in his arms as he pounded into her.

With her arms clinging to his shoulders, she knew the exact moment when he peaked. He groaned as his release shot inside her. He eased his hold and drew back to look up at her. She smiled at him and ran her hand through a bit of his long hair. She didn't want to leave their room to join the gathering below, wanted instead to retreat from reality as long as possible.

He lifted her from his lap, withdrawing from her, then set his clothes right again. "Finish putting my necklaces on me," he ordered, his voice quiet. "I will tell you what they mean."

She smiled, glad for the distraction—and the excuse to continue their private moment. "You mean they aren't just pretty?"

"Vanity has no place in a man's life. Everything I wear has meaning."

"And yet you chose a red silk vest—"

"Red is a powerful color. Since I cannot paint my face, I wear it in the way that I can."

She leaned forward and gave him a quick kiss. She sat in the V of his legs, with her legs over his thighs. "Tell me about this pouch." It was a small leather bag, about two inches by three, heavily fringed, and decorated with intricate beading, with symbols in each of the four corners and a patterned diamond in the center.

"It is my medicine bag." He looked up at her as he palmed the bag. "My full name is Hawk That Watches, as you know."

"Because of the hawk that visited your mother's tipi when you were born?"

He nodded. "And because of what I saw as a young warrior on my first vision quest. It was told to me that I would have eyes for what I do not want to know."

"What does that mean?"

"Such messages take a lifetime to understand. It is something to be known but not questioned. Because of that message, I carry a hawk's feather in this bag, along with a few other things that share their energy with me and protect me when I most need it."

"Like today."

"Yes."

Aggie picked up the next necklace. It was a long leather thong to which were bound the claws and canines of a bear in bands of blue and white beads. "Tell me about this necklace," she said as she draped it over his head.

"When I was newly married and my children small, the winter one year was long and harsh. My people were starving. We were happy when spring finally came, but still the snows did not stop. I went on a hunt. My search for game took me on a long journey.

One day, I came across a bear that had recently emerged from his hibernation. He sat at my fire to warm himself. I told him that my people were dying from hunger in the Winter That Did Not End. He told me he was an old bear who thought he had awakened too early and in the wrong season. He wished for a long sleep. He offered himself to feed my people, his fur to warm them. I was grateful for his sacrifice. This necklace reminds me to be grateful in all things. And it grants me the bear's spirit protection."

Aggie, still sitting with her legs spread out either side of him, caught his hands in hers, threading her fingers through his. "I love your stories. I think I should paint them so they can be told for long years to come."

"I would like that. And then I would tell the story of the turtle who painted."

Aggie took up the final necklace, a choker of long beige beads carved from bone. She rose on her knees to fasten it around his throat. "What of your choker? What is its meaning?"

He touched the four strands of long beads tied under his Adam's apple. "This is what I wear as a symbol of my intent to speak the truth. It is so that others who see me know that my words have no hidden meanings—they are what I say they are. They are my words. My words are the truth."

"We know that about you. Do you feel it's necessary to wear that with Logan's family?"

"It is always smart to wear it when you are among

strangers or enemies."

"Logan's family is friendly."

"I was thinking of my grandmother, but the sheriff is here. And Logan's brother is Shoshone."

"He is?" She shook her head. "I didn't know that. I look forward to meeting him."

He made a disgusted face. "The Shoshone are enemies of the *Lakȟóta*."

"Oh." She looked at him, wondering if he was teasing her. He wasn't. "Logan has been nothing but kind to us. It would be unkind of us to think of his brother as an enemy."

"I will keep an open mind on the matter. I have not met him." He got off the bed. Taking her hand, he drew her off with him. "It is time we went downstairs. Finish dressing." He sat in a chair at the small round table near the window, watching her. Aggie felt a warm heat rise to her face. She drew her stockings on, tied the garters, tied her corset on, stepped into her petticoats, then dropped the heavy blue calico skirt over her head. She settled it about her waist then buttoned the fasteners. The cotton shirt was made from the same material as the skirt. It had a wide white collar, matching white cuffs, and a mock kerchief tied above the top button.

Aggie stepped into her boots, then lifted her skirts so that she could see to tie them.

"I do not like those boots. They are ugly."

Aggie suppressed her smile. Chayton liked everything to be colorful and beautiful. "What would

251

you have me wear?"

"Moccasins."

She shook out her skirts. Only a little of her boots showed. "They would not match this dress."

"They would match any dress."

"If it means so much to you, I will find a pair and I will wear them."

He smiled and caught her hand. "You would do that for me?"

"I would do anything for you."

He came to his feet. She looked up at him, catching the way the lamplight spilled over his black hair hanging loose against the red of his shimmering silk vest. "I'm going to need to paint soon."

"I know. I can see you are wanting to walk out of your shell."

She wrapped her arms around his waist. "How is it that you know me so well?"

"I have watched you for a long time. I have hunted for you. I have fed you. I have made love to you. I have fought for you. You are the me that lives outside of myself. I know you as I know myself."

A knock sounded at the door. "Aggie?" White Bird called through the door. "Are you coming down to dinner?"

Chayton opened the door and smiled at his daughter. "Yes."

Aggie's tension deepened as the three of them went down the long staircase. The noise of the gathering below grew louder. She wasn't by nature a gregarious person. She was far more naturally a voyeur who'd rather watch and observe than engage in conversation. She was nervous for Chayton, too, and uncertain how he would handle an evening among a group of white people, three of whom he considered enemies.

The Taggerts' spacious parlor was filled with people. She looked around the room, hoping to spot Logan's brother. There was only one other man in Logan's age range, and though he was tanned and had long black hair, he looked more Spanish than Indian with his whiskey-colored eyes. She realized he had to be the brother, as he and Chayton were eyeing each other in a not-too-friendly way.

There was an older man whom Logan introduced as his father, Sid Taggert. He was tall, his dark hair graying at his temples. Aggie looked at the other people in the room. Chayton's grandmother and daughter, Sarah and Logan, several young boys about White Bird's age, and another blond woman, Rachel, who was married to Logan's brother, Sager. When Aggie was introduced as Chayton's wife, his grandmother sniffed dismissively.

Aggie looked at Mrs. Burkholder, wondering what, if any, impact her influence would have on the lives of the people in the room. Chayton didn't trust the older woman; she'd been the reason he was cut off from his people. The older woman's gaze settled on Aggie and a chill swept through her. She consoled herself with the fact that she and Chayton were independent adults who could make their own way in life. Nothing the woman could do, as rich and powerful as she was, would alter the truth of their love.

CHAPTER TWENTY-ONE

Chayton woke Aggie early the next morning. He was once again dressed in his traditional clothes. She felt the bed sink down when he sat next to her. He moved the pillows she'd burrowed beneath. The light outside was still pale lavender, lingering beside the window, too weak to fill the room. She looked up at Chayton. She remembered now that he was going back to the valley to retrieve their things, the bodies of the other bank robbers, and the bank money that was missing.

She touched his hair, holding a fistful of it as she slowly woke up. "Don't go."

He smiled. "I must. The Shoshone is going. We will see who is the better tracker."

"You're better. You're Lakota." He grinned at her. His teeth were white and straight, his brown face fiercely proud in the shadowy light of the room. "Come back to bed and spend the morning with me."

He leaned forward and kissed her, sending tingles

to her fingers and toes and heart. "They wait for me downstairs. You will see me tomorrow, day after at the latest."

"I don't want you to go."

He brushed his fingertips from her brow to her temple. "When I return, I will take you to the cabin, where you can step out of your shell and visit with the *Wakȟáŋ Tȟáŋka* as long as you like."

The thought should have comforted her, but it did nothing to ease the achy emptiness she felt inside. "I miss you already."

"And I miss you. Let me go so that I can return."

"Be safe. Come back quickly." Aggie watched him cross the room and quietly shut the door behind him. She stayed in bed, listening to sounds of the men as they left the house then saddled up and rode away. The silence in the wake of their departure was deafening.

She pushed the covers aside and went to the window, which looked out over the front of the house. The men were long gone. All that remained was the thick dust cloud kicked up by their horses. Aggie dropped the lace panel and turned to look at her empty room. What was it that had her so agitated? Chayton was in good company. Logan, Sager, Chayton, the sheriff, and his deputy would keep each other safe in the dangerous switchbacks and the remote valley beyond it. And in a few days, they would return. She made her bed and pulled out another borrowed dress.

Best thing to do, to make the time pass more

quickly, was to keep busy. She brushed and tied her hair, then washed her face and brushed her teeth. Maria had to be up working in the kitchen already. Surely she could use a hand.

She moved quietly through the hall and down the stairs. The house was dark, but a bright light spilled from under the kitchen door. People were talking inside, speaking Spanish, their voices sleepy and hushed. Aggie pushed the door open and stepped inside. The talking stopped. A short, heavyset man was sitting at the table, eating a plate full of eggs and fried potatoes. Strangely, the sight of such a robust breakfast made her feel queasy.

"*Buenos días, señora*. You are ready for coffee?"

The thought of coffee made Aggie's stomach clench. Perhaps she was coming down with something. She felt off, but not sick, exactly. More like homesick. She hadn't felt this way in a long time. It happened when she lost her parents and went to the orphanage. It happened when she moved in with Theo.

"Thank you, no. I couldn't sleep. I thought perhaps I could give you a hand in here. With such a full house, there must be much for you to do."

"No, it is not too much, *señora*. I am happy for the work. It means family is visiting. It is good."

Aggie went to the dish basin, but a wave of dizziness made her grab the sink.

Maria was instantly at her side. "Poor *señora*. It is bad in the beginning, no?"

"Beginning? I'm fine. I miss Chayton, that's all."

"Of course you do. Why do you not go sit on the porch outside? I bring you a piece of toast and some tea. It will settle your stomach."

"Thank you. I think I will. I didn't mean to trouble you."

"It's no trouble at all."

Aggie went outside. The sun still hadn't crested the horizon, but the high clouds were already aflame with pinks and roses. A soft breeze moved through the porch, easing some of the panic that held her in its teeth. Soon enough, Maria came out with a small tray. She set it down next to Aggie, then stood before her and smiled.

"When is the little *bebé* expected?"

"*Bebé*?" Aggie frowned as she looked up at Maria, then felt a furious blush color her face. "No. I'm not- I'm not. I'm just not myself. Thank you for the toast and tea."

"*Si, señora*. I think maybe you don't know yet. It's exciting time." She turned to go. "You will let me know if you need something more, *si*?"

Aggie smiled and nodded. She wondered if it could be true. It had only been a week or so since she and Chayton were first intimate. Pregnancy didn't happen that fast, did it? She wondered how he would take the news, if it proved true. To her, it seemed a miracle. Her own child. Someone who wouldn't have to grow up alone. Someone to love and cuddle and mold into a caring, productive adult. Aggie wrapped her arm around her stomach, hoping Maria was right.

Aggie lost track of how long she sat and daydreamed, but the sun was fully up when Sarah came looking for her. "There you are!" her hostess greeted her.

Aggie moved over and gave Sarah room to join her on the long bench. "I couldn't go back to sleep after Chayton left, so I wandered down here."

"Mrs. Burkholder and I have already eaten. I thought you were still asleep. I'm sure Maria could still put a plate together for you."

"I'm fine. I had some toast. Where are Rachel and the kids?"

"Sager took her and the boys home last night. White Bird is staying with them for a few days. Logan wanted me to ask you if you are ready to have your paintings packed up. We knew you wanted to return to Denver before the end of the season. We're not in a hurry for you to leave. As far as we're concerned, you and Chayton can stay here forever. We're just mindful of the deadline you set when you first arrived."

Aggie drew a deep breath. Sarah was right. It was time for the next step. "Yes. I'm ready. I'll do that today, while the men are out. It will help keep my mind off missing Chayton."

"I agree. I'll have Logan's foreman send men and the crating supplies you requested down with you."

Aggie started for the door, but stopped before she passed through. "Sarah, do you think Chayton will adjust well to living at my studio in Denver?"

Sarah walked toward her, her arms folded in front of her. "I don't know. Winter there has to be better than winter in his cave. I just don't know how he'll adjust to the white world." She reached out and squeezed Aggie's forearm. "We'll always be here. You two can come back out here anytime. He did all right at the cabin, didn't he?"

"We weren't there very long. And with the weather so nice, he didn't spend much time inside."

"He's resilient, Aggie. Look at all he's survived already. He'll be fine. He'll learn how to be fine."

When Aggie came back downstairs a few minutes later, she found only Mrs. Burkholder in the parlor. She could tell instantly from the older woman's tense posture that something was wrong.

"Good morning, Miss Hamilton. It's time we had a conversation about the future: your future and that of my grandson. His fling with you must end. I have extensive expectations of him which he cannot meet hiding away up here in these hinterlands. In short, you are a distraction he does not need. I am willing to compensate you generously for your time and inconvenience, but in return, you must not be here when my grandson returns."

Aggie felt a red burn of mortification seep upward from her collarbone, up her neck to her cheeks. "Mrs. Burkholder, I am your grandson's wife."

She laughed. "Nonsense. You're his paramour. You knew of me before you sought him out, knew that I was anxious to find him. You thought to capitalize on my situation—and my wealth."

Aggie frowned. "No."

The older woman looked at Aggie, her steel-blue eyes blade sharp. "I don't blame you. It is a strategy I might have taken, were our roles reversed. However, your little game is over. I will not have a trollop in my family. My grandson faces enough prejudice joining white society. He does not need to be burdened with you as well."

Aggie found it hard to breathe. A dull throbbing settled in her throat. "Perhaps it would be best to have this discussion when Chayton is here to participate. If he wishes me to leave, then I will go. Of course."

"My dear, you will be long gone before he returns. The Taggerts have arranged for your paintings to be crated and transported to town. You will travel with them. And you will have no further interactions with my grandson. In exchange, I will pay you the one-time sum of five thousand dollars."

"You want to pay me to leave Chayton?" Aggie was dumbfounded.

"No, I don't want to pay you. I'd much rather you just left. I *will* pay you, however, if that is the only way to secure your departure."

"I'm not leaving, Mrs. Burkholder. This is insane." Aggie came to her feet and walked to the door.

Before she could escape, the older woman stopped her with a last threat. "If you do not leave peacefully—and immediately—then you give me no choice but to take my great-granddaughter and return to Denver."

"Why would you take White Bird?"

"Her father's judgment has been compromised, distorted by his time among the savages who raised him and his time living as a hermit. I am her only other living relative. When I sue for custody, the involvement of his paramour in his child's life will make it easy for a judge to award custody of the girl to me."

Aggie frowned. "You're taking White Bird because of me."

Mrs. Burkholder did not answer. Aggie was stunned. It was true that she lived a Bohemian life, exempt from the influences of polite society. Never once in her life had she wished to conform to the rules of proper behavior, but it rankled that this supercilious woman claimed there was anything unacceptable about her marriage to Chayton. All of his friends— and even the sheriff—recognized their union.

"I have plans for my grandson that cannot be achieved with you in his life. I don't want the girl, but I will take her if I have to. And that is entirely up to you, Miss Hamilton."

"I'm Chayton's wife," she said to no one in particular. "He will not accept this."

"Leave my grandson to me. For your part, you must simply leave. Be gone before he returns, and I will provide you an even greater sum than I mentioned, one that will tide you over for years to come."

"I don't want your money, Mrs. Burkholder," Aggie said, though how she spoke with her heart breaking, she didn't know. "I don't want anything from you except for you to leave the Taggerts in peace. They've done nothing but help your grandson and his daughter. I will go with the men to pack up my paintings."

"If you are quick enough, you will be able to make the 5:00 p.m. train to Denver."

Aggie nodded. Perhaps it was best to leave. For now. Give Chayton time to get acquainted with his grandmother. She would leave him a note letting him know why she left.

"Don't think to communicate with my grandson again. Ever. I know of a boarding school that will take his daughter."

Aggie's heart tightened with pain. That would kill Chayton and be terrible for White Bird. She moved blindly into the hall and out of the house. Somebody spoke to her, but she didn't stop. She had to leave now, before she broke. Outside, a wagon was already waiting for her with Mrs. Burkholder's man.

There was no turning back.

* * *

Aggie watched the men unload her collection of paintings in their hard wooden frames. She had ten open-sided crates. Giles, the gallery owner, was at the window watching the activity on the sidewalk. She waved to him. Being here now was a bit like coming home. It was because of him that she and Theo had moved west. Though she'd known him since she was a child, she had no guarantee he'd accept her work for an exhibit. He opened the gallery's front door and motioned her forward. She burst into tears as she went up the steps.

"Oh! My dear." He held her in a tight hug. "Good heavens, child. I'm happy to see you, too, but I'm not crying."

"Giles," Aggie choked out, "my world has ended."

"Well. Then I suppose tears are required. Robin! Robin! Help us!" he called to his long-time friend and business associate. A beautifully proportioned and perfectly groomed man hurried into the front entranceway. "Be a dear and deal with the delivery man. We're having a crisis."

Giles whisked Aggie away to the kitchen at the back of the townhouse. He and Robin had bought the two townhouses years ago and now used most of the first floor as a gallery and the upper floors as their private apartments. When they'd reworked the lower floor to flow together as one unit, they'd kept one of the kitchens for use with their various gallery events.

"I'm so sorry to burst in on you like this."

"Think nothing of it. Theo was one of our own. Of course you would come here. Besides, Robin and I were hoping to hear from you before the end of summer." He set a water kettle on to boil. "Now start talking. Whatever has you broken up like this?"

"I just got back in town. I went to Theo's warehouse first. His work is everywhere. His clothes. It's as if I came back home after a short outing and everything was the same, but he's gone. He's never coming back." Giles handed her a monogrammed handkerchief. She pressed it to her face and spoke through its folds. "I spent the summer painting and painting."

"Did you? Good girl!"

She nodded. "I wanted to show him all of my work and he's not there. I knew he's not there. But being away from here, I could almost believe he was. But he isn't. And I fell in love and got married and I had to leave, and Giles, I can barely breathe."

Giles looked across the room to where Robin had joined them. The two men shared a look. Robin dragged over a chair next to hers and wrapped an arm around her. "Let it out, child. Of course you can't breathe with all of that noise inside you."

Aggie leaned into his shoulder, coughing and gasping as she sobbed. By the time Giles brought over a pot of tea, some mugs, and a tray of scones, the worst of the storm had passed. She was red-faced and swollen-eyed. She blew her nose a final time.

Giles drew a chair over and sat facing her. He leaned forward and put his hands on her knees. "I don't know what to address first. Could we start with 'you got married'?"

Aggie nodded. "I married a Lakota warrior."

Robin whistled. Sitting back in his chair, he gave

Giles a wide grin. Giles ignored him while he poured their tea. She told them about her summer. And Chayton, his daughter, his grandmother, and the Taggerts.

"You'll stay here," Giles announced. "I won't have an argument about that. I think you should absolutely get word back to your husband, regardless of what his grandmother said. He must be sick with worry."

"I can't. His grandmother will punish White Bird."

"Then send word to the Taggerts. Let them discuss it with your husband and determine how to handle the situation."

Aggie drew a fortifying breath. She nodded. "You're right."

"Of course I'm right. Now, let's go get a look at your work. We've got four weeks before our next show. If your work is what I think it will be, there's no reason you can't have the gallery for that time."

"Are you serious?"

"I am. I told you I would hang your work here when you got back."

She didn't tell him how many caveats he'd attached to that offer. The moment of reckoning was at hand. She'd know very shortly whether her work was good enough. Robin retrieved a claw hammer, then met them in the front room of the gallery. He carried the first crate into that room while Giles turned on the gas sconces. Robin used the claw side of the hammer to open the crates.

"Be careful, Robin," Giles said. "It doesn't take

such brute force."

Robin straightened and glared at Giles. "Would you rather open them?"

"No, of course not. You do it. But hurry. Have you seen her work? It's extraordinary. And she's an *unknown*."

Aggie's stomach clenched when Robin opened the largest crate with the two full-length paintings of Chayton. She heard Giles draw a sharp breath between his clenched teeth. Was that a good reaction or a bad one? He sent her a dark look over his shoulder as Robin leaned them against a wall at the far end of the room. Giles turned away and walked in the opposite direction, giving himself some distance to observe the two works.

"God damn. Goddammit. He's *gorgeous*." Giles shot her a look, but his eyes quickly returned to the two paintings. "Is he the one?"

Aggie found it hard to speak. She nodded.

Giles gave her a longer look. "You are in love with him." She didn't answer him.

"And you left him," Robin said, shaking his head. Aggie started to cry again. Robin put his arm around her. "Honey, if I'd left him, I'd be crying, too."

"Open another crate," Giles ordered. "I want to see all of them."

Over the next half-hour, each of her works were set out next to each other, lining three walls of the large exhibit room.

"These are beautiful. All of them." Robin looked at

the paintings as he moved slowly around the room. "She should have an exhibit all to herself. We could call it 'The Last Lakota.'" He glanced at her. "You said he's Lakota, isn't he?"

She nodded.

"Do you have more work?" Giles asked.

"Not finished. I have sketches for more pieces. He isn't the last Lakota, you know. His people still live, but on the reservation."

"Why isn't he with them?" Giles asked.

She shrugged. His reasons were too personal to share. "Many reasons. The people in the area he lived fear him. They think he's a renegade."

Giles and Robin exchanged a look. "'The Renegade: An Exploration of the Last Wild Indian,'" Robin said, spreading his hands as if to reveal a large sign.

"It will be a huge hit!" Giles responded.

Aggie sighed. "I want them to love him. Like I do."

CHAPTER TWENTY-TWO

Chayton hurried up the stairs to the room he shared with Agkhee. It had been a good journey. They found the stolen money. The Shoshone had found the trail, but Chayton had found the stash. Turned out he liked Logan's brother after all.

Agkhee wasn't in their room. He went back downstairs. Sarah stood there, with Logan, Sager, the sheriff, and the deputy. The air was heavy in the parlor, setting Chayton's nerves on edge. He looked at Logan, waiting to be caught up with the conversation.

"Aggie's gone. We boxed up her paintings, thinking to hold them until you two were ready to go to Denver to prepare for the show. For some reason, she went ahead." He held up a paper. "And she is not at her shop. Sarah sent a telegram to confirm her safe arrival, but it couldn't be delivered because no one was at her studio to receive it."

"Why would she leave?" Chayton asked Sarah.

Sarah shook her head. "I know she missed you. I told her you were both welcome to stay as long as you liked. I offered the men to crate up her work, not to hurry her on her way, but because she has that show to prepare for." She looked at Chayton. "I saw her the morning she left. She didn't seem herself."

"Do we know what gallery she was doing that show at?" Logan asked, looking at his wife and Chayton.

"She never said."

"I will go after her." Chayton took a step toward the parlor entrance.

"Hold on there." The sheriff stopped him, interjecting some logic. "An Indian alone in Denver is likely to get shot. That town'll make the Defiance folks seem downright friendly if you're by yourself."

"He's right," Logan told him. "I'll go with you."

"We will leave now."

"No. The train to Denver doesn't leave until 5:00 p.m. tomorrow," Logan said. "There will be plenty of time to make it. We'll get a good night's sleep, then head down to Defiance in the morning. Even if you left now for Denver, you wouldn't get there before the train. We'll ride down in the morning with the sheriff."

When it was time to leave the next morning, Chayton was stunned to see the entourage that had assembled. Apparently, Logan had told the Shoshone about the trip, and when the Shoshone told his wife about it, she wanted to join them, which meant bringing their three boys. Mrs. Burkholder was making the return trip to Defiance with them. Sarah and White Bird were going to ride with her in the carriage. Her guard was missing, but she'd explained to them yesterday that she'd sent him to accompany Aggie down to her studio in Denver. And then there was the sheriff and deputy bringing up the tail, driving the wagon with the dead outlaws.

Chayton glared at the Shoshone, who only laughed. "Don't look at me, Lakota. Your woman's already got you chasing your tail—she's why we're all here."

Chayton made a face and looked away. Logan clapped him on the shoulder. "Don't worry. Even with such a large group, we'll get to town in plenty of time to make the train."

The day inched along at a snail's pace. They stopped three times: once for lunch and twice to rest the horses. When they reached town, Chayton's mood had not improved. Though he rode sandwiched between the sheriff and Logan at the front of the line, he watched the townspeople anxiously. Their reception of him was never kind, and he didn't expect today to be any different.

Sager and Mrs. Burkholder's driver dropped the women and children off at Maddie's Boardinghouse to freshen up and await the 5:00 p.m. train. Chayton watched the crowd thicken as he, Logan, and the sheriff dismounted outside the sheriff's office.

"Finally caught him, did ya, sheriff?" one of the men shouted out. Others gathered to see what the excitement was about.

"Thought you'd bring him in dead," another

shouted.

Sheriff Declan held up his hands and faced the crowd. "That's enough, Mitt, Buckly." He climbed up the front steps to the boardwalk so that he could stand above them. "Chayton here single-handedly took down Skinner's gang of bank robbers and recovered the stolen cash. The Western Bank and Loan Company sees him as a hero." He looked around at the grumbling men, who were disappointed there'd be no fight today. "And I do, too. If any of you start a fight with him today, you'll be cooling your heels in jail overnight."

There were some jokes about how tearing an Indian apart would be worth any time in jail. Two men Chayton didn't know looked at each other and pushed forward. Chayton couldn't believe their foolishness in challenging the sheriff right in front of his jail. His eyes narrowed as he watched the men approach the boardwalk. One was a tall man, probably half a hand taller than Logan. The other was about the same size and height, but had the cool blue gaze of a white-eyes killer—and a pair of Colts hanging off his waist.

The Shoshone jogged over from the livery and pushed his way through the crowd, following the two men. Chayton sent a look to Logan; his friend was watching the approaching men with a tense face. The Shoshone cut the other two off at the stairs, but instead of blocking them, he moved to stand in front of Chayton on the boardwalk.

"Any of you got a problem with Chayton, then you

got a problem with me," he said, glaring out at the crowd.

The tall man walked up to the boardwalk and stood next to the Shoshone. "You men know who I am. I brought the railroad spur to town and I made damn sure you were charged fair prices to move your cattle and feed to the Denver stockyards. Chayton's a friend of mine. You know I take care of my friends—and my enemies."

Chayton could barely see around the big guy to watch the man with the Colts join them on the boardwalk. He said nothing, just spread his arms and let his hands hang over his guns as he faced the crowd.

Logan clapped a hand on Chayton's shoulder. "My friend, Chayton, is Lakota, but his fight with our people is over. It's done."

One of the men in the crowd spat a brown stream into the dirt road. "It ain't never gonna be over. What his kind did to my sister's family can't be undone." He pointed to Chayton. "I will know him and hate him all the days of my life. And if he thinks he can hang out here like any one of us, well, I won't cry if he mysteriously meets his end one night."

"A murderer is a murderer, Mitt," the sheriff said, answering the man's not-so-veiled threat, "whether he kills a white man, a Chinaman, a black man, or an Indian. I never cry when I see a murderer hang."

"I don't got a problem with him, long as he knows his place." The man spat again and walked off. His departure deflated the crowd. People began to thin out. Sheriff Declan came over to Chayton and held his hand out.

"Thanks for bringing down the Skinner gang. I'll get the paperwork started for your reward. When it's here, I'll send word to Logan." Chayton nodded at him. The sheriff went inside his office, leaving two of his deputies to keep the peace out front.

Chayton looked at Logan's brother and friends. The Shoshone shook hands with the tall man and the silent gunslinger. "What are you two doing here?" he asked.

The tall man glared back at Logan's brother. "Audrey got wind of the fact that Sarah and Rachel were going to Denver. She decided to let Leah know about it and make a summer party of it."

Logan laughed. "The kids with you?"

"Well, it wouldn't be a party without them. They're all down at Maddie's."

Logan shook hands with both men. "Thanks. I appreciate your help." He looked at Chayton. "These are my friends." He nodded toward the tall man. "Julian McCaid and Jace Gage." Chayton eyed them, then offered his hand. "You've probably seen each other around town," Logan continued. "Julian's only here in the summer and Jace runs the lumber mill outside of town."

"My railroad car's here," Julian told them. "We can head down to the station whenever you're ready— let's go get the ladies." He looked at Chayton. "Once we're settled, you can catch us up on what the hell's going on."

"Shoshone." Chayton stopped Logan's brother before he moved down the steps with the others. "Thank you."

Sager stared at him a long minute. "We're not enemies, you and I. I've been where you are. I know what it's like to lose your people and your family, and I know what it's like to move into white society. You aren't alone, Chayton. You have a new people and a new family." He held out his hand and took hold of Chayton's forearm. "You are a brother to my brother. That makes you a brother to me." He stared into Chayton's eyes. "I'm called 'Sager.'"

Chayton gripped Sager's forearm. "I am glad for your friendship. Sager."

They started down the steps to the street as a crowd of a different sort approached them. The men's wives were joining them, along with what seemed to be at least a couple dozen children. Chayton closed his eyes and let himself listen to the noise of their excited voices, the women laughing and chatting, the children chasing each other and teasing. It filled his heart with joy. For a painfully brief moment, he almost felt as if he had returned to his village from a lengthy absence.

Logan introduced him to Audrey, Julian's wife. She tried to point out the children that were hers, but there were so many of them that he couldn't keep them straight. He met Jace's wife, Leah, and their three kids.

Seeing the happiness on their faces made his heart ache for Agkhee. She would be both overwhelmed by the group and fascinated by it. His own daughter was no stranger to the other children. They accepted her among them as if she was but another beloved cousin and friend. Sarah looked over at him and caught him watching his daughter. She smiled at him, but there was a shadow in her eyes. He wondered if she regretted having only the one child to look after. She'd been a good mother to his daughter. It was a good choice he'd made.

He moved with the large gathering of Logan's friends and their families, walking with the men in the back of the group as Julian's wife, Audrey, led them to their private railroad car. His grandmother looked over her shoulder at him, glanced at the other men, then fell back and drew him aside with a hand on his forearm. For a minute she didn't speak, only watched him as if she was searching for the right words. Such caution was commendable. Words had power and should be used only with intent. He waited patiently for what she would say.

Before she could speak, a couple of men from the original group came forward. "Who said you could talk to anyone, Injun? Do your business and move on." He looked at Chayton's grandmother. "He bothering you, ma'am?"

Impossible, but Chayton could have sworn the old woman grew taller as she turned to face the men. "My good fellow, this young man is my grandson. I will

276

thank you to leave us be." Logan and Sager joined their small group, eyeing the men.

"He's a half-breed?" The man huffed a short laugh. "How 'bout that, Buckly? The white in 'im might keep 'im from scalping us in our sleep."

Chayton ground his teeth. The men nodded at his grandmother then moved along.

"Why do these people hate you so?" she asked.

Chayton studied his grandmother, wondering at the source of that question. He understood she lived in the area white men called Colorado, near the South Platte River, in a town called Denver. He'd been down there when he was boy, before it was so overrun with white men. How could she live there and be ignorant of the conflict that had caused such harm to his people? "These people, and mine, have been at war for years. I am their enemy."

"Are you? Have you harmed them?"

Chayton calmed his tongue. If it would free his people, he'd kill every last one of them. His grandmother included. But white men were pouring out of a hole in the ground like a hatched nest of spiders, filling the land from sunrise to sunset, as Logan had once told him. He could kill and kill and kill, and still they spread where they wanted, infecting the land that was so sacred to his people. He looked at his friend and his friend's brother. They awaited his answer, watching him.

Agkhee was white. She was as precious to him as Logan's friends' wives were to their men. The hatred

277

in his heart would end them, as it would destroy all white men, if he gave it life. Hatred was no man's friend. Having nothing more to say to his grandmother, he walked away. His mother would have scolded him for riding a dark horse. And he was. On a dark horse in a dark world. Agkhee was his only light. Where had she gone? She was a turtle out in the world without her shell.

He ached to find her.

The group walked down to the train station. There was a great gathering of Logan's tribe on the platform, clustered in two groups. One of Logan's immediate family, friends, and children, the other of trunks and luggage and uniformed people, men and women. Their features indicated they were mostly Hispanic. He wondered if whites took captives, too. Or had those people joined the fringes of Logan's tribe voluntarily? There was little he truly knew about Logan's way of life. The times they'd been together in years past, when they'd journeyed across the land alone or he'd visited Chayton's village, they'd talked much about Chayton's way of life and little about Logan's.

Chayton turned away from the noisy crowd and looked at the tracks. They ran parallel to the evening sun's rays, as far as the eye could see across the hilly terrain. Telegraph poles stood guard over the steel road. Logan said messages could be communicated through the wires that touched the pole. How that was possible Chayton didn't understand. He remembered when the tracks were being laid. Warriors he'd trained horses for had fought the relentless progress, foolishly thinking the white incursion could be ended.

Logan came to him, clapped a hand on his shoulder, and watched him with caring eyes. For a moment, neither of them spoke. "Life's about to get weird for you."

Chayton had no words to express the truth of that great understatement. "My wife went alone into this world."

"Aggie is from this world. It makes more sense to her than yours. You won't be alone in this, Chayton. Sager and I will be with you; we know both worlds." He nodded toward the big guy and the one with ice for eyes. "My friends will guard your back. We'll find Aggie and bring her home."

Chayton felt like vomiting. He had no home to bring his wife to. He was not a fit husband.

A deep, rumbling vibration disturbed the air and shook the ground. Logan's people looked excitedly down the track. Chayton glanced in the direction they did. Far down the track, a great, black iron beast came toward them, steam spewing from its head. Chayton kept his expression blank as the train rolled into the station. It went past them for a short distance to hook up with a special car sitting on a separate track. When it pulled forward and stopped, everyone knew what to do, where to go, except him. The women herded the children into a different car in front of an ornately painted one. It had more windows than the ornate one.

Logan's people standing with the luggage entered the same car and quickly loaded it up.

Chayton followed Logan into the long, ornate car. Inside, the space was a narrow room that looked like it could have been taken from Logan's house. The floor was carpeted in a golden color. The walls were papered with flocked green paper. The ceiling had green and gold striped paper. Several arrangements of clustered chairs and chairs around tables filled the room. At the far end of the car was a large window that looked out onto the tracks. Several lights were affixed to the narrow panels of wall between windows. Heavy, bunched fabric hung above the windows. In the middle of the car was an iron stove that was cold on this hot summer evening.

The men moved into the car around him, taking seats at the end of the car. "Make yourself at home, Chayton," the big man told him. The only place Julian could stand straight was in the middle of the car. "If you sit with us, we can discuss your situation and do some planning. We'll be in Denver in about four hours."

After a few minutes, the women joined them, taking seats at the other end of the car. The men who operated the train called back and forth to each other in a strange tone with words that Chayton didn't quite catch. And then the train pulled out, and the station grew smaller and more distant. Chayton got up and went to stand at the far window, watching his world recede at a mind-numbing speed.

CHAPTER TWENTY-THREE

It was fully dark by the time they pulled into their station in Denver. The children were sleepy and more subdued than when they boarded. Luggage was being unloaded at a rapid pace. A wagon and several black carriages were lined up, awaiting their arrival.

"Julian." The big man's wife came to them and slipped her arm through his. "Wasn't it a surprise finding our neighbor in Defiance? And then to learn that the grandson she's been looking for all these years was the very same man Logan's been friendly with for so long! It's sometimes a very small world."

Julian bent to the side so that she could kiss his cheek. "Hm-mmm. A very small world."

"Mr. McCaid, thank for your hospitality in sharing your railroad car with me and in seeing me safely returned to Denver."

"Of course, Mrs. Burkholder."

"Charles, let us take our leave." She took hold of Chayton's arm. He did not move.

"He'll be staying with us, ma'am," Logan told her.

"He has imposed on your largesse long enough, young man."

"Nevertheless, while we hunt for his wife, it's best if he stays with us so that he can participate in the search," Julian said.

Mrs. Burkholder frowned as she stared at Julian. "Well then, if you feel that's for the best, I will understand," she said, turning to Chayton. "I expect you to call upon me in the morning. We have much to discuss—far more than the missing painter."

"Until I have found my wife, I have nothing to discuss with anyone."

Her brows lowered. "Charles Burkholder, you will visit me in the morning."

"My name, old woman, is Chayton. If you wish to use an English version of my full name, you may call me Hawk That Watches. I will not answer to any other name."

"Charles was the name of your grandfather. It is what I have decided to name you. It is the name your mother would have given you if she'd been allowed to live among her own people and marry her own kind."

"My mother did live among her people."

"Mrs. Burkholder," Julian interrupted before she could dig in her heels further, "we'll bring Chayton to see you tomorrow. Please, go with my wife now. I know that she's as tired as you are, and we've yet to get the children settled."

Audrey smiled at the older woman and reached for

her, gently turning her away from the men. "Come along, Mrs. Burkholder. There is nothing as intractable as a man who has made up his mind. My husband will see that your grandson comes by tomorrow."

"I invented intractable, Mrs. McCaid. My grandson hasn't seen intractable yet."

"No, of course not. But the worst of your troubles are over, don't you think? You now know where he is. And he'll come to see you tomorrow. Did you ever, in your wildest imaginings, picture that happening?"

"I had begun to lose hope, I confess..." Their voices began to fade into the noise of the street.

Chayton looked at Logan with a grimace. "I would rather scalp her than see her again."

Logan laughed. "I know. But I'm not convinced she didn't have a hand in Aggie's disappearance—so you can't dispense with her yet. And I didn't want you to go home with her and run the risk of us losing track of you as well."

Chayton watched the chaos on the street resolve itself as the children, an older woman, and a couple of the younger women who'd been waiting with the trunks boarded what Logan called the McCaid Omnibus—a long coach with several windows. The luggage and remaining servants were loaded onto a wagon. And the wives and his grandmother stepped into a black carriage similar to the one the men were using.

Chayton again sat next to the window and watched

the buildings and roads and people of Denver as they moved away from the station and crowded buildings to streets lined with trees and manicured lawns. The brick construction gave the buildings such permanence that they couldn't be burned down, or blown down, or simply abandoned so that the land could return to the hills and prairie it had been before the *wašíču* invaded it. He had seen it in its wild state when he was a child. That state was long gone. Much like his people. How could such a massive change happen within the lifetime of a man?

Agkhee was lost in this forest of buildings. How would he ever find her? "It is true, then, what you told me about this city, Logan."

Silence met that comment. Julian was the one who answered him. "Denver is only one of tens of thousands of cities, all across the world. It is rare, in fact, to find so much undeveloped land as we find here in North America."

Chayton returned his gaze to the world outside his window. They followed the other vehicles as they stopped first at Mrs. Burkholder's mansion. He studied her sprawling home, at once curious about the structure and simultaneously dismissive of its regal situation—the very bones that gave it permanence. They drove a short distance down Sherman Street and pulled into the drive of another large mansion, this one built from red stone and lit with gas lights at strategic points along the circular drive leading up to the house. The wagon with the luggage disappeared around the back of the house while the omnibus and the two carriages stopped up in front.

People spilled out of the vehicles and milled about before walking up the paved path to the front steps. A uniformed man opened the large front door and stood aside to admit them. Yellow light spilled onto the front steps. Chayton followed the others into the house. The mayhem intensified for a few minutes as children were told to hug their fathers good night so that the women could put them to bed. Some of the older boys started up the stairs with quick waves, while the older maidens stayed behind to help with the younger children. Chayton wasn't really certain which children belonged with which father.

White Bird came over to hug him. "I am the luckiest of all of us, *Até*."

He smiled down at her and touched her soft cheek with his palm. "Why is that?"

"Because I have two fathers, and they are both with me here!" She pulled him down to kiss his cheek, then scurried up the stairs.

As fast as the noise had exploded, it receded, moving up the stairs and down a hall to some distant place. Chayton finally had a chance to breathe and look at his surroundings. The entranceway was wide and long. An intricately woven burgundy rug covered a large area of the floor. There was a room to his left that Logan called a "den." It had several panels of bookshelves, heavy leather armchairs and sofa, an enormous desk, and another desk, slightly smaller, off to one side.

Across the hall to his right was a room set behind open pocket doors. It was painted in a warm rose color and featured floral wallpaper and furniture upholstered in emerald-green silk. He liked the colors of the room to the right, but the men entered the one on the left, so he followed them. He went to stand by the dark window and look out at the lights that sparkled across the town. The men made small talk among themselves, but he did not join in.

After a while, the uniformed man who had met them at the front door came to speak to Julian. "Sir, I have a light repast of sandwiches and fruit prepared. Shall I serve you in here, or would you like to eat in the dining room?"

"What are the women doing?"

"They are already in the dining room."

"Ah. And you've fed the children?"

"Of course, sir. Their repast was awaiting them in the nursery when they arrived."

"Then we'll eat in here, Burns. Could you ask Sawyer to join us, please?"

"I'll send him. And I'll bring your supper right away, sir." The man stepped into the hall and walked quietly away.

Chayton frowned at Logan. Why was a man serving them food?

A few minutes later, another man—this one wearing a brown wool suit and high-collared shirt— paused at the threshold. "Good evening, Mr. McCaid."

"Mr. Sawyer, please come in. You know everyone here except for our new guest, Chayton. He is a warrior of some consequence in the Lakota tribe. It is his wife I asked you to help us track down." Julian looked at Chayton. "This is my secretary, an extraordinarily capable young man. When Sager requested use of my house here in Denver, I was naturally curious about the situation that necessitated your visit. When I heard what had happened, I knew we would not be able to begin our search for another day, so I took the liberty of asking Mr. Sawyer to assist us."

Chayton nodded to him. "Thank you."

"Mr. Sawyer, if you would, please update us with your discoveries."

"I've been to Miss Hamilton's studio on Market Street. Only one of her neighbors has seen her since her return to Denver. Apparently, she had her paintings unloaded at her warehouse. Then, not an hour later, she had them reloaded with a different driver. She left with that driver and she has not returned. The neighbor never spoke to Miss Hamilton, so she doesn't know any more details than that. As you requested, I checked with the police and the major hospitals. No one has seen a woman fitting Miss Hamilton's description. I also checked in with the ticket offices at all four train stations. To their knowledge, she has not purchased a ticket out of Denver. I have scoured the newspapers for the last few days, searching for a gallery announcement or

287

anything being reported that might involve your missing wife, sir." He met Chayton's gaze. "I have not been able to locate her."

"Thank you, Mr. Sawyer. Why don't you call it a night?" Julian suggested. "We'll be needing your services rather intensely over the next few days."

"Understood, Mr. McCaid. Mr. Chayton, I'm happy to assist in any way needed." He gave Julian a quick nod then turned and left the room.

"That's good news, Chayton," Sager told him. "It means that wherever Aggie is, she went there on her own—and she's likely still in town."

Julian nodded. "Tomorrow, we'll go to her studio and see if we can discover any clues that might provide some answers. I think you and Logan will visit your grandmother in the morning. If she had anything whatsoever to do with your wife's disappearance, you might be able to ferret that out."

Chayton looked around the room at the four men who had joined him on his quest to find his wife. They didn't know him, but, perhaps through Logan, they knew of him—and yet they did not hesitate to offer their assistance. It was the same kind of generosity the men of his own people would have offered him.

"I am grateful for your help," he told them.

Jace, the man with the ice-blue eyes, smiled. "We'll find her," he said, his voice raspy. "I've spent a lot of years tracking people. And Sager's like a dog. He'll track anything."

"True enough." Sager laughed. "I found your wife

when she went missing."

Chayton frowned. Burns returned with their sandwiches and glasses of water. "Your wife left you, too?" he asked when the butler left.

Jace nodded. "Those were dark days, my friend. I'll tell you the story."

Chayton sat on the floor cross-legged and listened to Jace recount the darkest few weeks of his life as he ate with the men. He liked Logan's friends, he decided. They were honorable men, people he would be glad to call his own.

* * *

"Hey."

Chayton looked up from the bed in the guestroom he'd been assigned to see Logan at his door.

"Got a minute?"

Chayton shook his head. "I do not know what that means."

"Yeah." Logan sighed. He came into the room and motioned for Chayton to move over. He sat on the bed next to him, both of them leaning against the headboard. "Remember when we first met?"

"When I almost killed you for stealing my horses?"

"I wasn't stealing your horses. I'd heard rumors of the ancient pictographs on the valley walls and wanted to go find them. But yeah. Then. Remember how I didn't know anything about the Lakota? You had to teach me things even Lakota children knew? Things like how to enter a tipi, and who smokes the pipe first and last, and what direction the pipe travels among a group of men?"

"I remember."

"Remember that you didn't laugh at me as I learned or the many times when I erred?"

"I did laugh. Now and then."

Logan shrugged. "You never made me feel foolish."

"It is not my place in life to make you less than you are."

"You're going to go through something similar here. The rules for social interaction in the white world are complex. They can take years to learn and master. Children spend ten or fifteen years learning them. Life at a remote ranch like mine or Sager's can be casual, but here in the city, people tend to be more formal. Different rules apply. Your grandmother is going to expect you to know those rules. I wondered if you would allow me to address your situation with her? I don't think she is well equipped to help you make the transition from your world into ours."

"I do not mind. The woman is"—he paused, trying to find a way to say what he wanted in English—"like a grain of sand under my eyelid. She is not a pleasant experience."

"She's annoying. True. But she's your grandmother. And I do think you, and White Bird, mean quite a lot to her."

"She wishes to rename me."

"When I was accepted into your village, I was given a different name, too." For a minute, neither spoke. "You know my story. You know how long and how hard my father searched for Sager—and the toll that took on our family. I think it may have been the same for your grandmother." He looked at Chayton. "Sager was an adolescent when he left the Shoshone. He knows something of how the things you're going to have to learn will affect you. You might not know that Julian is the grandson of a Cherokee and a slave—a foundation that put him at a disadvantage in the white world."

"And Jace? What is his tribe?"

Logan shook his head. "He's white. But he lives by his own rules. He has a highly refined sense of justice—he's one man you do not want to cross."

"He is a warrior."

"He is."

"I like your friends. And your brother. Despite the fact that he is Shoshone."

"They're good men."

They sat in silence for a few minutes, each lost in his own thoughts. "Logan, why did Agkhee leave?"

Logan made a face as he gazed at his feet. "I don't know. When we find her, you can ask her."

"Does she not want to be married to a *Lakȟóta*?"

Logan looked at him. Chayton calmed his features, hoping his friend didn't see the pain he felt. "The impression I got from the way she painted you is that she worshiped you. You can't fake that, not when she painted her love into her art. Maybe it's all a matter of miscommunication. She's an artist, an Other—they don't always live in this realm. Maybe she thought she told us when she was going down to the exhibit and we didn't listen. I don't know. Don't jump to conclusions until you have a chance to ask her."

Chayton couldn't stand the quiet in his room after Logan was gone. He left it to its unnatural silence and went to explore Julian's home. Though he'd been in buildings before, including the wide variety of structures that formed Logan's extensive ranch, and some of the stores in Defiance, he'd never seen a single dwelling the size of Julian's home. Many of the rooms on his floor had opened doors. He went through them all, exploring them in the eerie light of the moon. One door yielded nothing but a set of stairs. As big as the house was, he hadn't yet found the children, so he went up the stairs. More rooms in another maze of corridors.

Chayton wondered at the sickness in the white man's brain that he felt the need to surround himself with panels and doors of dead wood instead of simply living in a forest. Why was owning a hollow, empty structure worth invading Chayton's country? His people had died so that men like Julian could have these walls.

The door to one room was open. Rows of desks were arranged in rigid order facing the far side of the room, where a larger desk sat. Chayton lit a lamp and carried it to one of the desks. He lifted the top of the desk and retrieved a stack of books it held. He set the lamp down, then squeezed himself sideways into the tiny piece of furniture. The printed papers were full of words and images of happy white children.

His mother had wanted him to learn to read, but it was a skill she had left untouched far too long to teach him herself. And by the time he encountered Logan, he was far more interested in protecting his herd and courting Laughs-Like-Water to bother with learning to read.

"*Até*," a quiet voice broke into his thoughts, "what are you doing here?" White Bird slipped into the room and wiggled onto his lap.

"I was looking for you."

"I'm in the next door down, with the girls."

"With the girls? The boys don't sleep with you?"

"No. Their room is the other way." Her eyes lit up with mischief and humor. She drew breath to tell him some story, then apparently thought better of it. Among their people, though she'd been gone from them for half her life, the boys' activities and training were conducted entirely separately from the girls'. Chayton was glad such a practice was also respected here.

White Bird gripped a fistful of his hair and drew her hand down its long, sleek length, the gesture soothing to both of them. "Could you not sleep?" she asked him.

"No."

"You worry about Aggie?"

"Yes." He looked across their laps to the opened books. "White Bird, can you read this?"

"Of course. This is for babies. I read chapter books now."

Chayton felt ice in his heart at her confidence. Logan was right. He didn't even know what a white baby knew. Perhaps they were born reading and that was why they'd taken over his world. "Will you teach me, daughter?"

White Bird looked up at him, silence and wonder in her eyes. She laid her palm to his cheek. "I will. I will, my *até*. And you will teach other of our people. And we will make your grandmother proud."

"I do not care about my grandmother."

Her little face clenched in a disapproving expression as fierce as one Laughs-Like-Water would have given him when he said something stupid. How his heart ached. He couldn't save his people, couldn't do a thing to stop what had begun, but he had saved this one little spirit, the biggest part of his soul.

"*Até*, there are many ways of helping our people," she said in a voice older than her years. "I have spoken to Logan-*p'apá* about this. And I think I understand. He says the best way is from within the machine of our enemy. He means—"

"I know what he means. It is true there are many ways of helping our people, however, that is not the best way—it is but one way. The best way is to remain *Lakȟóta* as you move into the skin of our enemies. Tell the stories of our people, remember our history, adhere to our values, and use the language of our fathers." He shook his head. "I cannot live in my grandmother's skin and keep joy in my heart."

"I can, because I know why I do. I will do this for us."

"How will this help our people?"

"Grandmother has very much money. Money can buy countries. The chief in Washington paid money for our land. If I earn money, I can buy it back."

"Money is but another kind of blood, daughter, one paid for in the souls of the living."

"Money is blood, and power, and it is the only thing the invaders value. I will take what they value and give it to our people." She climbed off his lap, then bent to kiss his cheek. "Good night, *Até*. When you are ready to begin your studies, I will be happy to help you."

He watched her carefree stride carry her from the room. If anyone could conquer the white world, surely it would be his daughter. He worried how she would do as she said and keep her soul.

CHAPTER TWENTY-FOUR

Ester rose with the sun the next morning. After slipping into her robe, she summoned her maid. She threw open the heavy brocade curtains on her bedroom windows and paced across the pools of sunshine, feeling the press of time.

"Good morning, Mrs. Burkholder!" her maid greeted her cheerily after entering the room. She immediately went to the large canopied bed and began setting it to rights as she chattered at her mistress about her breakfast order.

"Never mind that now. I need you to send Harry to me. Right away. After my visit with him, I'll have tea and toast. Be quick about it, girl!"

Ester continued pacing as she waited for her servant. He'd proven himself to be indispensable over the years and had become as much an advisor as a secretary and guard. He was indefatigable in any activity she assigned him. His only shortcoming was his rigid moral imperative. There were times when she'd rather he didn't question her but simply accomplished the mission she set for him without debate.

This was such an occasion.

A short knock sounded at her door. "Enter!"

"Morning. What can I do for you, ma'am?"

"I'm afraid, Harry, that we haven't sent the girl far enough away. I need you to find her before my grandson does. We must send her abroad. Or to the East Coast. Or perhaps South America. Somewhere, anywhere, where Charles will not find her."

Harry grinned. He folded his arms and watched her, his head tilted in that way he did when he was about to argue with her.

"If you fail in this, I will fire you."

"You're not going to fire me, or you'd have done it a long time ago. Someone has to be your conscience. Did it ever occur to you your grandson loves this woman? And she loves him. Would it be so bad to have an artist in the family?"

"I don't pay you to think. I pay you to do."

"Don't worry. I'll find her."

"I don't want her harmed. I just want her to disappear. I am willing to pay handsomely for that to happen."

"And if she doesn't want to go?"

"Make her want it, Harry."

"Okay. I'll take care of it." He grabbed the door, but looked back at his employer and shook his head. Ester returned his dark look, lifting her chin—and a brow—as she did so. She didn't need a scolding from a man younger than her grandson. It was for Charles' own good that she did this. It would be hard enough for him to enter society as it was. He didn't need to start his new life burdened with a bad choice from his old life.

A little voice she'd rather not listen to whispered from the back of her mind that she'd married the man she loved. It was that love that had carried them through the tragedies they'd seen. But theirs had been an entirely different situation, she argued with herself. She'd had the great fortuity to not only marry a man she cared about—indeed loved—she'd found in him a man who'd been able to carve for himself and their heirs, of whom only Charles and his daughter remained, an important role in the western expansion of the United States. Marriage was more than an affair of the heart; Charles was the inheritor of a vast fortune. He wasn't starting with nothing, as she and her husband had. He needed a wife equal to his place in society, and in industry, that was already his.

* * *

Harry picked the lock on the heavy iron door and stepped into the enormous warehouse studio where he'd dropped the artist off several days earlier. He left the door open, hoping a neighbor would be curious and come to see who was here. The studio was on the second floor of a large brick industrial building. Long white sheers covered the windows on both sides of the building, softening the light that pierced the tall windows.

Tucked in a corner to the right of the front door was a two-floor apartment complete with a parlor, dining room, kitchen, washroom, and several bedrooms. The space was out of place in the cavity of the studio, but had obviously been fully lived in, as it was full of rich furnishings. Paintings were everywhere, stacked several pieces deep in some places, leaning against walls and furniture.

"Hellooo! Aggie! Honey, I'm so glad you're back in town! I've brought your mail. How was—"

Harry turned as a matronly woman in a blue dress with a white apron came to a full stop, alarm gathering in her expression as she saw him and not Aggie. He smiled at her in an off-handed way. "Mornin'. Didn't mean to scare you. Aggie is getting ready for an exhibition and sent me to collect a few things—her mail being one of them."

The woman moved the mail behind her back and her eyes narrowed. "How do I know what you say is true?"

Harry held up his keys. "She wouldn't give the key to her place to just anyone, would she?"

"Well, no." She looked askance at him. "Are you one of her models?" Harry smiled without actually answering. "Oh, she is a lucky girl."

"She is," he agreed. "She's been given a chance at winning a space in a juried show, but there is so much competition for the remaining spot that she couldn't spare the time to collect a change of clothes or grab her mail. You should see the work she did over the summer. Truly awe-inspiring and fresh."

"Oh. Well, here." She handed a small stack of mail to him. "Don't let me delay you. Which gallery did you say she was showing her work at? I cannot wait to see it! I know how much it meant to her to secure a place for herself in a show."

Harry made a face and shook his head. "I'm a rotten friend. I don't remember the gallery name. It was over on the other side of town. There was a cafe near it, and that steak restaurant, and I think a jewelry store…" He looked at her as if for help reaching a thought that was just out of his grasp.

"Oh! You mean the Giles Gallery! Did she make it into a showing there? He was a dear friend of her father's, but even so, he only shows the very best artists' work. It was her dream to show there."

Harry snapped his fingers. "Yes! That's the one! You'd think I'd remember that." He held up the mail. "Many thanks. You've been a great help!" He started to move deeper into the apartment, going toward the stairs as the woman went to the door. "Oh! One more thing. It's a secret about her show. Since there is only one place left available, she doesn't want other artists to know about it. Would you be a love and keep this conversation to yourself? There are some men one of the other artists is sending around to threaten her at the fringes of the show, hoping to bully her into not showing. If you see them, best avoid them entirely."

"Oh! My. Yes. I won't speak to them. I'll watch, though, and let her know if they come by. Thank you for telling me!"

* * *

Ester made Harry repeat himself. He'd found the painter's gallery and, perhaps, the painter herself. She set her pen down and put her letter, mid-sentence, away in the drawer of her escritoire. She stood. Patting her hair to make sure its pins were still in place, she nodded at him. "Please have my carriage brought around."

"It's already waiting for you."

"Where's the gallery?"

"The Giles Gallery is across town. They are still putting the show together, but I know her art. It's phenomenal."

Ester gave Harry a quelling look. Let the girl take her paintings and be famous somewhere back east or overseas or on the moon. This corner of the world was too small for the both of them, and far, far too much was at stake for the woman's continued presence in her grandson's life.

She walked into the foyer. Thomas, the butler, handed her the lovely summer bonnet that complemented her linen ensemble. She faced the small mirror in the ornate hatrack beside the door. "I am expecting visitors this morning, Thomas, one of who is my grandson. As I explained earlier, he looks like a wild Indian; do not let his appearance frighten you or any of the staff. He and his friends are to await my return."

"Very good, madam."

She went outside, into the sweltering late summer heat, and stepped into her carriage. The ride to the gallery didn't take long. It was nestled into a block of multi-floor red brick buildings. Her carriage shifted as Harry climbed down from his seat beside the driver and opened her door. She took his hand and stepped down the short steps to the hard-packed dirt road.

The morning was well advanced, the street already bustling with busy people moving about. There was a distant, persistent sound of hammering and men calling to each other as they constructed more buildings farther down in both directions. Oh, how she loved this town and its booming growth. The more it became a center for expansion in the west, the greater the population in small towns upstream, the more in demand her wholesale business became.

Harry opened the gallery door for her. When it shut behind them, the noise of the growing city became muffled. A handsome young man in a neatly tailored suit came forward to greet them. "You weren't exaggerating your excitement over our exhibit," he said to Harry. "Thank you for returning so quickly!" He switched his attention to Ester, greeting her with a polite head nod. "And you must be Mrs. Burkholder. How do you do? I'm Robin Daniels, assistant to the proprietor Prescott Giles. As I explained to your man earlier today, we are very excited to showcase Miss Hamilton's work exclusively. And I am willing to give you a preview, but you must understand that the exhibit is not fully completed yet. The works are still being arranged. It will be a more pleasing experience for you to await the show on its opening day."

Ester waved him away. "You are wasting my time, young man. I'm expected at another engagement and have only moments to spare."

Robin bowed gracefully. "As you wish." He stepped to the threshold of the exhibit and clapped his hands, ordering the workers to vacate the room. They left their tools in place. The pieces that weren't yet hung leaned in place against the wall. The gallery was composed of three connected rooms, each featuring a different color theme on the walls and a tasteful arrangement of Aggie's works.

The first room Ester entered was longer than it was wide, drawing the visitor's eyes all the way across the room to the large piece she'd seen in Aggie's painting tent. Seeing the painting hanging on a wall in a building deep in the heart of decent civilization caused a momentary paralyzation within her. Her legs wouldn't move. Her lungs ceased to pull air.

Her grandson looked out at her from his portrait, a man who was a master of his destiny, proud, regal— even wearing his savage clothes. His black eyes glared back at her as they had so often in real life in the short time she'd known him. He stood against a rocky hill as if one with it beneath the cerulean-blue sky, his black hair lifted by the breeze. Ester could almost scent the wind that swirled around him.

He was magnificent. The piece was magnificent.

"That piece is titled 'Hawk That Watches.' Miss Hamilton said it's the warrior's name. He is a focal point of this exhibit."

"What is the asking price for that piece?" Ester asked.

"It's not for sale. She has already gifted it to her patron, Mr. Logan Taggert. If you like it, however, she has many sketches of this particular subject. I have no doubt you could commission another unique piece."

Ester dismissed the man as she stepped deeper into the room, walking slowly from painting to painting. The girl had talent. Each work showed a deep realism, using light and color to reveal the emotion of the land and the details of her grandson. Even in the pieces that didn't feature him, there were echoes of him everywhere.

She moved into the next room, slowly becoming aware of her grandson's changing expressions, from anger and distrust to thoughtfulness and even joy. She'd never seen him happy in the short time she knew him. She wondered if she ever would. Miss Hamilton saw in her grandson something Ester herself hadn't.

These works weren't dispassionate studies of some wild red man. Miss Hamilton had painted her grandson's soul. A pain sliced through Ester's heart. She clutched her cane. A person couldn't see another's soul without loving that person. She'd been so blindly certain that Miss Hamilton was after her fortune, but these works proved her heart was true—or it had been before Ester had sent her away.

She'd come here thinking to buy up the paintings and shut the exhibit down. But the seeds of another plan had begun forming. Her family had founded a dynasty around America's Manifest Destiny. How fitting for her to reclaim her lost grandson and transform him from his savage upbringing into an urbane, educated businessman. She could make an example of him, and use his transformation to grow her market share.

Perhaps she'd been looking at his attachment to the artist in the wrong way. The girl could be an integral part of documenting his domestication. What a triumph he would be for Ester. She would show the world that not only could she turn a savage into a decent citizen, so could she conquer the savage west, turning it into a safe place for businesses to thrive, he would become the symbol of her success.

She turned to leave, but something caught her attention. A price. A ridiculously low price. She went from piece to piece, shocked at how little the gallery was asking. This would never do. These works were important pieces of history.

Mr. Daniels returned to her side. "What did you think of the paintings?"

"I'm astounded at the quality of them. There are several I'd like to purchase, but I refuse to pay those ridiculous prices."

He frowned. "Ridiculous? The artist specifically requested that we keep the prices low."

She made a dismissive sound and waved her hand. "It devalues the works. Your clientele are my friends. We visit each other's houses. We display our art acquisitions proudly. It is a matter of personal achievement that we are able to enjoy fine art in our own homes. If anyone were to see these paintings being offered for such a pittance, not one of them would deign to own the works, much less display them in a place of honor."

Mr. Daniels' cheeks deepened in color. "I can see your point. I will discuss this with Mr. Giles as soon as he returns. The prices were extremely low, but it was at the author's request and aren't indicative of the quality of her work."

Ester showed Mr. Daniels the pieces she wanted and the prices she was willing to pay. She handed him her card. There was a small satisfaction to be had in seeing the exact moment when he recognized her name.

"You're the Indian's grandmother."

"I am. However, that isn't why I'm demanding you increase your prices. I have bought several works from you and I've never paid less than the amounts I proposed for the two I wish to purchase. It is slightly insulting that you devalue works featuring my grandson. And when you add to the mix Miss Hamilton's extraordinary skill, I think you would offend any connoisseur."

Mr. Daniels smiled at her. "As I said, I will discuss this with Mr. Giles. And I'm delighted that you were able to find a couple of works to make your own. I won't be able to release them until after the show. I'm sure you'll understand."

"Of course. Good day, Mr. Daniels." She started toward the entrance, but paused before leaving. Looking back at him, she asked the question that had been pestering her mind: "Why is it that Miss Hamilton settled on the prices she did?"

Mr. Daniels smiled. "She's an artist. She isn't driven by money. She loves your grandson on a level very few people ever get to experience. She requested these prices so that more people might have access to your grandson and could love him as she does. It is for that reason that I do not know if we will be able to honor the change in prices you've suggested."

"If you are not able to, sir, then I shall acquire the entire collection and close the exhibit. Good day to you."

CHAPTER TWENTY-FIVE

Chayton watched the town slip past the small coach window. They'd stopped at Agkhee's studio earlier. Someone had been there at some point after Agkhee's quick arrival and departure, because there was a stack of mail that included a postmark more recent than her return date. They'd found a woman in the stairwell, but she took one look at them and refused to talk. Julian had taken over the questioning and managed to get from her that Aggie's assistant and model had asked that she not speak to anyone.

Julian, Sager, and Jace were going to make a round of visits to all the gallery owners in the city once they dropped Chayton, and Logan, off at his grandmother's. With every street they crossed, every building they passed, every vehicle they went around, Chayton's temper grew. Sarah had said that Agkhee was upset the morning she left. Logan had said he wasn't convinced his grandmother wasn't involved in Agkhee's disappearance. Was it possible that the old woman had hidden Agkhee somewhere in her house? What better way to keep her under control?

When Julian dropped them off at his grandmother's house, Chayton followed Logan to the front door and waited with him to be admitted.

"Logan, my grandmother said her man drove Agkhee down to Defiance and saw her safely home. We have only her word for that. He was the last to see her. What if he kept her? What if she is somewhere at my grandmother's house?" Or worse, the thought he couldn't bear to speak—what if his grandmother had harmed Agkhee?

Logan nodded, but did not have a chance to answer him before a middle-aged man in a uniform opened the door. "Good day, gentlemen." He stepped back and widened the door to admit them.

Good day, he'd said. It was *not* a good day.

"Where is my wife?" Chayton asked. The butler looked at him as if he didn't understand. Chayton repeated himself. This time, Logan, too, gave him an odd look. Chayton broke. He stepped forward and grasped the little uniformed man by the throat and lifted his face close to his own. "Where. Is. My. Wife." He spoke slowly, forcing each word out from clenched teeth.

The man sputtered. His arms flapped about. His mouth opened and closed. Chayton thrust him aside and took the stairs two at a time. He heard the man cough and gasp. Logan followed him up the stairs.

"Shall I summon the police?" the butler asked.

"No. He won't harm anyone," Logan said. "Tell the staff not to resist or impede. And they must not hurt him. Mrs. Burkholder would be devastated if her grandson were injured."

"Yes, sir. I will gather the staff in the kitchen…"

Chayton heard nothing more as he entered the first room. It was full of furniture and textiles. A thick carpet covered the floor. Heavy drapes covered the window. Curtains framed the bed. He looked under the bed, in the armoire, anywhere large enough to contain a small female. He went into the next room and the next, increasing his speed and desperation as he went. He opened one room where a uniformed woman was changing the linens on the bed. She screamed when she saw him, then just stood there and screamed and screamed.

Logan moved around him and ushered her from the room, urging her to hurry down to the kitchen where the others were gathering.

Chayton went from room to room, down corridors, up stairs, sweeping the entire house. Each room was larger than the area inside most tipis. This building held enough space to house a small *Lakȟóta* village. And it was empty.

His grandmother, and her people, had invaded his country, sweeping away the homes of his people, so that she could build houses empty of any occupants—except for the uniformed people who served them. How did that make sense? How could anyone exist in this upside-down world?

He shoved his way into the kitchen, the last room in the house he had to inspect. A woman screamed. The others gasped and huddled in a corner. Some of the men stood with the women as if in fear of him. Other men stood between him and the quaking group.

"I am searching for my wife," he told them.

Logan turned his back to the room and whispered to him. "English, Chayton. English."

Chayton glared at his friend, then let that gaze of hatred sweep those in the room. Before he could speak, the kitchen door was thrown open and his grandmother entered. She banged her cane on the hardwood floor.

"What is the meaning of this? Charles, why on earth are you frightening my staff this way?"

Chayton turned on her, prowling closer as he spoke. In English. "My name is Chayton. Or Hawk That Watches. Use it, old woman. I will not answer to any other. What have you done with my wife?"

His grandmother took a couple of long breaths, pulling air through her flared nostrils. He wondered how well she would breathe with his hands around her throat.

"We will not discuss this here. Follow me to the library, please, gentleman."

"Madam—" her butler started, but was cut short by the orders his grandmother issued as she walked out of the room.

"Not now, Thomas. Have the staff return to their duties. Mr. Taggert, please join us."

311

Logan held the door for them, giving Chayton a quelling look as he passed. Chayton knew words and thoughts held a power of their own that once expressed could never be revoked. Right now, he was at a breaking point. He did not want this life. Not without Agkhee. His temper was restrained by a tie that was fast unraveling.

His gaze swept the heavily paneled room as he entered behind his grandmother. It was cluttered with books, vases of cut flowers, heavily padded furniture upholstered in floral prints. He wanted to sweep the shelves bare, break the china, burn the house. He turned blazing eyes upon his grandmother.

"Tell me what you have done with my wife."

"I have done nothing with your wife."

"Then we have nothing to discuss." He started for the door.

"I have not given you permission to leave."

He pivoted to face his grandmother. "And I have not given you permission to breathe, yet you do."

"I will not tolerate your insolence."

"And I will not tolerate your arrogance."

His grandmother visibly collected herself. "The woman you call your wife is not, in truth, your wife. A wife is an asset to her husband. This may not be a concept you are familiar with. A man in your position in life does not marry for love. He marries to strengthen his dynasty. The woman you claim to have married is not an asset to you."

Chayton held himself utterly still as he absorbed

the meaning of her words.

"Chayton…" Logan quietly urged caution.

Chayton ignored his friend as he slowly returned to stand in front of his grandmother. "I have no dynasty. I have no people, no country, nothing other than my heart. It is mine. You cannot own it. You cannot buy it. You cannot relocate me from it. It is mine. And I have given it to my wife. Where is she?"

"She isn't fit for you."

"I will find her."

"You are my grandson."

"She is my wife."

"I want more for you. You are socially handicapped in having been raised by savages. You need every advantage that can be afforded you. A proper young wife from another powerful family. An entire education. You need to adorn yourself in the attire expected of a man of your social status—and groom yourself accordingly."

"I need my wife. Nothing else."

"You cannot have her."

Chayton's eyes widened. "What have you done with her?"

"I sent her away."

"Where?"

"She doesn't matter."

"She does matter. She is all that matters. She is my people."

"I am your people." She thumped her cane. "I am what matters. I am a wealthy woman, Chayton. A very wealthy woman. And though it aggrieves me terribly, I will not live forever. If you are alive when I die, you will inherit my wealth."

"I care nothing for your money. It will not undo what has been done to my people."

"No. It will not. However, what you choose to do with my money after I pass is entirely up to you. You could use it to help your people, in ways that only you would know how. Or, without your compliance to my wishes, I will likely bequeath my fortune to the widows and orphans of some cavalry unit—the very men whose sacrifice made this wild land safe for us to settle. I will not take care of the woman you call your wife. And I will not acknowledge my great-granddaughter."

"You would aid my enemies?"

"The war is over, Chayton. Your people lost. They've been conquered. They must do what all conquered people do: assimilate or die. As you must. If you comply with my wishes"—she held up her hand and swept it through the air—"all of this will be yours. You can use it to aid your people, the people who stole my daughter from me, the people who killed your uncle and whose cruelty sent my beloved husband to an early and terrible death, sickened as he was by all he had lost. It will be yours, that is, only if you step into the role your grandfather built for you. You must learn to behave within the boundaries of a civilized gentleman; you must accept the challenges of the education you must receive to own and run the enormous business I've kept alive for you. You must groom yourself and dress appropriately. And you must cut your hair. If you comply, you will inherit my estate to use as you wish—perhaps to help your people."

Chayton glared at the old woman, who behaved as if she held the power of a great chief. He drew his knife from its beaded sheath. It was satisfying to see her eyes widen and her pale face grow even paler. He took hold of one of his long, leather-bound braids and cut through it. He tossed the useless lump on the plush carpet at her feet then cut his other braid and dropped it next to the first.

His world had ended and he must mourn it, so it was an appropriate action. He would comply with the old woman's wishes. He would wear the clothes of a white man. He would learn things white children learned. He would take up the reins of her cursed business.

But only so that he could use the profits to help his people—and only if he did so with Agkhee next to him.

"I will step into your white world, Grandmother, but only if you return my wife to me."

His grandmother sighed. She closed her eyes. When she opened them, she sighed. "She is at the Giles Gallery on 16th Street."

* * *

315

"Aggie—can you come down and join us?" Robin said through her closed door. "There are some men downstairs anxious to speak to you."

Aggie opened the door. "Men?"

"They said they were friends of Chayton's."

"Is he here? In Denver?"

"Come down and ask them."

Aggie didn't need to be asked again. She'd sent Logan a letter the day she arrived, but so far hadn't heard back. Had he come for her? She flew down the back stairs, then hurried through the kitchen to the foyer, where Robin had asked the men to wait. She came to an abrupt stop when she saw them. She didn't recognize two of the men, but Sager, Logan's brother, was with them. Her gaze settled on him. He slowly smiled.

Aggie's eyes watered. "How is he?" she asked without preamble.

"Man's goin' out of his mind looking for you," Sager told her.

"What of White Bird? Is she still with Logan?"

The men frowned at her. The tall one answered her. "She's with us at my house."

Aggie lowered her gaze and drew a relieved breath. The door opened. She looked between the men's shoulders and saw Chayton and Logan come into the shop. She pushed through the men and rushed to Chayton. He caught her up in a tight grip. She couldn't hold her tears back. Through her sobs, she heard Chayton murmur something in Lakota. Even without understanding his words, his voice was the most comforting sound she'd ever heard.

"I have been so sick with worry," she choked through her tears.

"Why, *mahasani*? Why did you leave me?"

"Your grandmother said she would take White Bird from Sarah and Logan if I didn't go." She drew back and looked up at Chayton. "She's a powerful woman, Chayton. She could do it."

"No, she can't." Logan patted Aggie's back. "No one's going to take White Bird anywhere. I'm her legal guardian."

Aggie sighed and lowered her head to Chayton's shoulder.

"Are you well, Agkhee?" he asked.

"She hasn't been eating. And what she does eat doesn't stay down," Giles said as he stood a few feet away from the gathering. Aggie hadn't heard him join them.

Chayton's arms tightened around her. "Who is this man, Agkhee?"

She straightened. "He was my father's closest friend. He is like an uncle to me. He let me stay here when I had nowhere to go. Chayton, this is Prescott Giles and his assistant, Robin Daniels. Giles, Robin, this is my husband, Chayton, and his friends, Logan Taggert, Logan's brother, Sager…" She looked at the other men, but didn't know their names.

The tall one offered his hand. "Julian McCaid. And this is Jace Gage." The men shook hands.

317

Chayton registered the words Giles had said. He looked at her and frowned. "Why haven't you been eating?"

She sent a quick look around at the men, irritated with the hot wash of blood that colored her cheeks. The men were staring at her until a flash of intuition hit the tall one and he started to grin. "Food doesn't sit well with me right now. And I've been so worried about you and White Bird."

Chayton shook his head. "Worry does not change the taste of food." He looked at the men, all of whom were smiling at him. Aggie saw his expression change when understanding hit him. She didn't think her cheeks could become any hotter, but they did at that moment. "Agkhee, are you pregnant?"

She sighed and kept her eyes locked on his bear claw necklace. "It's early yet. I cannot be sure, but I think so."

He put his hand on her stomach, which was still flat. He spread his fingers wide, their span nearly reaching from hip to hip.

He bent his face to her hair. "You will not leave my sight. I will feed you. You will eat. And you will paint. You are my life, Agkhee. If you ever wish to leave me again, I will give you my knife so that you can kill me outright." The lines around his mouth deepened as he spoke his edict. She reached up and touched his cheeks, then noticed his hair was short, ragged thongs still binding his truncated braids.

"What happened to your hair?"

"It does not matter."

"It matters."

"When a *Lakȟóta* mourns, he cuts his hair."

"What were you mourning? Not me?"

"You. And everything that is no more."

"Let's go home," Logan said.

"Where is home?" Aggie asked him.

"My town home," the tall man answered. He withdrew a card from his breast pocket and gave it to Giles, setting a hand on his shoulder. "Thank you for taking care of her."

"I could do nothing less. She is like a daughter to me. Aggie—we still need to finalize a few things about the exhibit."

She left Chayton's side and went to hug both Giles and Robin. "Set the prices that you wish. I will concede this issue. This time."

"My painting isn't for sale, is it?" Logan asked.

"No, of course not. It's only on loan for this show," Aggie assured him.

Logan looked at his friends. "You have to see her work. She's extraordinary." He led the men into the exhibit rooms. Giles and Robin followed them. She glanced at Chayton, then stepped toward him and eased her arms around him.

He lifted her chin as he stared down into her eyes, then bent and pressed his lips to hers. She circled her arms around his neck as he deepened the kiss. After a moment, she broke the kiss. "I love you, Chayton."

He bent his forehead to hers. "You are my life,

Agkhee. If you throw our marriage away, what remains of my life will have no meaning for me." He let his gaze sweep across her face. He caught her cheeks in his hands. "There may be bad things in our future—it is life, after all. But I need to know that we will face the good—and the bad—together. I am not strong enough to live without you."

Aggie nodded. "I agree."

"And you must eat. I wish for a strong, fine son."

"Or another beautiful daughter."

"It will be as it will be, but only if you nourish our child."

She smiled. The men came back, buzzing with commentary as Logan herded them to the door. Something was different in their eyes when they looked at her now, as if they were trying to understand how she did what she did. They helped her into the carriage as if she were the most precious of creatures. Giles and Robin came outside to see them off. She waved to them from the open carriage window.

For the first time in days, she finally felt as if she could draw a full breath. The carriage swung as it moved into the road. She slipped her hand into Chayton's and smiled up at him. "Thank you for finding me."

He nodded toward the men with them. "Our friends helped. We are not without a people, I have learned."

CHAPTER TWENTY-SIX

Aggie stepped out of the dressing room, tightening the sash of her dressing gown. White Bird sat on the foot of the bed, facing her father. They were speaking rapidly in Lakota, but stopped when she entered. She sent a look between them, wondering if theirs was a private conversation. She smiled at White Bird, then asked Chayton, "Would you like some time alone to talk? I can go—"

He reached up and took her hand. "No." He looked at his daughter. "Let us speak in English. We are deciding what will become of my daughter now."

Aggie slipped her arm around White Bird and sat next to her. This choice was not Aggie's to make, but she wanted to be sure that White Bird's preferences were fully considered. "What is it that you wish would happen, sweetheart?"

White Bird sent a worried look to her father. "I don't want to hurt anyone. I understand grandmother wants me to live with her."

Aggie checked Chayton's reaction to that. "I have heard this also," he said.

"Do you want to live with her?" Aggie asked.

"No, but it was kind of her to offer."

"Do you want to live with us?" Aggie asked.

White Bird sent a pained look toward her father. "I don't want to hurt my *até*."

Chayton took her hand. "You wish to stay with Sarah and Logan?"

White Bird nodded. Her eyes were wide, and she looked about to cry. Chayton offered a reassuring smile. "This is a good decision. If it makes you happy, I know it will also make them happy. You are very important to them. Agkhee and I will be nearby much of the time, though I expect we will also have to spend time here in Denver, with grandmother."

"White Bird, you know our home is yours. Wherever we are, you have a home with us, too." Aggie looked at Chayton's daughter, wondering if this was the right time to tell her their news. Better that they tell her than she hear it from someone else. "I believe your father and I are going to have a baby sometime in the late spring."

That news took a moment to sink in. When it did, White Bird hugged Aggie, then Chayton. She whispered something to him as she hid her face in his neck. A tear spilled down his cheek. He pulled her in tightly against him. "She said she misses her brother and hopes we have a boy."

"Oh, White Bird." Aggie couldn't keep the tears

from her eyes. Weeping was terribly easy lately.

Chayton's daughter wiggled around to face her as she sat on her father's lap. She swiped a hand across her face. "I'm glad I don't have to leave my cousins. And I think Sarah and Logan are going to have a baby, too."

"They are?" Chayton looked surprised.

White Bird nodded. "For some reason, Sarah can't have children, but she is going to adopt one from Aunt Audrey. I heard them talking."

Chayton wrapped his arms around White Bird. "Your family is growing, little bird."

She nodded. "I'm glad. I thought we were dying, *Até*. But we aren't. I will teach my new brothers or sisters how to be *Lakȟóta*." She looked up at him. "The kids here think I should have a white name. What do you think?"

Chayton thought about that for a minute, then nodded. "It is a good idea. Have you chosen your name? Or would you like me to give you one?"

"I like the name Skylar. It sounds like a bird soaring."

"It is a good name." He nodded. "I have decided that we will take grandmother's last name. In the white world, last names are given from the father to the children. My father did not need a last name. But my mother received her last name from my grandfather. We will be Burkholders. You will be Skylar White Bird Burkholder. I will be Chayton Burkholder. And Agkhee is Agkhee Hamilton

Burkholder."

Aggie smiled and reached a hand over, threading her fingers with Chayton's.

"Grandmother and I have much to discuss, but I have decided these will be our names."

A knock sounded on the door. Aggie opened it to find a maid holding a heavy tray. She opened the door wide to let her set it down. "Mrs. McCaid thought you would prefer to dine in the quiet of your room tonight. She wanted me to be sure to let you know if you preferred to eat with everyone else, they'd be sitting down in about an hour." She looked around Aggie. "White Bird, the children are gathering in the kitchen now for supper."

"Thanks!" Skylar hopped off the bed. "I have a new name now! I'm to be called Skylar Burkholder."

"Very well, miss. Skylar it is."

Aggie and Chayton shared a warm glance with each other. "Please let Mrs. McCaid know a private dinner is perfect for us tonight. Thank you."

"Yes, ma'am. Set the tray outside your door when you're finished with it."

Chayton got off the bed and went to push the heavy drapes wider apart over the window so that they wouldn't interfere with either the breeze or the sunset. He set the tray on the floor next to the bed. He'd bathed earlier and was wearing an open cotton shirt and blue denims.

"You're wearing white clothes."

He looked down at himself. His necklaces hung

against the dark column of skin his opened shirt exposed. "Logan's brother provided these to me. They are comfortable." He threw back the coverlet and removed the cotton blanket from the bed. He wrapped it about himself, then faced Aggie. "Agkhee, would you stand with me in my blanket?"

She smiled and stepped into the cover of his open arms. "The first time you asked me that, did you do it to trick me?"

Chayton grinned. "How could I know that you knew so little of a man's desires that you didn't understand what it meant to be with him inside his blanket? White women are foolish."

"Maybe. But this white woman was smart enough to get the man she wanted."

His eyes grew serious. "Will you let me feed you? My baby is hungry. I can hear him growling. He is a bear in your belly. If we do not take care of him, he will eat you, then come out and fight me."

Aggie laughed. "That sounds positively horrible, but yes, I will, because I'm starving."

He sank to the floor next to the tray. Leaning back against the bed, he indicated she was to sit in front of him between his legs, facing the window so that they could both see the sunset. The window extended from the floor to the ceiling, giving them an unobstructed view of the Rocky Mountains.

"I asked the cook to provide us some light food that would not upset your stomach."

"That was thoughtful of you."

"I have been a father before. My wife was pregnant when she was killed."

Aggie grabbed his hand that rested on her stomach and squeezed it. "I wish she was still here with you. And your son, too. I know that, if she were, you and I would never be. I would never meet you, and I would never know why my heart was so empty. But I also know the shadows in your eyes would be gone."

He held her hand in his. When he spoke, his voice rumbled against her back. "I think we do not get to know why the *Wakȟáŋ Tȟáŋka* sends to us the experiences he does. We may never know, until we get to our final sunset and look back on the days our lives have seen, and then only if we have clear eyes to see." He drew a breath, then kissed the side of her head. "For now, I am grateful to have another chance to know joy, to share my heart and my life. Thank you, Agkhee, for your kind words. I know they were spoken from your heart."

He lifted a cucumber sandwich, made with white bread and a hint of butter. He offered her a bite, then took one himself. The sandwich was tiny, so a couple of bites finished it off. He lifted a drumstick of fried chicken and held it for her to bite. "I like chicken prepared this way. Do you know how to make it?"

She nodded.

"Good. Then you can show me so that I can make it for you when you are painting." There was a bowl of gazpacho soup. Chayton sniffed it, then sipped it. "It is good. You try it."

Aggie sipped from the bowl. He was right. The cold tomato soup was tasty on a hot, late summer evening.

"How is that sitting with the bear?"

She laughed. "He is still hungry and threatening to eat me."

Chayton rubbed her stomach. "Let him settle. He cannot expect to win every battle."

Aggie leaned back against Chayton, absorbing his contentment. "How is it that time seems to stand still when I'm with you?"

"I spoke to the sun and asked him to slow his descent. He agreed. See? He is only now painting the sky with the colors of sunset." His arms tightened around hers. "You are mine, Agkhee. I am in no hurry for this time to pass. We will eat slowly. We will enjoy the show. And then I will make love to you. You, too, must learn not to race ahead."

"I'm anxious to meet the bear."

"I look forward to that as well. But everything is unfolding as it needs to. And that is a very nice feeling."

Aggie tilted up to look at him. He was so strong, so steady, so certain of them and of life. She reached up and cupped the back of his head, bringing his mouth down to hers. He held her neck and chin in his big palm as his mouth took hers. His lips were firm, warm. She leaned back, and he followed her down to the carpet. His ragged hair fell forward but wasn't long enough to curtain their faces. Still, she ran her hands through it.

He leaned on one elbow and used his free hand to trace the curves of her face. He had such extraordinary eyes, full of hunger and love. He drew his fingers down her neck to the place where the lapels of her robe overlapped, touching her bare skin with the tips of his fingers. He pulled the tie free, then pushed the two sides of fabric apart, baring her body. His gaze slowly swept from her eyes, over her breasts, her waist, to her hips.

His eyes was filled with awe. He reached forward and cupped a breast, then leaned over and kissed her ribs, her belly. His face lingered below her navel, pressed against the soft skin between her hips. He murmured something against her skin.

"What are you doing?"

He looked up at her and grinned. "I'm meeting my son. I told him he'd better grow sharp teeth; he'll need them in this world."

"And if you're son's a girl? Would you still want sharp teeth?" The look of horror that filled his face made her laugh.

"It is bad to make such jokes about an unborn child." He sat up and began removing his necklaces.

"You're not wearing your choker."

"No. I was unsure what I faced in this day when I dressed. I knew I would lie, cheat, steal, and kill to get you back."

Aggie put her hands behind her head as she watched him disrobe. "Ah. So, if we argue when you are not wearing your choker, I shouldn't trust your words?"

He frowned at her. "You will always trust me. I am your husband." He took his shirt off, exposing his broad, tanned shoulders. When his hands went to the buttons of his fly, Aggie's gaze was locked on them. He pushed the denims down his lean hips. She felt a warmth creep up her neck when he stood before her in only his cotton underwear. He was already erect; she could see the wide, dark column of him the thin cotton barely constrained.

His gaze held hers as he released the tie at the top of his drawers. He pushed the thin cotton down his hips. She couldn't resist any longer; she had to look. He was magnificent. He took hold of his heavy erection, stroked it, moved its head in and out of his fist. Aggie's lips parted. She could feel every inch of her body tensing in anticipation of what would happen next.

He reached over and grabbed a couple of pillows from the bed, then set them next to her head. "Move down so that we don't kick the tray. I will feed you more when we're finished."

She scooted sideways, never taking her eyes off what he was doing with his hands. She slipped her legs between his spread ankles, lifted herself up, then set a hand on his fist and drew his member down to her mouth. The only part of him exposed to her was the crown. She swiped her tongue across the hot, smooth surface.

Chayton sucked in a sharp breath, then took his hands away so that she could have full access to him. She stroked his length with both hands, learning his shape and size. She leaned forward, grazing him with her closed mouth, up one side, down the next. She looked up at him as she repeated the gesture with her tongue. Impossibly, he seemed to grow with every touch.

"Agkhee, I like that very much. Very much. But I cannot take more." He knelt in front of her, between her legs, and bent down to kiss her mouth. His lips were hungry, seeking. His tongue pushed into her mouth. He did with his tongue what his penis would shortly do between her legs. She ran her hand down the smooth flesh of his torso and then back up again. When the kiss ended, they were both breathing heavily.

He leaned over her, kneeing her legs wider apart so that he could have access to her core. She held herself up on her elbows so that she would watch as he entered her, joining their bodies. He rubbed the heavy head of his member over her delicate flesh, stroking and stroking her sensitive places until she was all but whimpering for him to take her.

She closed her eyes, certain she would die if she had to take another second of his torture. No sooner had she done that, a soft, warm, wet, nibbling sensation pierced her mind. Her eyes flew open to find his face between her legs, his nose buried in her dark feminine curls. His tongue was firm and soft at the same time. When he reached around her thigh and thumbed that special spot, her body took over, bucking and thrashing against his mouth.

He forked his fingers between hers, holding one of her hands until her passion began to ebb. Then he took hold of her hips, keeping her still as he sucked that nub above her opening, pressing her core ever more tightly against his face as her body convulsed in violent waves of hunger and desire.

When it ended, he grinned up at her from between her legs. She was breathing heavily, gasping for air. He crawled over her body, kissing the soft skin between her hips, nibbling around her belly button, pressing his mouth to the flushed underside of a breast. He lifted up and looked down at her, still grinning. "It is good we are alone. You would wake an entire village. And then one of the elder women would be chosen to speak with you about your intimate manners."

Aggie groaned. She couldn't remember making any noise. She only remembered feeling the extreme sensations he'd given her.

"But I would tell you to ignore the elders," he continued. "And the stares of our people in the village. I would only smile at them, for they would all know the pleasure I give you every time we are together."

Aggie drew him down to lie on top of her. "You talk too much. Give me what I want. *Now*, husband."

He drew his hips back, then positioned himself at her opening.

"Yes."

When he eased himself into her, she groaned again. She rubbed her hands up and down his arms, feeling the strain in them as he moved over and in her body. She stroked his back, absorbing the feel of his tension as he thrust into her. And then passion pushed all other rational thoughts aside. All she could do was surrender to the needs of her body. She arched up to meet his thrusts, silently urging him to greater speed, harder thrusts. She cried out when she peaked, and this time she heard him groan as his release found him. He went deep, burying his face in her neck as his hand grabbed her bottom and held her firmly against his last, pulsing thrust.

When their bodies calmed a bit, she took hold of his face and kissed his cheek, his mouth, his nose. "Guess who woke the village that time?"

He laughed. "*Mahasani*, you give me great joy."

"It is the same for me." She sighed.

CHAPTER TWENTY-SEVEN

Aggie sat next to Chayton on a settee in the McCaids' parlor the next morning as his grandmother was announced. The room was filled with Logan's friends. The men stood as she entered. Chayton stood last. After the greetings were over, he asked his grandmother to join him in Julian's den. A knot formed in Aggie's stomach. Sarah moved to sit next to her in Chayton's vacated spot. She reached out to hold Aggie's hand.

"All will be well, Aggie," she said. "Chayton needs to come to terms with his grandmother."

"What if he doesn't? What if they speak from places neither can understand or respect?"

"They'll find common ground," Sager said. "Chayton was raised to respect his elders. And she wants progeny. It is only through him that the dynasty she built will live on. It is her arrogance that will lead her to meet him where she must."

"And if they don't come to terms, the world won't

end." Logan's steady voice was reassuring to her. "You still have your studio. You have the cabin up by the Circle Bar. In a way, should the worst happen, there are no changes you need to make."

"And should we hear her scream," Jace smiled, "we're only a hallway away from rescuing him before he can commit murder."

Aggie couldn't help but laugh. "Thank you." She looked around the room at the four couples who'd dropped everything in their lives to help her and Chayton through this crisis. "Thank you all for everything you've done for us."

Sarah touched her forearm. "Aggie, Chayton talked to Logan this morning. He said you're expecting." Sarah smiled at her. "I'm so happy for you. It's a wonderful new beginning. Thank you for letting White Bird stay with us. I was afraid...I was afraid you would take her."

Aggie's eyes welled up in response to Sarah's emotions. She reached over to hug her friend.

Sarah laughed after a minute and took a delicate lace handkerchief from her pocket. "I have some news, too." She looked around the room. "Logan and I have decided to adopt. Audrey will be helping us find the right child or children."

Leah and Rachel jumped up, hurrying to hug both women. Rachel joined them in crying happy tears. Leah shook her head. The men were shaking hands and congratulating Logan. Aggie felt a wonderful sense of belonging. Chayton had been right. They weren't without a people now.

* * *

Chayton closed the door behind his grandmother. She walked into the room, strolling to the bookcases, ignoring him. He did not speak. She sent a look over her shoulder, then casually made her way to the big leather sofa. When she had herself arranged to her satisfaction, she sent an expectant glance toward him. She lifted a brow. "It's rude to stare, young man."

"It was rude to send my wife away, old woman."

His grandmother drew a deep breath. "I did what I felt I had to for your benefit."

"It was not for my benefit that you did what you did."

"It was. You have no idea how important I am. How important the Burkholder name is."

"Which may be a reflection of how unimportant you and your name are to me."

His grandmother gasped. She thumped her cane on the ground several times. "You said yesterday you would comply."

"I said many things yesterday."

His grandmother rose to her feet. "You are my grandson." He did not reply to this, which left her at a loss. She sighed. Her shoulders slumped. "I will accept the artist as your wife. However, I must ask that you marry her according to the rules of polite society. In a church, with witnesses. A proper

335

wedding will go a long way toward your acceptance into society."

"I will agree to this request."

His grandmother studied him as if gauging his intent to keep the treaty they were negotiating. "I would also like you, your wife, and your daughter to live with me so that I can oversee your entry into civilized life."

"My daughter will be staying with my friends, Logan and Sarah. They have raised her since she was five summers. It would be cruel for me to take her from them. I have discussed this with them, and they have agreed."

She pressed her lips into a fine line and reluctantly accepted his change to her terms.

"My wife needs to travel for her work," he continued. "I will accompany her. I know I have much to learn about your world, so I will accept living here with you for the winter months, but in the summer months, we will go where she needs to go to find the content she needs for her paintings." He looked at his grandmother, watching for her reaction to his next request. "You will provide her with the space she needs for her work. An area dedicated for her use which no one will disturb without her permission."

His grandmother nodded. "She may have the attic. And if that is not satisfactory, I will have a wing built for her." Her shoulders lifted a bit. "In exchange, you will agree to undergo intensive lessons in everything you need to know to take over the reins of our business. You must be able to read and write in English. You must understand complex math and bookkeeping. You must study contract law and governmental policies. You must take dance lessons and learn our rules of social etiquette. It will take you years of study to be ready to run the company. You will do this in your winter months. The summer months are yours to do with as you wish."

Chayton considered her terms. He nodded. "I find this acceptable."

"Then we will begin with your wardrobe—and the manners you will need to see you through a formal affair such as your wedding. This will take time. I believe we should plan for a winter wedding."

"Grandmother, my wife is expecting a child. I must consult her before setting a date for our wedding."

"Oh, dear Lord." His grandmother dropped heavily onto the sofa. She sat in silence for a moment before looking up at him. "Then I will have to move the timeline up significantly. And I will acknowledge the fact that you have already married her in the way of the savage. Yes. Your formal marriage will be your first step in your transformation. It will make quite the success story, I believe. I must speak with Aggie and get things moving along." She looked up at Chayton. "Do bring her in to join us."

When Chayton entered the parlor, it was buzzing with noise. Agkhee was sitting with the women, who were weeping and laughing. He shut the door with an audible click. The men turned to look at him, but he only had eyes for Agkhee. Silence blanketed the room. She stood, clasping her hands in a tight grip. He smiled at her.

"My grandmother has accepted our marriage. However, she would like us to be married again in the white way. I have agreed to this. It requires much discussion, apparently. She would like you to join us so that she can make plans."

Aggie crossed the room, feeling a bit as if she'd been summoned to the headmistress's office while she was at the orphanage. She forced herself to breathe as she crossed the hallway to Julian's office.

"Come sit beside me, dear," Ester said. "I do not like to shout."

Aggie did as requested, grateful that Chayton stood so near her.

"I owe you an apology." His grandmother's words shocked her into silence. "I thought what I did was in the best interest of my grandson. I see now that I was wrong. And I ask for your forgiveness."

Aggie smiled. That couldn't have been an easy thing to admit. "Thank you, Mrs. Burkholder. I do forgive you."

"You will call me 'grandmother' or 'grandmamma.' As I have told my grandson, I choose to accept the fact that you are married within the terms of his savage tradition. But you must also marry according to our customs." She looked up at Chayton. "Do sit down and quit hovering."

Chayton brought a chair over so that he could sit next to Aggie. She reached to take his hand.

"Please tell me about your family," Ester said. "I know very little about the Theo Hamilton line."

"My original family name was Hofsteader. My parents died in a cholera outbreak when the war started. I was sent to an orphanage in Virginia. I lived there until I was twelve, when my foster father adopted me. I don't know anything about my parents' families or where they're from. Or even if I have other relatives."

"I see. Perhaps we should look into that. A person doesn't spring from thin air. You may not have living relatives, but you might. Perhaps you have a matron like me who is searching for you even now."

Aggie smiled. "If I do, I would love to know."

"Very well. We shall see what we can find out." She sent Chayton a sharp glance. "We have not discussed the matter of names. It is imperative that you take Burkholder as your last name. And because I am recognizing your Indian marriage, you, my dear, will henceforth be known as Agnes Hofsteader Hamilton Burkholder or Mrs. Charles Burkholder. You, young man, will be Charles Burkholder."

"I will be Chayton Burkholder."

"You must take a civilized name."

"I will be Chayton Burkholder, or I will not be your grandson."

Mrs. Burkholder's brows lifted as she settled a glare on Chayton. "Very well. You will be Charles

Chayton Burkholder, but you may go by your middle name if you wish. I will have my lawyers draw up the proper papers. I believe we should select a proper name for my great-granddaughter as well."

"We have chosen her name. She is to be known as Skylar White Bird Burkholder."

The old woman considered that. "That isn't my preferred first name, but I will accept your choice. Are you certain she shouldn't come live with us?"

Aggie didn't miss the slight change in Mrs. Burkholder's imperial tone as she deferred to her grandson. The shift made her aware of several things. What a lonely existence Chayton's grandmother must have had, losing all of her children, one by one, and then her husband, learning she'd had three other grandchildren but that they had not survived the Indian wars. Aggie could understand her wishing to gather all of her remaining family around her.

"I'm sure she will come to visit frequently, Grandmother," Aggie said. "It is nice to know she is welcomed here."

"Indeed, this is where she belongs. I must speak to Mr. Taggert to ensure she is being given the proper education and social opportunities." Ester looked at her grandson. "I will also make arrangements to reimburse him for his expenses on her behalf. I don't agree with your decision, Chayton, but I understand that you feel it is in her best interests."

He nodded.

"Now then, about the wedding. I feel we must act

very quickly, because you are soon to give me another great-grandchild, my dear." Aggie blushed and smiled. Mrs. Burkholder pursed her mouth. "I also have the impression that the two of you have close ties to the backwater town of Defiance."

"We do. It's where our friends live," Aggie told her.

"I was shocked to see the town's reception of my grandson. It is unacceptable that he be treated like a criminal. He is not a renegade Indian: he is my long-lost grandson. This, regrettably, causes me to believe that it would be best to hold your wedding in Defiance. I know how provincial ranchers can be. A show of elegance and wealth will go a long way toward quelling their ignorant fears and lifting my grandson in their esteem, which I believe will benefit you should you wish to spend any time at all there, especially with your children."

Aggie smiled at that, but saw that Chayton was having a difficult time unraveling her convoluted reasoning. "Yes. A wedding in Defiance would be wonderful."

"Very good. Then I will make the arrangements. We will have the ceremony within the month. In the meantime, I will have you both visit with a tailor and a dressmaker so that you may have a wardrobe befitting your status. No more savage clothes. No more borrowed clothes."

Chayton looked about to argue, but held his silence.

His grandmother stood and marched to the door. "If you both wish to stay here until the wedding, assuming Mr. McCaid is agreeable, I will not argue. After the wedding, you will move in with me. Aggie, your husband has requested that I provide you with the proper space you'll need for painting. When it is convenient for you, please visit with me to discuss that."

Aggie caught up to Mrs. Burkholder at the front door and gave her a hug. "I look forward to that. And thank you for being so wonderful."

"Indeed." The older woman held her emotions in check, her face stiff. "Good day, then, children. Please keep yourselves available to assist me as needed and to help with your wardrobe and the wedding preparations."

When the butler closed the front door and stepped out of the foyer, Aggie turned to see a frowning Chayton.

"What is it?"

"I am not going to like this new life."

She slipped her arms around his waist and looked up at him.

"I am lost in this world, Agkhee. In my world, I could read the colors in the sunset sky and from them determine the night's weather. I could gauge the moisture in a wind and know if the coming rain would be a drizzle or a deluge. I knew how to hide in a snowdrift if a blizzard caught me while out hunting. Elk and deer stepped in front of my arrows so that I could feed my family. My family, my village, we never went hungry.

"Here, it is a different forest—as wild, but without rules. There are no stories that guide how things move, how a man is to behave with discipline and morals. It is complex and confusing." He stroked her face. "There was nothing I did not know in my world. I had no doubt that I could provide for you and protect you. When I first met you, I thought you were the turtle without a shell. But here...here it is I who am without a shell. I am inside out, Agkhee. I do not know that I will survive in this land."

She touched his chest. "I'll be your shell. And you'll be mine."

He nodded. "I need you by my side."

Aggie smiled at him. "We'll do this together. I will not let you lose your soul."

CHAPTER TWENTY-EIGHT

Chayton dismounted and left his pony freestanding outside of Leah and Jace's house, where Logan and Sarah were staying while they awaited the wedding. Logan had sent word for him to come down. Jace jogged over from another building a little way down the lane.

"Chayton! Good to see you!" They shook hands. "How are the wedding plans coming along?"

Chayton frowned. "It is busy. So much fuss for a thing that is already accomplished."

Jace laughed. "Well, what did you expect? Women are running the show."

"Agkhee and I went to Denver for a few days when her exhibit opened. We are back now for the wedding."

"We were reading about it up here. She's become quite the celebrity. Apparently you have, too."

"At least the townspeople no longer pull me from my horse when I ride down Main Street."

Jace smiled and clapped him on the back. "That's always a good thing."

Logan, Sarah, and Skylar came out onto the front porch. Sarah waved at him as Logan came down the steps to join them. Skylar ran ahead to greet him.

"Hello, *Até*!"

Chayton hugged her. Every time he saw her, she'd grown taller. "Hello, my daughter."

"Logan, hurry back! I can't wait to show Chayton. Skylar—stay with me!" Sarah called from the porch.

"I will!"

"I'll leave you to talk." Jace excused himself and started up the front path to the house with Skylar. "We'll have coffee and pie when you return."

Chayton looked at his friend. "What is it that we have to discuss?"

Logan's expression grew grim. They walked in silence a short distance before Logan stopped to lean against a split rail fence.

Logan sighed. "I have a gift for you." His posturing conflicted with his words, which put Chayton on edge. He pulled a thick envelope out of his pocket and handed it to Chayton. He looked at Logan, then opened the envelope and withdrew several papers. He couldn't read the words on them. He'd been learning the English alphabet and its phonetics, but he couldn't yet make sense of the papers. He gave Logan a frustrated look.

"It's a land deed. To the area south of the ridge by your cave, down to the cabin, over to your pass, and half of the Valley of Painted Walls."

Chayton frowned. "How can you give me land that already belongs to my people?"

"It no longer belongs to your people. My government bought it from them. I bought it from my government. *Our* government, Chayton. I'm giving it to you for a wedding present."

Chayton sighed and propped himself up against the same fence. This made him sick in his stomach. He owned the land because this paper said it was so, instead of owning it because his people had been stewards of the land for time beyond time. Instead of owning it because his people had defended it from their enemies for generations. Instead of owning it because it was etched into his soul, he owned it because the paper said so. "Thank you."

"It's a total of five thousand acres. I wish I could have given you more."

"It is an unexpected and generous gift." Chayton set a hand on Logan's shoulder. "I thank you for it." They walked together in silence back to Jace's house. Chayton's heart was heavy. They paused at the gate. "You are a true brother to me, Logan."

Logan smiled. "Yes, I am. And I always will be." He opened the gate. Skylar saw them approaching the house. Chayton heard her announce his return. He sent Logan a questioning look. His friend only shrugged and smiled.

Skylar came to the open door and took his hand. "Hurry, *Até*!" The house smelled of coffee and something sweet, like the pie Agkhee had made him. Sarah stepped out of Jace's parlor, blocking his access to the room. Leah was there with Jace. He frowned and looked at Sarah.

"Chayton, you know that we love you very much," she said.

He nodded, watching her warily.

"You remember that Logan spent many years trading with your people. Some of his favorite pieces were the ones Laughs-Like-Water created. When she passed, Logan never sold or traded the items she made. We've saved them for Skylar. And for you."

"I do not understand, Sarah."

Skylar took his hand. "Come with me, *Até*." Sarah, Jace, Leah, and their kids all made way for him to enter. There, spread across the sofa, chairs, and tables were the moccasins, leggings, breastplates, medicine bags, warshirts, dresses, cuffs, sheaths, pouches and so much more that had comprised Logan's last trade with Chayton's wife.

Chayton couldn't restrain his reaction to the sight of all of her hard work. He could hear his wife singing and hear her praying over the pieces as she wove their energies into them. The trade the year she died had been large, for she'd had the help of several apprentices through the winter, maidens who had died with her that day Landry and his men leveled Chayton's village.

He looked over at Logan and Sarah. Words failed him.

Sarah took up one of the warshirts with its extravagant beadwork. "I know that your grandmother has ordered a special suit for you for the wedding, but I thought perhaps you might prefer to wear this. We know your story, Chayton. I think of this as Laughs-Like-Water giving you into your new life, your new marriage to Aggie."

Chayton took the shirt from her. He sat down hard in the chair where it had been. Lifting the shirt to his face, he drew a deep breath and, in his heart, thanked Laughs-Like-Water for her gift.

Skylar hugged him. "I didn't know, *Até*, that Sarah-*m'amá* and Logan-*p'apá* had these. My mother was very skilled."

Chayton smiled and reached a hand out to stroke her hair. He nodded, then looked up at Sarah and Logan. "Thank you." He gazed in wonder at the large collection they'd kept of her work. "Would it be too much to ask for a couple of pieces for Agkhee?"

"These are yours, Chayton," Sarah told him. "And Skylar's. Do with them what you will."

"I would like to give her a pair of moccasins and a medicine bag."

"I will help you pick them out, *Até*. We will give her the prettiest ones." Skylar brought him the only pair of moccasins that had been made from white deerskin. The beadwork was done in a design that looked like ribbons of lavender, blue, and red. He remembered camping near a source of the white clay Laughs-Like-Water used to treat several skins that spring, giving them their extraordinary color. These moccasins went partway up the calf and were topped with long, finely cut fringes.

"Yes. These are the right ones for Agkhee. You have chosen well. I will select her medicine bag." He looked at several that were in the collection, choosing one that had a hawk done in red, yellow, and black beads and was surrounded by a background of white beads. He held the bag for a moment, catching the energy that his wife had woven into the piece. He wondered if she'd known when she made it that one day Chayton would find a way to live without her. Skylar smiled up at him. He hugged her, then looked at the friends around them.

"Thank you."

* * *

Aggie had spent the last hour hiding behind the lace curtains in her room at Maddie's Boardinghouse, watching her friends enter the church, all of them in lovely dresses and fine suits. Several of Chayton's grandmother's friends and business associates had made the journey from Denver and even as far away as Washington, D.C., to attend their wedding. It was rumored the governor of Colorado and his wife were late additions to the guest roster and that the territorial governor of Wyoming had sent an envoy to represent him.

She heard someone walking toward her door. Sarah

had said she and Logan would come for her when it was time to go to the church. She looked at herself one last time in the mirror. She and Chayton's grandmother had spent many hours examining different fashion plates for wedding dresses. All of them had tightly fitted bodices. The one they'd selected and which she now wore had a square-cut neckline and cutaway three-quarter sleeves. It was made of ivory silk in a cream color with swaths of bobbin lace around the neckline, cuffs, and hips. There was an overskirt of silk, then from her knees to the hem, two rows of the bobbin lace frothed down the front of her gown. It was elegant and stunning. Aggie was so glad she could fit into it still without being uncomfortable. It was hard to believe it had only been three weeks since she had met with Chayton and his grandmother in Julian's home. So much had happened since then.

And now the wedding. A knock sounded at her door. She spread her veil out over her bustle, then walked slowly across the room to open the door. It wasn't Logan standing on the other side. "Chayton!" She quickly ducked behind the cracked door. "You can't see me yet!"

"Why not?"

"Because the groom isn't supposed to see the bride before she walks down the aisle." She didn't tell him it was bad luck. He was superstitious enough to call off the wedding until another day.

"Agkhee, I have seen you many times. And you are

already my wife. Let me in. Please."

She opened the door. He was not wearing the handsome gray suit Mrs. Burkholder had selected for him. Instead, he wore a gorgeous ensemble of Native attire. His tunic was elaborately embroidered with patterned beads from the front to the back, and down both sleeves. The leggings bore a wide, complementary beaded panel. His moccasins matched his leggings. He wore his medicine bag, bear claw necklace, and choker. He was magnificent.

"Chayton, why aren't you dressed? What's happening?"

"I am dressed. I will be wearing this for the ceremony."

"Oh, no! Your grandmother will be furious."

"I am a man of two cultures. She must learn to embrace both, as I also must learn." He handed her a pair of soft white moccasins. The beadwork that adorned them looped and rolled like fine ribbons. "My first wife made these, Agkhee, for us. Would you please wear these?"

Aggie's eyes welled up. She took the moccasins from him and moved deeper into the room. "What do you mean she made these for us? How is that possible?"

"They were in the last set of items Logan received in trade with her. Remember I told you she wove energy into her pieces? Yours were the only pair of white moccasins she made. And there was no other warshirt as fine as this one in the group. I think she knew we would find each other. I feel that she made these for us and that she will be with us in spirit today."

"They are so beautiful. I will happily wear them, but I can't bend down to put them on. This dress is too stiff."

He led her to a seat. "I will help you." He knelt before her and removed the high-heeled ivory satin shoes his grandmother had selected for her ensemble, then slipped the soft leather moccasins on her feet and tied the laces.

She stood up to test them out. "Oh, these are like slippers. I love them."

He looked up at her. "There is one other thing." She sat back down. He drew a small pouch from his waistband. "This is your own medicine bag. Usually, we would have a ceremony so that it could be blessed. I thought today's ceremony might serve that purpose."

Aggie took the little pouch. It was elegantly beaded and bore a raptor with spread wings. She stroked the image. "It's a hawk. Like you."

"You must give some thought to what the source of your medicine is, then put in this pouch something that represents that medicine. It will be an energy source for you. It will guide and protect you. It doesn't have to be done today."

She touched his short hair. His grandmother had demanded he have it properly trimmed, but he had insisted the barber leave it long. It brushed the collars of his new cotton shirts. "Chayton, you are my medicine. You are what keeps me strong and guides me."

He took out his knife and cut a slim lock of his hair. "Then put this in there."

She went to the dresser to find a small ribbon. She cut a narrow strip of it and used that to bind his lock of hair. When she finished, he lifted the bag over her head and fitted it under the lace that followed the square cut of her bodice top, tucking it between her breasts.

"You must wear this all the days of your life, Agkhee. Then you will never be without me."

She pressed her hand to the little bag, hidden inside her cleavage. "I will. I love you, Chayton."

He lifted her chin and touched a kiss to her mouth. "I love you, my Turtle Who Walks Out Of Her Shell."

Aggie jumped when a knock sounded on her door. Sarah's voice called through the door, "Are you ready, Aggie? It's time!" She opened the door and popped her head in. "Chayton!" She pushed the door fully open. "You can't be in here! It's—"

Aggie grabbed Chayton's arm and drew him to the door, interrupting Sarah before she could finish that thought. "He was just leaving!"

He turned and walked backward the last few steps, grinning at Aggie. "In a few minutes you will be my wife in my world and in yours."

"Yes. Yes. If your grandmother doesn't kill you for wearing that outfit."

His smile widened. "She will not. I would not be a

man if I let a little old woman kill me." He stepped over the threshold into the hall, then looked as if he might come back in. Logan blocked him with an arm over the doorjamb.

"Go, Chayton," his friend ordered.

Sarah held two bouquets. Both had been made in a Denver greenhouse and sent up here yesterday, as were dozens of other bouquets that decorated the church and the tables in the reception tent that had been put up in the field next to the church. Such extravagances the town had never seen.

Sarah handed the bouquets to Logan, then adjusted Aggie's long veil that draped down over her bustle. The original design had called for a train that gave the back of the dress the elegant effect of a waterfall of silk and lace. But given the realities of where they were being married, and that much of the day would be spent outside in a tent set over a dirt field, Mrs. Burkholder and the seamstress decided to leave the train off and to shorten the dress up to her ankles.

Sarah handed her her bouquet of lilies, baby's breath, and white roses. "It's beautiful." She felt like a true princess. The dress and the flowers were stunning; she wished she could spend the day doing a portrait of her and Chayton rather than entertaining all the important people his grandmother had invited to their special day. She sent a panicked look to Sarah.

Sarah caught her arm. "You're beautiful, Aggie. I can see the artist's madness crowding your eyes, but there is no time now to stop and do a sketch.

Tomorrow, we can put you back in this dress, then you can sketch and paint to your heart's content."

Logan was leaning against the doorjamb. He smiled at her. "I dunno. I'd rather a painting than a party, any day."

"Logan Taggert, you're Chayton's best man. Your job is to help this day go off without a hitch."

He straightened, still grinning. "Yes, ma'am." He handed Sarah her small bouquet of irises and daisies, then extended his arm to Aggie. "Shall we go?"

They went downstairs and into Maddie's kitchen at the boardinghouse, then crossed the street and followed Chayton into the church. There was a sudden shift from joyful chatter to silence to a collective gasp. Aggie saw Chayton wink at Skylar, who waited in the anteroom with her basket of flowers. He started down the short central aisle. His grandmother was in the front row. She sent a look his way and realized what their guests were reacting to. She stood and faced him, blocking his passage the last few steps to the dais.

"What is the meaning of this?" she hissed. In the silence of the church, her voice carried.

Chayton continued until he'd moved a step past her. He turned to address her—and the entire gathering of her people. "I am *Lakȟóta*. And I am your daughter's son, Grandmother. These two facts will never change. I ask you to accept both truths."

"You said you would take your place as my heir." She lifted her cane and swooped it through the air, indicating to his traditional garb. "This is an

355

abomination. On such an important day."

"Aw, hell," Logan groaned to Aggie under his breath. "Should have known Chayton would treat this as a council meeting."

"What do you mean?" Aggie whispered as she looked at him with worried eyes.

"A gathering of this type among the Lakota is meant to address rights and wrongs and future plans." He tore his gaze from the drama in the room and looked at her. "Chayton is forcing his grandmother's hand—and that of those she's gathered. After this morning, they will stand with him. Or against him. The lines will be drawn."

"Logan! What do we do?"

"We honor him by letting him say his piece." They focused again on what was happening in the room. Chayton was explaining why he wore the clothes he chose.

"The pictures woven into my shirt and leggings tell the stories of my people. It brings my ancestors to this important day with me and allows me to honor them. The clothes you would have me wear exist only to please the eyes, not to honor the lives of all who have gone before me." He looked around the room at the silent and worried faces of his grandmother's assembled guests. He lifted a hand, gesturing toward the back of the church, where Aggie waited with Logan.

"My wife is from the same world as my grandmother. She will be a bridge connecting our worlds. I have already married her according to sacred *Lakȟóta* traditions. Today, I marry her according to the traditions of my grandmother. In this way, I honor my grandmother." He gave Mrs. Burkholder a solemn look, then glanced at her guests. "Today, my grandmother has a choice that she must make. She must accept that I am *Lakȟóta* and I am her grandson. Or reject both facts."

Aggie felt chilled by Chayton's ultimatum. His grandmother sent an embarrassed glance at her guests. At the front of the room, Sager stood up. He made eye contact with Chayton and his grandmother, then went to stand on the dais behind where Chayton would exchange his vows with Aggie. Jace stood and silently moved to stand with him. Julian followed. Sheriff Declan joined them, as did the shopkeeper, Mr. Kessler.

Before the dust could settle on that shocking display of support, Rachel stood and moved behind Sarah. Then Leah and Audrey. Maddie, the boardinghouse proprietress, stood with the women. As did Mrs. Kessler, who'd been so afraid of Chayton when Aggie first met her. There wasn't room for all of them on the dais, so they stood in two rows at the front of the church.

A man in an elegant suit stood in the row behind Chayton's grandmother. He clapped, and the seated guests slowly followed his lead. After a moment, he held up a hand, requesting silence as he stepped out of the pew and into the aisle.

357

"Who is that?" Aggie whispered to Logan.

"That is the territorial governor of Wyoming's envoy."

The politician placed a hand on Chayton's shoulder, then addressed Mrs. Burkholder. "Madam, your grandson is one the rarest of beings: an articulate savage and a skilled diplomat. I understand your pride in him. It is a fine thing you're doing, bringing him into your world as your heir. It's a step toward the peace we seek in this region." He bowed to her. "Thank you for allowing me to witness this."

Mrs. Burkholder contained her burgeoning distress under the mask of a composed expression. She nodded at the envoy, then turned her attention to her grandson, her gaze steely as she observed him. "I accept the two facts you present without contest, my grandson. Had I not, we would not now be where we are. And while I don't understand your deviation from our accepted traditions on a day like today, I understand your choice has significance for you, and is therefore not meant as a repudiation of the new world into which you enter." She looked at Chayton, the governor's envoy, and Aggie. "Please, let us continue."

Chayton smiled. Aggie could see in his eyes the victory he'd extracted from his reluctant grandmother. This was not a step toward peace, but a skirmish in the coming war of wills between two very proud people.

"Who is going to win, Logan? The dragon or warrior?"

"Time will tell, Aggie. But I do know whose side

I'm on."

Chayton took his place in front of the preacher and turned to await her. The music started again as Skylar went down the aisle first, beaming as she sprinkled a trail of rose petals. Then Aggie and Logan stepped out of the entryway and made their way toward Chayton.

Aggie looked at Chayton standing in front of the preacher. She could barely hear the instructions the preacher gave her to remove her gloves and set her hands on Chayton's. Fortunately, Sarah took her flowers and gloves, then reminded her what to do. When the preacher invited anyone who felt their union should not be permitted to speak up, her heart started a vicious hammering. She kept her eyes locked on Chayton's in the lengthening silence that followed. He was not afraid. He was determined.

When the ceremony was finished, the preacher closed his Bible. "Well, son, kiss your wife!"

She laughed, but Chayton didn't. He said something in Lakota, then translated it for her. His words were whispered, meant only for her ears, though she knew others around them heard him as well.

"I am your husband. I am your protector. I am your shell. Your joy is my joy. For as long as I breathe."

Aggie nodded, feeling as if his vow was even more sacred than those the preacher had led them through. "And I am your wife, and the bridge between your worlds, and your shell. Your joy is my joy. For as long as I breathe."

Chayton leaned forward and gently kissed her on the lips.

EPILOGUE

Valley of Painted Walls, August 1884

Chayton looked across the lower draw of the valley where his herd lived. He'd bought the rest of the valley the year he married Agkhee. How easy life was when one had the benefit of privilege in the white world. No one had questioned his intent as the heir to the Burkholders' vast fortune in buying the land. Of course every gentleman needed land for hunting.

Spread out before him were dozens of white tents scattered over the northeastern end of his valley. It was hauntingly similar to the days of his boyhood in this valley, but these little dwellings were tents, not tipis, and the people were white, not bronze. Those gathered were, nonetheless, his people. And for that he was grateful.

The McCaid clan, the Gages, the Declans, and the Taggerts, with all their attendant offspring, had taken over his valley for the week in what had become an end-of-summer tradition for them over the past few years. Soon afterward, the children would resume their schooling for a new season. The McCaids would travel to their other properties. And the rest of the adults would return to the work awaiting them. His friends accepted his grandmother as a respected, if not quite cherished, elder. She and Rachel's father rarely got along, so Sid was often the peacekeeper between them.

Chayton looked for his grandmother now and found her sitting comfortably in an armchair outside the entrance to Logan's large tent, where the women prepared the meals. His youngest son was on her lap. Chayton couldn't tell what they were saying, but given that his son did not yet speak either *Lakȟóta* or English, it had to be an interesting conversation.

Aggie came up to him and reached her arms around him. With her big belly, the gesture was no easy feat. It had been a busy summer visiting the different towns where she'd been showing her paintings. He was glad winter was coming. His turtle needed quiet time. They'd built a larger house on their land south of Logan's Circle Bar Ranch, one with a proper studio. They'd spent the last five winters at his grandmother's house. He'd made good progress stepping into the management of her empire. This winter, they would be staying at their new house, giving Aggie a chance to recuperate from their third child—and an opportunity to dive into an intensive work cycle in preparation for a tour of shows on the East Coast next summer.

He watched his daughter leading her brothers to a circle of children. Agkhee had given him two beautiful sons, and now a third child was on its way. "Look at our people, *mahasani*," he said in a soft voice as he wrapped an arm around his wife. He lifted her hand to his chest. "I cannot tell you the joy I feel at this moment."

"You don't need to. I see it in your eyes."

"Will you and the baby be safe while I travel with Logan for our autumn trade at the reservation?"

"We'll be fine. We'll be at your grandmother's and have her enormous staff at our disposal. The baby isn't due until October. You'll be back by then." She looked out across the valley. "It will be good to come home this winter. To our home."

He kissed her forehead. "It will, but not until you and the baby are ready. Grandmother enjoys the children. I think she enjoyed seeing the Valley of Painted Walls today. She is nowhere near the deathbed she mentions so often."

Agkhee laughed. "She'll outlive all of us."

He gave her a solemn look. "None of this would have happened without you. This valley is alive again."

She smiled. "None of this would have happened had you not survived to save this valley." She squeezed his waist, then let him go. "Supper's being served. Join us when you're ready."

He nodded, then reached out and caught her hand.

"Agkhee—I love you."

She met his gaze. "I love you, Chayton."

ABOUT THE AUTHOR

Elaine Levine lives on the plains of Colorado with her husband, a middle-aged parrot, and a rescued pit bull/bullmastiff mix. In addition to writing the Red Team contemporary romantic suspense series, she is the author of several books in the historical western series, Men of Defiance. Visit her online at ElaineLevine.com for more information about her upcoming books. She loves hearing from readers! Contact her at elevine@elainelevine.com.